SWIFT AND SADDLED

By Lyla Sage

Done and Dusted

Swift and Saddled

SWIFT AND SADDLED

A Rebel Blue Ranch Novel

LYLA SAGE

The Dial Press
New York

A Dial Press Trade Paperback Original

Copyright © 2024 by Lyla Sage
Dial Delights Extras copyright © 2024 by Penguin Random House LLC
Excerpt from *Lost and Lassoed* by Lyla Sage copyright © 2024 by Lyla Sage

Published in the United States by The Dial Press, an imprint of Random House, a division of Penguin Random House LLC, New York.

THE DIAL PRESS is a registered trademark and the colophon is a trademark of Penguin Random House LLC.

DIAL DELIGHTS and colophon are trademarks of Penguin Random House LLC.

This book contains an excerpt from the forthcoming book *Lost and Lassoed* by Lyla Sage. This excerpt has been set for this edition only and may not reflect the final content of the forthcoming edition.

LIBRARY OF CONGRESS CATALOGING-IN-PUBLICATION DATA
Names: Sage, Lyla, author.
Title: Swift and saddled / Lyla Sage.
Description: New York: The Dial Press, 2024. | Series: Rebel Blue Ranch; 2
Identifiers: LCCN 2023047065 (print) | LCCN 2023047066 (ebook) |
ISBN 9780593732434 (trade paperback; acid-free paper) |
ISBN 9780593732441 (ebook)
Subjects: LCGFT: Romance fiction. | Novels.
Classification: LCC PS3619.A384 S95 2024 (print) |
LCC PS3619.A384 (ebook) | DDC 813/.6—dc23/eng/20231127
LC record available at https://lccn.loc.gov/2023047065
LC ebook record available at https://lccn.loc.gov/2023047066

Printed in the United States of America on acid-free paper

randomhousebooks.com

2 4 6 8 9 7 5 3 1

Design by Virginia Norey

This book couldn't be dedicated to anyone but you,
dear reader, for running alongside me as
I chase my dreams.

And for Corrine, Leo's sweetheart.

Our sunsets glow with color,
And in the pearly dawn of morn,
The pungent scent of sage drifts down,
On a breeze that's mountain born.

—"This God-forsaken Land," Juanita Leach,
cowboy poet, circa 1940s

SWIFT AND SADDLED

Chapter 1

Ada

I've come in contact with a lot of liars, but none quite so big as Google. I'm not trying to discredit the search engine, but I am trying to bring attention to its most annoying inaccuracies. In this case, telling me that the dive bar I was sitting in—because it was the only establishment in the small town of Meadowlark, Wyoming, that was open past ten o'clock on a Sunday night—served food.

It did not.

Google's stupid bar-graph busy-meter also said that the Devil's Boot—not sure if that's actually the name of the bar, considering that there's not a sign anywhere that indicates that—wasn't busy.

It was.

Not insanely busy, but busy enough to at least get the "moderately busy" designation on Google.

There was also a very boisterous cabal of old men at the bar—Google couldn't have told me that. But if there'd been any pictures of this place on its business page, I probably could've deduced that for myself.

And avoided the Devil's Boot altogether.

Stupid Google.

This place was exactly what I thought of whenever I pictured a small-town dive bar. There was old-school country playing on a jukebox and an excessive number of neon signs; it smelled like stale cigarettes, and there were spots on the floor that my Doc Martens stuck to when I walked.

I'm not a snob. I've got nothing against a good dive bar. I just didn't think I'd end up sitting in one. Not today.

When I left San Francisco yesterday and started making my way to Wyoming, a dive bar would've been the last place I wanted to be the night before I started the biggest job of my career.

But I was hungry, and the small but weirdly quaint motel I was staying in tonight didn't have the best Wi-Fi, so I left in search of sustenance and internet access, but I only found one of those two things. What kind of dive bar has no food but good Wi-Fi?

The kind with a very tall and very hot bartender who took pity on me when I asked about food and fished out a snack-size bag of Doritos from behind the bar and gave them to me with my whiskey and Diet Coke. I didn't ask how old they were—I didn't want to know—but I had a pretty good idea, considering they were almost soft. They tasted like the bag had been open for a while, though it was still sealed when I got it.

After that, I settled for a high-top table in the corner. On the wall behind it, there was a neon sign of a cowboy riding a beer bottle like a bull. The ridiculousness of it tugged at the corners of my mouth, and I liked that feeling.

Honestly, I didn't know if eating the Doritos that could probably qualify for a senior citizen discount was better than eating nothing, but here I was, eating them.

I wiped the nacho cheese dust off my fingers so it wouldn't dirty my iPad screen. I had pulled up the email threads between Weston Ryder and me, double-checking the time I was supposed to be at Rebel Blue Ranch tomorrow morning and making sure I had the map downloaded to my phone, just in case.

That was me, Ada Hart, nothing if not prepared.

I didn't know much about Rebel Blue—just what Teddy had told me over the past few months. I knew Teddy from my first year of college. We went to the same school in Colorado—at least for my first year. After that, I ended up transferring to be closer to home.

Going home was now a decision that I deeply regretted, because it had led to what would forever be known as "the incident" to me, but also known as my wedding to others.

I shook any thought of *that* and *him* out of my head.

After I left Denver, I stayed in touch with Teddy—mostly on socials—and I was grateful for that now. She was the one who'd referred me to Weston, who I thought was the owner of Rebel Blue, but I didn't know for sure. When you google it—again, stupid Google—you only get the information that it's a cattle ranch and that it's nearly eight thousand acres.

I guess I could've asked Teddy, but I didn't want to bug her. She'd done enough for me.

I didn't know how to conceptualize eight thousand acres. *Fucking massive* is what I was thinking, when I heard one of the old men at the bar giving the bartender a hard time.

"What kind of bar runs out of ice?" he growled incredulously.

"The kind that has a bunch of sad old men who drink whiskey like water," the bartender fired back. I looked up at them. The bartender had a small smile on his face, so he couldn't be too upset with the jabs. "Gus is bringing some, so make that drink last for the next ten minutes." He pointed at the glass in front of the man, and the man scoffed at him.

I felt my phone vibrate on the table and picked it up.

> Teddy: Hey! Did you make it okay?
> Me: Yeah—just doing some prep before tomorrow.
> Teddy: EXCELLENT.
> Teddy: This is going to be so fun.
> Teddy: I'll stop by this week.
> Teddy: Can't wait for you to shine!

I saw that I also had a text from my business partner, Evan—he was the contractor—and my mom, who was no doubt telling me that I was wasting my time in Wyoming.

Maybe I was, but for some reason, I really didn't think so.

I slid my phone back onto the table and flipped it facedown. I needed to focus. Over the past four months, I'd exchanged hundreds of emails with Weston. We'd discussed his vision, we'd decided on timelines, crews, and costs. People always thought that tearing down walls was step one, but it was actually like step three hundred. I was going over steps one through two hundred and ninety-nine when a giant ball of white fluff appeared at my feet.

"Waylon! Goddammit," I heard the bartender yell. I assumed Waylon was the dog sitting at my feet and staring up at me with his tongue hanging out and a crazed look in his eyes.

What an angel.

I leaned down and gave him a scratch on his very soft and furry head. Huh, less than a few hours in Meadowlark and this place was pulling smiles out of me at a record-setting rate.

"Seriously?" I heard the bartender whine. "Who the hell brings his dog to a bar?" I looked up just as a man walked in the door.

Damn. What the hell were they putting in the water in Meadowlark, Wyoming?

From here I could see that he wasn't as tall as the bartender, but close. His open flannel shirt covered a white T-shirt that clung to his chest. My eyes glided over him until they hit his worn-out cowboy boots.

Maybe it was because I'd been surrounded by tech bros in Patagonia vests for too long, but this man was doing something for me.

I bet he had rough hands. Working hands. For a split second, I imagined what they would feel like if he dragged them across my body.

Nope. No. Definitely not.

Do *not* go there.

We were not about to have fantasies about the mystery cowboy in the dusky dive bar—no matter how good-looking he was.

I was here to *work*.

I got snapped back to reality by my new furry friend licking my hands—probably tasting the elderly Dorito dust.

I couldn't help but listen to the exchange between the bartender and the cowboy. Eavesdropping was one of my favorite hobbies. "What kind of bar runs out of ice?" the cowboy shot at the bartender. The group of old men whooped in agreement.

"Where's your brother?" the bartender asked.

"Busy." The cowboy shrugged his shoulders.

"Where's my ice?"

"Truck."

"You couldn't bring it in?"

"I figured you could do that part." The bartender shook his head but came out from behind the bar and walked out the door. It was obvious that there was some sort of bond between these two. I didn't think they were brothers—they didn't look alike—but there was something.

Not brothers, but definitely bros.

"Get your dog," the bartender said on his way out. "Please."

The cowboy's eyes started scanning the bar—probably looking for his dog—but landed right on me. Me, whose hand was currently getting a thorough licking, and who was unashamedly and unabashedly staring at the cowboy.

I should've looked away, but I didn't.

I couldn't tell what color his eyes were from here, but I wanted to.

We stared at each other for way longer than was socially acceptable, and he flashed me a small smile that hinted at a dimple on either side of his face.

Not fucking dimples.

Those should be illegal.

Or at least require some sort of warning before flashing them at people.

Warning: Dimples may appear and cause panty-dropping.

It looked like he was about to start toward me, but our weird and intense stare-off was interrupted by the bartender putting an ice cube down the back of the cowboy's shirt.

He made a distinctly unmanly noise that made me laugh. Everyone's hot and badass until there's an ice cube down their shirt.

"Brooks! What the hell!" he exclaimed and did this little shimmy thing as he tried to get it out. It was cute.

Really cute.

The bartender—Brooks—just laughed as he made his way back behind the bar, bag of ice in one hand, and said, "Get your dog, and I'll let you stay for a drink."

The cowboy adjusted his shirt and ran a hand through his sandy brown hair. "Fine."

He took a step toward me, catching me with his unrelenting eye contact again. Why was he coming toward me?

A warm tongue licked my hand again.

Oh. The dog. Right.

I looked down, breaking his stare. I had to. I couldn't be held responsible for what might happen if we maintained eye contact for much longer. There was something about it—the confidence it communicated—that felt electric.

"Sorry about him." His voice was close to me now. My fluffy companion wagged his tail as his owner's footsteps approached. "He's got a thing for beautiful women." My eyes snapped up, and yet another smile was pulled from me, but this one was directed at the man who was now less than two steps from me.

"Has that line ever worked for you?" I said with a laugh. My voice felt foreign—not quite comfortable. Like when you talk for the first time after waking up.

"You tell me," he said. His eyes were bright. And green. *So* fucking green.

"Not bad," I responded, "but I feel like the delivery could be improved."

There was another flash of dimple. "How so?"

"You've got to mean it," I said.

His expression changed. He looked confused. "Of course I meant it." *Huh.* He was so convincing. Maybe if I'd had better experiences with men, I would've believed him.

"Hey!" Brooks's voice cut through our conversation, and the cowboy looked back at him. "Bottle or draft?"

Instead of answering, the cowboy looked at my table—the iPad must've made it obvious I was working on something, because instead of trying to sit or insert himself, he looked at his dog and said: "Let's let the beautiful woman work, Waylon." Waylon obeyed and went to his owner, whose eyes were back on me. "I'll be at the bar when you're done—if you want company."

Wait. He wasn't going to pressure me? Try and make his way into my space? He was just going to . . . let me work?

Damn. I guess men were built different in Meadowlark.

The cowboy gave me one last dimpled smile before turning back for the bar. My new friend, Waylon, followed him.

I watched him walk away, and it took effort for me to tear my gaze away from his back.

Trying to get back on task, I shook my head a little—like I was trying to shake off every thought about the handsome stranger.

It felt good to be noticed by him—to be the object of his stare. Right after my divorce, my self-esteem had been at an all-time low. Even now, more than a year later, it wasn't great.

So I couldn't deny that I liked someone looking at me like I was the only person in the room.

My ex-husband had never looked at me like that.

Now *that* was a train of thought I was not dealing with today. I pushed it down and went back to my iPad, and noticed a new email from the owner of Rebel Blue.

> *Ada,*
> *I hope your drive was okay and everything went smoothly. Excited to meet you and get started tomorrow.*
> *Best,*
> *WR*
>
> *Sent from Mobile*

Chapter 2

Ada

I looked at the time: 10:32 P.M. A couple of hours had passed since I arrived at the bar. I was meeting Weston at nine-thirty, so I really needed to get back to my motel soon. I started back in on my work, making sure I wasn't missing any important files or information that I needed to review with Weston tomorrow.

Once I got into a groove, it was easier not to think about the cowboy sitting at the bar, but I couldn't shake the thought entirely. Every time I looked up, his eyes were on me. Again and again we made eye contact for a second too long, and then I would get back to work.

It was a seemingly harmless cycle, but it was getting me all keyed up.

I didn't quite know why, but I was . . . drawn to him. The way he joked with the bartender, the old men at the bar occasionally slapping him on the back, and how he kept one hand on his dog—all made me wonder who this man was and what he was like in the light of day.

I was curious.

That's why I did it.

At least that's what I would tell myself later.

I got to my stopping point in my work, gathered up my stuff, and slid it into my tote bag. I didn't need to look up to know that his eyes were on me, but I looked up anyway—just as he took a swig of his beer.

We stared at each other again as I stood up. His eyes followed me, and I hoped that his body would too. I had no idea what came over me, but I didn't want to fight it.

I broke eye contact when I got closer to the door, but as I walked, I could feel his eyes on my back. Instead of walking out the door, I turned down the hallway right before it.

Ada, what the fuck are you doing?

Are you actually inviting a stranger to follow you down a dark hallway in a dingy dive bar? Is that what you're doing?

Yeah, that's what I was doing.

I stopped when I reached a door halfway down the hall and leaned against it. Waiting to see if he would come to me.

He did.

His shadow appeared in the entry to the hall, and my heart kicked at my rib cage like it was trying to escape.

I could feel his footsteps as he approached me, because as he was coming toward me, the world that I knew was shaking and crumbling to make way for him.

For something new.

He stopped a few steps from me, and his green eyes cut through the dark. They were heated as they drank me in—but also concerned, maybe?

That made two of us.

"You okay?" the stranger asked, not letting me break his gaze. He was close now, so I had to crane my neck to look at him. I stepped toward him and nodded. I didn't trust my voice. It would give me away. It would tell him that I wasn't okay and whatever this trance was that both of us were in would snap.

I didn't want that. I wanted something new.

I wanted him—the man who looked at me like I was worth looking at.

"Are you sure—" I cut him off when I fisted my hands in his shirt, pushed up on my toes, and hauled his mouth down to mine.

He was still, stunned, but only for a second before he brought one hand up to cup my face and the other to twist in my hair.

Yes, I thought. *I need this.* His hand against my face was rough, just as I thought it would be, but he was soft—like he was savoring this.

My mouth moved against his, and he dragged the hand that was against my face down the side of my body to grip my hip. His hand left a trail of electricity behind. It was like I could feel the air crackling all around me.

I needed to be closer to him.

I dropped my bag and wrapped my hands around his neck just as he pushed me back against the door with a delicious amount of force. I thought my head was going to knock against the door, but the hand that was in my hair cupped the back of my head, making sure I didn't hit it. Then he used that hand to grip both of my hands and pin them above my head.

Our bodies were flushed and our tongues tangled. When he gently nipped at my bottom lip, I couldn't help but moan and hope that the sound was drowned out by the jukebox.

His other hand traveled from my hip to my ass, and he slid his hand into the back pocket of my jeans. "Is this okay?" he asked against my mouth.

"More," I breathed. He gripped my ass. Hard.

"Fuck, who are you and what are you doing to me?" he groaned. My hips rolled involuntarily, needing more, and I could feel his hard dick under his jeans. When was the last time I'd turned someone on? When was the last time *I'd* been turned on?

A loud cough came from the end of the hallway, and both of us froze. I looked up at the cowboy, who kept his eyes on me before dropping my hands and turning to address our intruder.

"I need to get into my office—if you don't mind." It was Brooks. The bartender. He sounded like he was smiling, but I didn't look at him to confirm. My cheeks were hot, and I wanted to crawl under a rock and never come out.

This was so stupid. I was so stupid.

I always did this. No matter how hard I tried, I couldn't totally get rid of that part of me that thrived on rash, impulsive decisions. Impulsive decisions themselves weren't the problem. I'm sure some people made great ones, but I wasn't one of them. When I made an impulsive decision, I usually ended up paying for it for a while to come—my failed marriage being the prime example of this Adanomenon.

"But you guys are welcome to continue against the other wall," the bartender continued. Oh god. This was so embarrassing. I couldn't take it.

So I did what I'd come to Wyoming to do.

I ran.

Chapter 3

Wes

I stared at the bag on the kitchen counter in the Big House. It was my only tangible proof that last night had actually happened—my own glass slipper or some shit.

The woman from the bar was heavy on my mind. I hadn't slept at all. I was awake all night wondering about her.

Who was she?

Where did she come from?

Why didn't I go after her after she kissed me?

Brooks was the answer to that last one. After she ran off, Brooks stood in the hallway of the Devil's Boot, blocking me, with a stupid cocky smirk on his face.

"Honestly, the shit I find in this hallway stopped surprising me a long time ago," he had said. "But this? This was unexpected."

"Shut up," I said. Not caring that he'd just seen me with a woman pressed up against the door, getting more fucking desperate by the second.

"Do you even know her name?" he'd asked. No, I didn't know her name.

But I really fucking wanted to.

"I swear to god, if you tell Emmy about this, I will punch you in the face," I told him. Even though I wouldn't. But it was the only threat I could think of at the time. Lighting him on fire felt too aggressive. I also knew he was absolutely going to tell Emmy.

I didn't think those two had a single secret between them at this point.

"I've already been punched in the face by a Ryder—that doesn't scare me." I thought back to when my older brother, Gus, had punched Brooks in the face when he found out that him and our little sister, Emmy, had been sneaking around behind our backs.

Brooks and Gus were best friends, so the sound of that punch was probably heard around Meadowlark. It took a minute, but they were good now. Even though I knew Gus still felt pretty damn guilty about it.

"On that note, don't tell Gus either." The last thing I needed was my siblings ribbing me about getting caught making out with a girl in a bar like I was a horny twenty-one-year-old kid.

"All right, I'll make you a deal." His smirk got bigger. "I'll only tell Emmy, and she'll probably tell Gus."

"How the hell is that a deal?" I asked.

"Because I won't tell him."

"You are so annoying, you know that?" He just shrugged. At that point, I grabbed the woman's bag off the floor, not knowing what I was going to do with it, but I didn't want to leave it there.

So here it was on my kitchen table.

And I still didn't know what the fuck to do with it.

I could ask Emmy. Or Teddy.

Actually scratch that, definitely not Teddy. I would never hear the end of it. Emmy would let it go after a while. Teddy would bring it up at my funeral. Teddy was my sister's best friend and had been since Teddy's dad moved her to Meadowlark when she was only a few months old. She was a notorious shit-giver, which I enjoyed when her sights were set on other people, but I didn't need her coming after me.

A memory of the way the mystery woman had clutched at my shirt flashed through my mind. She was so . . . bold.

It was fucking hot.

And the way she moaned when I bit her lip? Goddamn. I might've gotten carried away, but everything in that moment just felt so *good*. The bass line coming from the jukebox, the dim hallway, my hand on her ass.

I felt my jeans tighten.

Get your head in the game, Ryder. You have a big day. You can't be having spontaneous boners.

My dreams were becoming reality today. Just to be clear, my dreams were not the spontaneous boners.

It was technically Day One of Project Rebel Blue Guest Ranch. I'd been referring to it in my head as Project Baby Blue, but I wasn't about to tell anyone that. Even though it was Day One of the designer, Ada, being on-site, we'd been working together through emails since October.

I looked at the clock on the oven—avoiding looking at the bag again. Half past six. I had a good three hours before Ada was supposed to arrive. I had a feeling it was going to be the longest three hours of my life.

I'd been waiting all winter, and now I was in the home stretch.

We had a bunch of cattle near the entrance of Rebel Blue, so this morning, some of the ranch hands and I would drive them to another spot. At least I wouldn't be spending the next few hours sitting on my ass waiting.

The anticipation was killing me.

When my dad and Gus had finally agreed to the guest ranch, it'd felt like more than just them trusting me with a big responsibility.

It felt like they saw me.

Between Gus, the hard-ass but also dedicated, efficient, and hardworking oldest son, and Emmy, the fierce but also kind and caring champion barrel racer, it felt easy to get lost. I didn't have an identifier like they did.

I was just Wes.

And that was fine. I didn't mind, but I was still excited to have something that was mine.

I heard the floorboards behind me squeak.

"How are you feeling about today?" Amos Ryder's gravelly voice came from behind me.

"Good," I said. "It feels weird that it's finally here." My dad rounded the kitchen counter and stood across from me now.

He was wearing his classic Wranglers and cotton button-down. Before he started work, he always rolled the cuffs of his shirt up so you could see the faded swallow tattoos on his forearms.

"What time is the designer getting here?" he asked.

"Nine-thirty. Are you coming back here, or do you want to meet us at the site?" I asked.

"I'll meet her here," he said as he took a sip of his coffee—without letting it cool. I didn't know how he drank it when it was still scalding. "This is your project, Weston. You don't need me to be at the site. You can do this."

If there was one thing that Amos Ryder always did, it was believe in his kids. And Brooks, too, I guess. And we didn't even do anything to earn his unconditional support for us. He just did it. I mean, I guess that's how some parents were. But still.

I was fucking terrified of letting him down.

I rubbed a hand down my face. "I know. It's just—" I paused for a second, trying to think how to word my thoughts. I'd always been second in command—third, if we were getting technical. I lived in Gus's shadow, knowing that he would end up running the ranch one day. I'd never done anything on my own. "It's a big deal" is what I settled on.

My dad nodded. I think he understood the part I wasn't saying. "What's that?" he asked, gesturing toward the bag on the counter.

I didn't really want to tell my dad how the bag came to be in my possession, so I just said, "A friend left it at the bar last night."

Amos raised his eyebrows in question. "A friend?"

I swallowed. "Yeah. I brought it home because I didn't want it to end up permanently smelling like cigarette smoke," I said nonchalantly, I hoped.

My dad's eyes narrowed, just a little, before he shook his head and took another sip of his coffee. "All three of you need to get better at lying."

Chapter 4

Ada

I've made a lot of stupid decisions in my life—really stupid decisions—so you'd think that I'd understand that stupid decisions have consequences.

For example: If you choose to marry an asshole, your marriage is going to suck. If you choose to eat nothing but old Doritos for dinner, you're probably going to wake up hungry. And this is my new favorite: If you impulsively decide to kiss a stranger in a Wyoming dive bar, you will lose your iPad.

Which you need. For your job. That you start today.

Excellent.

Now I had to show up for the first day of my biggest job to date without my planner, renderings, color schemes, product spreadsheets, and basically everything else I needed. Because not only did I leave my tote at a bar after kissing a stranger, I left it at a bar that doesn't even have a phone number. Which honestly feels kind of illegal.

But the whiff of cigarette smoke coming from my hair told

me the Devil's Boot didn't care too much about the legality of having a phone number.

So not only would I look like an idiot on my first day, I would also have to return to the scene of the crime and risk running into the handsome cowboy stranger, which would lead me to another stupid decision.

Because goddamn.

I could not get that kiss out of my head. I dreamed about what would've happened if the bartender hadn't caught us. Would he have kept going? In my dream, he slid his rough hands under my shirt and dragged them up and down my body. I undid his belt. He lifted me off the ground. I wrapped my legs around his middle. He pinned me against the wall and—

"Double shot vanilla latte for Ada!" The barista's voice shook me from my inappropriate nine A.M. fantasy.

Right. Coffee. That's what I was doing. Not getting pressed up against the wall by a hot cowboy in a dusky dive bar.

Which was a bummer, but probably for the best.

I went up to the counter, picked up my latte, and nodded a quick thank-you to the barista. She looked at me for just a little too long—like she couldn't figure out why I was here. The eyes in the coffee shop also lingered on me a little too long. It was like I was wearing a giant neon sign that said NOT FROM HERE.

I never realized how grateful I was for drive-thru coffee places until this moment, but even so I had to admit this place was cute. Also, it was called the Bean? Needlessly adorable.

Once I got back outside, I snapped a quick picture of my coffee cup with the mountains as a backdrop to post on my socials with the caption "Day 1. New project coming soon."

I started @homeiswherethehartis after failing out of my interior design program. Honestly, I wasn't really built for school. Starting my own business helped me realize that that was okay—that just because I wasn't good at school didn't mean I couldn't be a good designer and that I could learn my trade in a different type of classroom.

What started as volunteering to declutter and organize people's closets had turned into something that I was proud of.

Too bad I was the only one in my life who was.

Still, the community I built on my profile was one of my favorite things. There were people out there who didn't even know me who liked to follow along on my projects.

And I had a feeling this one was going to blow everything else I'd done out of the water.

My red 1993 Honda Civic was waiting for me in the parking lot. Honestly, I was surprised she'd made it to Wyoming in one piece. I should've had more faith in her. After my divorce, she was the only car I could afford. She had her flaws. The power steering fluid leaked, so I had to refill it once a week if I wanted to be able to steer. She also didn't have air-conditioning. But she was the only thing that had never let me down. I sat in the driver's seat and pulled up the map to Rebel Blue on my phone. Thank goodness I'd kept that in my pocket and not put it in my tote. I didn't quite know how I was going to approach the day without my iPad, but at this point, I didn't have a choice.

Play stupid games, win stupid prizes, Ada. And your stupid prize is looking like an idiot on the first day of your new job.

Google Maps said that Rebel Blue was about twenty minutes from the town center. It was nine o'clock, so I was running right on time.

You would never catch me going anywhere without at least a ten-minute buffer.

Honestly, I'd prefer fifteen, but the coffee was a necessary stop.

I took a quick second to look at myself in the rearview mirror. The first thing I noticed was that I looked tired. The dark circles under my eyes were not doing me any favors.

Rebel Blue Ranch, here I come.

I grew up in California, so I wasn't a stranger to the mountains, but I'd never seen mountains like these before. My mountains were mostly dry, dull, and brown. Plus, I'd grown up in the suburbs of San Francisco—not in the heart of the Wild West. The winding roads that led me to Rebel Blue were carved into what felt like the entrance to another universe. It was the beginning of April, so there was still a good amount of snow packed onto the mountains, especially the higher up I looked. The stark white of the snow against the big blue sky was incredible.

I swore the Wyoming blue sky was way bigger than the California one.

My favorite spots were the places where the snow had melted enough that you could see the greens and browns underneath. It felt like a promise—that no winter could last forever.

Damn, it was crazy what these mountains were doing to me. One beautiful view, and I was contemplating my entire existence. Even though I felt small, the moment felt . . . big. Really big.

"In point five miles, turn left," Siri's voice blared through the speaker, and I trained my eye on the left side of the mountain road, looking for the entrance. I didn't know if it would be clearly marked or if it would appear out of nowhere.

After a minute or two, I saw a massive wooden arch and gate. "Arch" wasn't the right word—it was more like three sides of a square with a gate at the bottom. I slowed the car and pulled off the road, coming to a stop in front of it. Near the top of the square, big iron letters spelled out REBEL BLUE RANCH. Above that, burned into the wood, was an outline of what I thought was probably a bull skull. Or a steer? Is that what it was called?

The gate was open, and beyond it was a dirt road that seemed to go on forever. I looked down at my phone. The address that Weston had given me was apparently about a mile up the road.

I really hoped my car's shocks would make it. I lifted my foot off the brake, took a deep breath, and crossed the threshold into Rebel Blue.

Here we go.

Chapter 5

Ada

For some reason, it didn't occur to me that a cattle ranch would have so many cows. In theory, I knew there would obviously be cows. What I didn't know is that a bunch of them would be blocking the road to Rebel Blue's Big House, which is what Weston called it in the email.

I should've given myself a fifteen-minute buffer.

Don't get me wrong, I love cows. I am a firm believer that if you pass them while you're driving, you're legally obligated to point at them and say "Cows!" But that's the only way I've ever seen a cow—through the car window, in a field, far away.

Now the cows and I were up close and personal. They were swarming my car like bees at a hive. I didn't know how it happened—or what to do now. My windows were rolled down, and I figured I would start with just asking them to move.

"Could you guys please move?" I said loudly. "I really need to get through." I honked my horn once to emphasize my point.

Nothing.

If I slowly moved forward, would they get out of the way? Or would I accidentally become a cow murderer? Could I kill a cow going one mile per hour? Or would I just injure it? Would I have to pay the vet bill? I couldn't afford the vet bill for a cow.

And what if I hit more than one?

Oh god.

I looked at my phone. It was 9:25. I thought that I could reverse and go around, but that idea went out the window when I looked through my rearview mirror and saw more cows.

All right, Ada, these cows are standing between you and your future. How are you going to get through?

I scrambled for my phone, which was plugged into my aux cord—well, one of those tape things that had an aux cord—quickly found my early 2000s playlist, and cranked up the volume.

Within a few seconds, "Move Bitch Get Out da Way" was pumping through my speakers. This was going to work. If they wouldn't listen to me, they might listen to Ludacris.

I put both hands on the wheel, ready to speed through the opening that would inevitably appear once the cows realized what I needed.

I was ready.

But . . . nothing happened.

I was still stuck and now—I looked at my phone again—officially late.

I dropped my head onto the steering wheel and let out a huff. The last twelve hours had really not been great for me.

I kept my head down, contemplating my entire existence, until I heard a voice.

A man's voice. And it wasn't Ludacris.

I peeled my forehead off my steering wheel and saw two men coming my way on horseback.

There was also a white ball of fluff with them.

The cowboy who was on a gray-and-white dappled horse came closer to my driver's-side window, and I quickly turned my music down. I really hoped he was here to get the cows out of my way.

When I looked up at him, I was met with the same green eyes that had captured me at the bar last night.

My eyes went wide. "Oh, fuck" slipped from my mouth before I knew what I was saying.

I was met with those license-to-kill dimples that were even more perfect in the light of day. In my head, he had been a cowboy because I was in Wyoming and he was wearing cowboy boots. It didn't occur to me that he was *actually* a cowboy. But the man in front of me was a cowboy through and through—down to the brown hat and leather chaps.

And the horse.

Obviously.

"Fancy seein' you here," he drawled. My mouth went dry. What were the chances that the one time I make out with a stranger, he turns out to work on the ranch that's also the site of my project? "We'll get these guys out of your way." He paused. The other cowboy was working on the cows, who had started to move away from my car. They were taking their sweet-ass time, but at least they were moving. The white ball of fluff, which I now recognized as Waylon—the dog that got me into trouble in the first place—was also contributing. "We don't get a lot of visitors this way—are you looking for something?"

Silence was no longer an option. "I—I'm here to meet with Weston Ryder," I stammered. "I start work here today."

The cowboy's smile widened. He was looking at me like he knew something I didn't, and it made me uneasy.

"You're Ada Hart?" he asked.

Apparently the whole ranch knew I was coming. "Yeah," I said shakily.

"You've got about a quarter of a mile until you get to the Big House. I'll meet you up there." He tipped his cowboy hat at me, and a shiver went down my spine.

My attraction to him clearly wasn't dulled by the daylight.

Before I could respond, he started shouting to the other cowboy and moving his horse around the car. I tried not to watch him—tried not to notice the way his gloved hands tugged on the reins or how his legs tightened around his horse's middle.

After a few minutes, the cows had moved from the path and I was in the clear. The cowboy gave me a nod, and I took that as my cue to continue driving down the dirt road.

Leaving the cowboy in the dust . . . for now. I didn't know why *he* had to meet me at the Big House. There was no way he was the owner—he couldn't be more than thirty.

Did that matter?

I didn't know anything about ranches. Why hadn't I watched more *Heartland*?

In my head, I tried to work out a plan. I would get to the Big House, talk to Weston, and then at some point I would find the cowboy again and tell him it was a one-time thing.

All it was ever going to be was a one-time thing.

Last night, I wasn't myself. I was tired, hungry, nervous, and faced with the world's cutest pair of dimples. The entire thing was an out-of-body experience that would never happen again.

Ever.

I came here to get away from my problems—not give myself new ones.

If I wasn't so keyed up over the cowboy, I probably would have been more awestruck by Rebel Blue Ranch. "Beautiful" didn't adequately describe the landscape surrounding me.

Honestly, it was fucking majestic—like a painting come to life. I'd never seen anything like it.

But I had other things on my mind. Green-eyed things with dimples.

As I got closer to the Big House, the trees got denser, until I saw a large ranch-style log cabin in the distance—which I assumed was the Big House. There was a loop that created a sort of driveway, and I parked my car close to the front door. There weren't any other cars in the loop, so I figured it was okay.

Now that I'd stopped the car, my heart picked up the pace. It was first-day jitters. It was I'm-not-good-enough jitters, and it was also dimpled-cowboy jitters.

When I ran out of the bar last night, I almost regretted it.

Now I needed to get as far away from that man as possible. I didn't want him, his dimples, or his cute-ass dog anywhere near me.

Right then, as if summoned by my thoughts, the white ball of fluff appeared in my peripheral vision. I looked at him through my window. His tongue was hanging out and his tail was wagging so hard his entire body was wiggling with it.

Why did his dog have to be so cute? He shouldn't get to have a cute dog *and* dimples.

I got out of my car, and Waylon was ready. He continued to wiggle his entire body, and I reached down to scratch behind his ears. I should've kept my eyes on the dog, but I looked up just in time to watch Dimples ride up to the house.

When he brought his horse to a halt, I looked back down at Waylon and thought how strange it was that I knew this dog's name—I even knew the bartender's name—but I had no idea what the cowboy's name was.

Maybe I could get away with never knowing it. I'd be okay with that.

I heard the no-name cowboy's boots hit the dirt, but I kept my eyes on the dog—I didn't want to make any more eye contact with this man than was necessary.

Prolonged eye contact is what got me into this mess.

"We can head in," he said, then gave a short click of his tongue. Waylon left midpet and went to his owner, who was waiting for me by the front door. He had wrapped his horse's reins around a post a few car lengths away, which I was happy about.

I loved animals, but horses scared the shit out of me—they were so big.

As I approached the front door, Cowboy John Doe opened it and Waylon ran inside. Both Waylon and his owner were so at ease—they must be here a lot. I realized that he was holding the door open for me, so I scurried past him, being careful not to look him in the eye.

Once inside, I took a look around. For some reason, I thought it would feel more like a business, but I was immediately struck by how cozy it felt.

This was a home.

There was a place for coats and shoes near the front door. There were even special hooks for cowboy hats.

The entry was open, and I could see down a wide hallway to a living room and kitchen. The house smelled like pie crust, cedar, and leather conditioner—not a combination that I would ever put together, but in here it was perfect. If they ever wanted to sell this, they wouldn't have to use the cookies-in-the-oven trick because this place smelled like home all on its own.

"My dad is waiting for us in the kitchen." His voice came from behind me. I knew he was close. The same electricity that surrounded us in the bar was humming now. It almost distracted me from what he said.

His dad?

That explained why he was so comfortable. His dad was Weston, the owner of the ranch. I groaned inwardly. Hopefully his son didn't have much—if anything—to do with the project.

The Cowboy Heir walked past me and down the hallway, and I followed—trying to pull myself together and slip on the mask of professionalism that was normally a permanent fixture on my face—especially in situations like this.

I didn't like that this man had unnerved me—made me

unsteady. I didn't want anyone to have the power to do that anymore, let alone a stranger.

A very nice stranger who'd left me alone when I needed to work and kissed the hell out of me afterward, but a stranger nonetheless.

When I walked into the kitchen, there was an older man—probably in his midsixties—doing a newspaper crossword puzzle at the long oak table. He was wearing faded blue jeans and a button-down shirt with the sleeves rolled up. I could see faded tattoos, but I couldn't tell what they were.

His salt-and-pepper hair was longish—it curled at his neck—and it matched his neatly trimmed salt-and-pepper beard. He looked up at us, and it was obvious that he was related to my mystery cowboy. They didn't look very much alike—just enough that you knew they belonged in the same family tree. When I saw him, I felt . . . calm, like I'd just found shelter from a storm.

All right, Ada. Get your game face on.

The man stood up and said, "You must be Ada Hart. We're happy to have you." He stretched out his hand, and I took it.

"Thank you so much for having me. It's a pleasure to meet you, Mr. Ryder," I said, trying to keep my voice level and failing not to think about the fact that I could feel someone else's eyes on me.

"Call me Amos, please." Amos? Who the hell was Amos? Where was Weston?

I paused for just a beat too long. "It—it's a pleasure to meet you," I stammered. Great first impression, Ada. "Sorry, I was just expecting to meet Weston, since we've been in contact." Amos's eyes shifted to the cowboy behind me, and a crease appeared between his eyebrows.

Was he confused? Well, that made two of us.

The cowboy behind me cleared his throat. "I'm Weston," he said.

Had I heard him right? No. No. No. Absolutely not. This could not be happening to me.

"But most people call me Wes."

Chapter 6

Wes

Holy shit. The woman from the bar was standing in my house. Not only that, she also happened to be the woman I'd been waiting for all winter—the one who was going to turn my dream into a reality.

Holy *shit*.

"I'm Weston," I said—just then realizing that I hadn't introduced myself earlier. I didn't know why. Maybe I just felt like she already knew me. "But most people call me Wes."

I would say that it was a hell of a coincidence, but I didn't really believe in those.

I'd thought she was a stunner in the Devil's Boot, and I thought she was a stunner now. Her wavy black hair hit just above her collarbone. She was wearing loose black jeans and a tight long-sleeved black T-shirt—which was way too thin for April in the mountains—and her brown eyes were looking everywhere but at me.

I didn't know how to process the fact that I wanted her to look at me. I wanted to hold her gaze again, like I did at the bar, until we ended up in the same place we were last night—caught up in each other.

"I'm sorry my son has bad manners, Miss Hart." My dad's voice cut through my thoughts. "But we're thrilled to have you here." He shot a pointed look at me as if to say *This is your thing, Weston. Pull your weight.*

Right.

Focus.

"Do you wanna sit?" I asked, and gestured toward the table. "We can go over ... uh ... everything." Well, maybe not everything. I made my way past her and pulled out a chair for her across from where my dad was sitting. She looked apprehensive but sat down anyway.

"I'm sorry," she said. "I misplaced my iPad last night—left it somewhere—so I had to write everything down in a notebook, and I might've missed something. I'm going to grab it tonight, so is it okay if we meet tomorrow? I really apologize."

She was talking to my dad, not me, but the disappointment—in herself—that I could hear in her voice triggered a small pang in my chest.

I guess there was a reason I'd grabbed her bag off the floor of the bar last night. Instead of sitting, I went over to the kitchen counter and grabbed the canvas tote, then came back to the table and placed it gently in front of her.

Ada looked up at me, brown eyes wide. I rubbed at the back of my neck and explained, "Things that get left at the Devil's Boot might as well get sucked into a black hole—never to be seen again."

I tore my eyes from her and looked at my dad. I hated that

this was happening under his gaze, but his expression was blank. His eyes were narrowed a little bit, but that was his only tell that the wheels in his head were turning.

The man always cleaned house at his standing poker game, and it was easy to see why.

"Uh . . . thank you?" she said, like she didn't quite know how to react. If I were her, I wouldn't know how to react either. Earlier, I thought this could've been a glass slipper scenario, but now that the situation was unfolding, I felt kind of creepy for taking her bag.

That's probably what she was thinking—that I was fucking creepy.

"I didn't look in it or anything—I just didn't want it to get ruined. I know the bar owner, and he was going to help me track you down to return it."

She nodded slowly, still unsure.

"Funny how things work out, isn't it?" That was my dad. He was smiling a bit now—always so fucking observant. "Weston is right about the Devil's Boot—it's where things go to disappear—people included." Ada pushed out a laugh.

"This is great," she said. It seemed like she was starting to find her footing. I could almost see a mask slipping over her features—what kind of mask, I didn't know, but damn, I wanted to find out. "Thank you," she said to me. "You saved me a trip down that dirt road. I don't think my car would've survived." As I sat down, Ada reached into the bag and pulled out her tablet and stylus.

"So, normally I start by making sure that I answer any questions about the contracts. I know you've signed them"—

she looked at me and then at my dad—"but, Amos, do you have any questions?"

"No. Weston and I reviewed them with our lawyer before signing, and everything looks great." Cam was helping us with the legal stuff. My dad had had another lawyer for years, but he had a soft spot for my niece's mom. She was family, and Amos Ryder took that seriously.

She hadn't yet passed the bar exam when she reviewed the contracts, but she'd taken it in February and there was no doubt in any of our minds that she would. Her results would probably come any day now.

"That's great," Ada responded. She sounded more confident, more professional now. Like she was getting into a groove. "So, we'll finish up any demo that you've already started, then we'll start with the largest undertakings: the kitchen, living spaces, and bathrooms. Once we finish those, we'll start on the bedrooms and the exterior at the same time. If all goes according to plan, we should finish up by June fifteenth, but the end date on the contract is July first because the only thing that's ever certain in a renovation is that something will go wrong." Ada laughed a little.

If I hadn't heard her real laugh at the bar last night, it would've been believable. But this laugh was practiced, calculated.

"My contractor, Evan, will be arriving tomorrow. He'll help manage the project and the local crews." I knew about Evan—he was included in some of the emails, and I'd coordinated his extended stay at the Poppy Mallow Inn just outside of town—but hearing his name fall from her lips now made my nostrils flare.

What the fuck? No, I did not get to be jealous of another man's name on her lips when I'd known her for less than twelve hours. That was asshole behavior, and I tried really fucking hard not to be an asshole.

"I emailed Evan's accommodation reservation to both of you last week, so he should be good to go when he arrives," I said, trying to be helpful.

"Speaking of accommodations," my dad chimed in, "Ada, I know you said that you preferred to stay on-site for long projects when possible." Ada nodded. Where was my dad going with this? I'd already prepped the cabin closest to Baby Blue for her. "Weston prepared one of our cabins for you, but we've been having some water issues due to this year's heavy snowfall. I got word this morning that the cabin has flooded."

Shit. I didn't know that—it must've just happened.

"We'll work on getting it back up to standards, but until then, you're welcome to stay here—in the Big House."

"Oh." Ada seemed caught off guard. "This is your home— I could never impose."

"It's not an imposition, I promise. We've got plenty of space—I've already made up a room for you—and plenty of food, and this way, you can still stay on-site." My dad was smiling. He loved it when people were in the Big House. It was usually just him and me. "Plus, the Big House is closer to the project site than your cabin would've been, and you're welcome to our four-wheelers and side-by-sides, so you don't have to drive your car through the ranch's terrain. And when your cabin is ready, you won't have to go very far."

"Um . . . that's very kind of you . . ." Ada was stumbling over her words. "I do appreciate it, but . . ."

"It's temporary, Ada," I said without thinking, but I had a feeling she didn't want to take the offer because of me. If she preferred to stay on-site, and if that's what helped her set herself up for success, then I didn't want her to have to give that up. "We can probably get your cabin squared away in a week or so."

"This isn't the first time we've flooded," my dad added. "Plus, I make a mean pot of coffee." He winked at her, and it pulled a smile out of Ada—a real one. My dad had a way of putting people at ease.

Ada looked down at the table for a moment before saying, "As long as you're sure it isn't an imposition."

My dad clapped his hands together. "It's settled, then. Now if you'll excuse me, I've got to get back to work." He stood from his chair, and Ada and I stood with him. "Weston can take it from here." He reached out to shake Ada's hand again. "I've got a good feeling about you, Ada. Welcome to Rebel Blue."

And with that, Amos Ryder grabbed his cowboy hat off the table and, looking every bit the rancher he was, headed out the door.

It was like the air knew it was just the two of us now, because it started to hum.

"I'm sorry if that was weird," I said, looking at Ada, who was back to avoiding eye contact. "Finding out who I am, and the fact that I grabbed your bag, and my dad offering to have you stay here—that was a lot of content for a ten-minute conversation."

"Yeah," she breathed—still not looking at me. "Thank you, though, for the bag thing. That place doesn't even have a phone number, so I wasn't holding out hope for a lost and found."

That made me laugh. "How did you even find the Devil's Boot? I don't even know if it shows up on Google Maps. The road you go down to get to it doesn't even have a name."

"It shows up," Ada said—a ghost of a smile was hinting at her lips. "I was looking for somewhere I could get some food, and it was the only place that was still open." Her smile got bigger—like she was sharing a joke with herself.

"But it doesn't. Have food, I mean." I knew it was in Brooks's plan to start bringing a food truck in on the weekends during the summer, but not yet.

"Yeah. Google is a filthy liar." She finally looked at me then, and my heart caught in my chest the way it had last night. I smiled at her, but as soon as I did, she snapped her gaze away.

"Well, the pantry here is always stocked, and if you have any favorites, just let me know and we'll get them for you. Evan is welcome to the pantry too." I tried to shake off the disappointment I'd felt when she looked away. I didn't like how weird it felt between us. "I can show you your room, so you can get settled, and then I can take you over to the job site?"

"That would be great. Thank you."

I assumed that my dad would put her up in Emmy's old room because it had its own bathroom and it was the most private.

It also had a damn good view.

I led Ada down a hall, where we passed my room, and then toward the back of the house where Emmy's room was. My dad had left the door open.

"This is where you'll be," I said. "It used to be my sister's room, but it's got the best view, so my dad likes to leave it for guests when he hasn't taken it over as his yoga studio."

Ada let out a little snort. "I wasn't expecting that," she said.

"If there's one thing about Amos Ryder, it's that he's full of surprises," I said with a smile. Some days I wasn't very proud to be me, but I was always proud to be my dad's son.

I motioned for Ada to go ahead of me, and she stepped into the room. "That door there"—I pointed—"goes to an en suite bathroom, and if you round the corner just outside the bedroom door"—I gestured toward the door—"there's a sitting area with a similar view. That's the very back of the house." It was where I liked to draw whenever I had a chance.

"This is great. Thank you for letting me stay here. I just feel better when I can be the first one on-site and the last one to leave, and staying close by makes that easier. I would sleep on-site if I could."

"We're happy to have you," I said sincerely. Not because I felt pulled to her, not because she was beautiful, and not because I'd kissed her. I was happy she was here because her being here meant that I was on my way to having something at Rebel Blue that was mine.

And that was priceless to me.

Chapter 7

Ada

At this point, it was very hard to believe that my life wasn't just some big cosmic joke. Weston Ryder was a hot, age-appropriate, and seemingly kind cowboy—not the weather-beaten old rancher I'd been imagining.

And I'd kissed him.

Well, "kissed" was the benign term—especially when I thought about the way he'd pushed me against the wall and pinned my hands above my head, or when I remembered how he felt pressed up against me.

And the memory of it would be all I was going to have, because it would never happen again.

Not only was my job *his* project, I was living under his roof, and he was technically my *boss*.

Oh god.

I made out with my boss.

Which was bad enough on the surface, but it got a hell of a lot worse when I realized that I had unknowingly placed myself on the wrong side of an unfair power dynamic with a man.

Again.

Stupid decisions have consequences.

And now I was going to be forced to spend the next four months working for him, and in the closest of quarters. Even now, I was closer to him than I wanted to be—in the passenger seat of a side-by-side and wearing one of his big Carhartt jackets.

It was a lot colder in Wyoming in April than I'd thought it would be, but I was just planning to grin and bear it until I could grab some more layers. However, Weston the kind cowboy grabbed this jacket out of the coat closet as we walked out the door because he didn't want me to be cold.

Now not only was I warm, I was enveloped in a masculine cedar scent that I wanted to bottle. Weston—who told me several times he preferred Wes, but that felt too familiar—was taking me to the job site and giving me a tour of Rebel Blue along the way.

It was even more striking now than it was on the drive in.

"So, the job site is what used to be the Big House," he was saying. "It's the one that my dad grew up in. He built the one we live in shortly after he married my mom." I appreciated the history lesson—I liked knowing about the places I was working on. It helped me create something that the owners or residents would love. "This part of the ranch is where most of the original structures are. Toward the east we have our family stables, and toward the west is where you'll find the ranch hand cabins and the larger stables."

"How many people work here?" I asked, genuinely curious about the workings of something as massive as Rebel Blue Ranch.

"Give or take forty—depending on the time of year—but we're having another growth spurt, so that number will probably be higher this time next year. Especially with the guest ranch. We'll need wranglers and another cook, at least."

"And does your whole family work on the ranch?" The family photos in the house gave me the impression that the Ryders were a close bunch.

"Yeah. My brother Gus is the oldest, and he's my dad's second in command. He'll inherit the ranch someday." I tried to place the shift in his voice. It wasn't envy or jealousy—maybe it was just respect? "And my little sister, Emmy, does the riding lessons, horse training, and ranch hand work—tending to cattle, maintenance on the grounds—that sort of thing. And Brooks is here a few times a week and fills in where we need him, usually odd jobs."

Brooks. I knew that name—the bartender. I knew there was something familial between them, but he didn't say "brother." "He's the bartender, right? How does he fit in?"

"I forgot you'd met him already." A blush was creeping up Wes's neck. "He's . . . Well, he's my brother's best friend, and he and Emmy are together." I wonder how that all went down. I never really saw myself living in a small town. I'd never even been to one before now, but I bet the gossip was fun.

"So they're dating?" I asked.

"That feels like too normal a word for them," he said. I waited for him to continue. "When you meet them, you'll get it. It's easy to see that they're a forever type of thing." I looked over at Wes, who had his eyes on the dirt path ahead of us. One of his dimples had appeared. It was obvious he held a lot of love for the people in his life. "So to describe them as just 'dating' feels weird. They're not anything I can really describe—they just sort of *are*. You know?"

I didn't know, but I'd take his word for it.

"And where does Teddy fit in?" I asked, because she had to have some sort of pull with this family to convince them to hire a no-name designer from San Francisco.

"Teddy is Emmy's best friend—they've been inseparable since birth, basically. And they roomed together at college." Why didn't Emmy's name sound familiar to me, then? I'd never met Teddy's best friend, but I'd heard about her off-handedly.

"I feel like I remember Teddy's roommate in college having a weird name," I said, mostly without thinking. Wes laughed, a big, loud laugh. The type of laugh that would cause me to wonder how the hell a person could be that happy.

"Emmy's full name is Clementine," he said, still laughing a little. "But she usually goes by Emmy. My dad is the only one who uses our full names regularly." Clementine. That was the name—I knew it was fruit-related.

"Clementine like the song?"

Wes's smile got bigger. "Yeah, but don't say that to her. Sore subject."

Luckily, the side-by-side came to a stop before I had to attempt to cover the fact that I'd just inadvertently insulted Wes's sister, who he was obviously extremely fond of.

I didn't have any siblings, so I'd never really understood the bond.

Honestly, I didn't really understand a lot of bonds. I loved and respected my parents a normal amount, but I don't think I would live on a ranch in Wyoming with them.

As far as friends went, I didn't really have any—not because I didn't want them, but because making friends as an adult is hard. Honestly, I enjoyed solitude, but there's a difference between that and being lonely.

For a long time, I've mostly been lonely.

My divorce was more than a year ago, but I felt lonely before that.

Now that I was thinking about it, I didn't remember a time when I hadn't felt lonely.

Damn. That was a harsh realization for ten o'clock in the morning.

I swallowed the prickly sensation in my throat and looked up at the house we had stopped at.

It was big and beautiful, but in an unassuming way. Its paint was chipped and it looked a little haunted. Even if I hadn't seen the photos of the inside, I would be able to tell that it was going to take a lot of work to make this thing not only livable but also a desirable place to stay.

That didn't scare me.

When I looked at the house, I didn't see the sinking roof, the plywood doors and windows, or the overgrown weeds around it.

I saw my dream.

This house was not only my golden ticket out of California, it was also my pit stop on the way to something bigger.

I didn't know what that something bigger was yet, but I knew it was out there. I'd worked so hard to get out of my home state, I wasn't about to just do this project and then go back.

Wes—I mean Weston—got out of the driver's side, and I followed on the passenger side, more slowly—not able to take my eyes off the house. Seeing the house in person was like lighting a match and my brain was gasoline. Once the two met, they couldn't be stopped.

I was in the middle of a thought about exterior paint colors—white was classic but overdone, a version of baby blue was calling to me—when Weston—whose voice was entirely too close—said, "We've maintained her the best we could, but this winter took a heavier toll on some of the older structures than we were expecting."

"She's beautiful," I said. Yeah, she was showing her age, but she wasn't decrepit or in disrepair. She just needed someone to believe in her.

"Yeah, she is," Weston said. His voice was still so close, but I didn't want to find out how close, so I started walking toward the house. The air was cool on my face. It felt nice, but I was grudgingly grateful for the warm jacket.

I knew how big the house was from the specs that Wes had sent me—around thirty-five hundred square feet—but it didn't look or feel that big. It wasn't gaudy or overbearing. It almost felt like it had grown here instead of being built, like it was meant to be in this field, on this ranch, with the big blue sky kissing the mountains as its backdrop.

I loved it.

Before I knew it, I was at the front steps. This place called to me. What's that saying? The mountains are calling and I must go? Well, the old house in the mountains was whispering, and I needed to get inside.

I heard Wes's voice behind me as I started up the stairs:

"Watch out for that third step, it's tricky—" He didn't get to finish his sentence because when I got to the third step, the top of the stair flipped up, and I started going in the opposite direction from where I wanted to go.

I shut my eyes as I braced myself to hit the ground, but I didn't hit the ground. Instead I hit something firm and warm that smelled like cedar.

Wes caught me.

One of his arms was at my waist, and his other hand was cradling my head. When I opened my eyes, I was staring up at him. The way we were right now reminded me of last night. My tongue involuntarily darted across my bottom lip, and I watched Wes's eyes track the movement.

The air around us started to hum—the same way it had last night at the bar and in the Big House kitchen this morning—and I was desperate to let go again—to lose control for just a second.

"You okay?" Wes asked. His voice was low. "I tried to warn you." He smiled, and I had a prime view of those dimples.

I felt a cool breeze against my face and remembered where I was. Outside. Wyoming. Rebel Blue Ranch. I looked past Wes's face and saw the house.

My dream.

My chance.

That was enough to jolt me out of the trance that only this man was capable of putting me in. I scrambled to my feet and out of his arms. I didn't know how to recover from that situation, so I dusted myself off, even though I'd never actually hit the ground.

"I'm fine," I snapped with more annoyance than necessary. I hoped my tone would push this man further away, because when he was near me, I was liable to do stupid things, and I couldn't afford any more consequences.

When his dimples disappeared, I immediately wanted to apologize—an unnatural impulse for me—but I didn't. I couldn't.

"Right. Okay." He looked at the ground. "When you walk up the steps, just make sure you step in the center of the third one so it stays in place, or skip it altogether." I gave him a nod and let him lead the way this time.

I watched as he removed the large slab of wood from the front door with a grunt, and desperately tried to ignore the butterflies in my stomach.

Honestly, the reaction I was having to him was cause for concern.

I didn't *want* to react this way. My body didn't typically respond to people like this—not even my ex-husband, although he didn't want me either, so that could've been part of it. Still, this wasn't normal for me, and I didn't like it. It made my head fuzzy, and I needed that little asshole to be crystal fucking clear.

Wes turned back to me and I quickly looked away, avoiding eye contact as I moved into the house.

When I got inside, I looked around and felt the same feelings I'd felt outside, but there was one that was so unexpected that it made my heart jump into my throat.

Hope.

Chapter 8

Wes

I was an idiot.

But at least I was aware I was an idiot.

In this situation, though, I would've lost no matter which decision I made. I either could've let her fall, or I could've caught her. I would've felt bad for weeks if I'd let her fall, but I also felt bad now for touching her—even if it was to keep her from hitting the dirt—when she very obviously did not want to be touched.

My hands had reached for her before I even knew what they were doing. Then she was in my arms and my world stopped again.

Just like it did when she'd rolled her car window down today.

And just like it did last night.

I didn't know how to deal with this. I'd been attracted to people before, had a few girlfriends, but not for years.

And honestly, I didn't mind. At the risk of sounding like an asshole, I knew there were women in Meadowlark who wanted me—for either a fling or some sort of relationship.

The older ladies in Meadowlark were always dying to set me up with their niece or their granddaughter, saying I needed to find a nice girl and settle down, and the Meadowlark gossip mill could never figure out why I hadn't done that.

It was that word "nice" that frustrated me.

It wasn't a bad word, but to me it didn't feel like a good one. I'd always been called a "nice" guy. It didn't matter the context—with friends, with women, with strangers—I was always "nice."

Again, not bad, not good—just there.

Maybe that's why the thought of a nice girl from this nice town didn't feel like . . . enough for me.

But sometimes I wanted it to be.

The truth—at least part of it—was that I liked my life as is. I never felt that because I wasn't in a relationship I was missing out or anything.

The other part of it was more personal. It was deep-rooted insecurity that came from having a brain that I sometimes felt like wasn't my own.

I'd been diagnosed with major depressive disorder about five years ago. At this point, I'd learned to live with it, and I had a regimen—medication, therapy, physical activity—that worked for me, which meant that things didn't get as dark as they used to. It's why I liked to draw too. Drawing helped my brain be kinder to me.

Logically, I had the depression bull by the horns.

But depression wasn't a logical disease. It was an unexpected cold front in the middle of July. It was impossible to predict, which meant that I spent much of my time worrying about when the other shoe was going to drop. Not if, but *when* I would sink into another dark hole and have to decide to claw my way out of it.

Even when I was happy, I was thinking about when I wouldn't be.

Honestly, it was exhausting. It took up so much of my brain even though I recognized that there wasn't very much I could do about it.

That's what I meant when I said that my brain didn't feel like my own sometimes. It felt like it belonged to my mental illness instead.

And, frankly, that sucked.

"This place is incredible." Ada's soft voice brought me back to Baby Blue. She was standing in the middle of what used to be the living room and staring up at the vaulted ceilings. "How long did you say it's been empty?"

She was looking at the old Big House the way I looked at it—like it was a dream. Yeah, I wanted a guest ranch, but I also wanted this place to *be* something. Not just a building that *used* to be something. I wanted it to stand on its own.

It was a part of Rebel Blue, and Rebel Blue was a part of me.

"My parents moved into the new Big House before my brother was born, so probably around thirty-five years."

"It's in good shape for being empty for that long," she responded, running her hand across the kitchen wallpaper. "But that does mean that we're probably going to be in for some surprises."

I smiled at that. "Honestly, I'm just hoping that I don't see any more animals in here—dead or alive."

Ada's brown eyes widened. I liked her eyes. They were dark, but they had a variety of light and dark rings—like the inside of a tree. The rings—they were like those hypnosis circles.

"Yeah," I responded. "The raccoons are almost as fond of this place as I am. I had the raccoon guy come, but those fuckers are ruthless."

A laugh bubbled out of her—not like the one in the kitchen and not like the one last night. This one was like she didn't want to laugh, but she couldn't stop it.

Who didn't want to laugh?

"The raccoon guy?" she asked on the end of her laugh.

"Yeah. Wayne."

Ada raised one of her dark eyebrows. "What exactly does the raccoon guy do?"

"He takes care of the raccoons," I said, a little confused. "He comes to get 'em and then safely relocates them." What else would a raccoon guy do?

One corner of her mouth twitched. "Of course there's a raccoon guy," she said. More to herself than to me, I think. She walked toward the workbench that I'd set up between the kitchen and living room. "All right," she said. "Let's go over what this week is going to look like."

As she pulled her newly returned iPad out of her newly returned bag, I walked up next to her, making sure I kept a professional distance. I didn't want to make her uncomfortable, but I saw her stiffen anyway, so I took another step away, and her posture eased a little bit. She pulled up a few different files, flipping to what looked like a schedule.

"So, Evan will be here tomorrow, and he'll be overseeing the rest of the demo. From the look of the place now"—Gus, Brooks, and I had spent the last few weekends getting a head start, neither of them ever said no to hitting shit with a hammer—"it shouldn't take that long.

"The construction crew is set to start next Monday, right?" I asked, trying to show her that I'd done my homework. She nodded. "Thank you for accommodating my request for a local crew," I said. "My dad—well, my whole family, really— is happy about that. It's important for Meadowlark."

"No problem," she said, looking at me this time. "I never thought about it before, but it makes sense to utilize the local economy—especially for a project like this. I'm assuming you guys are a big part of it." I nodded. That was true. "Honestly, I've never thought too critically about that before you mentioned it, but it's something I want to incorporate into my future projects."

"It is very much appreciated in this small town," I said, locking eyes with her again. Finally. Her eyes were like magnets, and when she wasn't looking at me, my eyes searched all of her until they could find hers again.

I felt it then, my heartbeat. I heard it too. When our eyes locked in like this, something unlocked in me, and my whole body remembered what it was like to get lost in this woman—this stranger—and it craved that feeling.

I think she felt it too, because she took a step toward me.

So I took a step toward her.

In the silence of the room, I heard her breath hitch.

Fuck, I wanted to hear that sound a million more times.

We stepped toward each other again—toeing the line.

Ada was a stranger to me, but I didn't want her to be. Maybe what happened in the bar last night was fate.

Maybe Baby Blue wasn't my only chance at something bigger—at something that could be mine.

I wanted to touch her—to reach out and cup her face. I almost did, but when I went to take the last step, the old floorboard under my feet creaked loud enough to shock us both back a step.

Ada's eyes snapped away from mine, and she shook her head. "Listen," she said. Her tone was harsher than I'd heard it. It wasn't the cool professional one she'd been using with me all day. This one was angry. "I didn't come here for some stupid 'Cowboy Take Me Away' fantasy. I came here to do a job."

"I'm sorry," I said quickly, not thinking too hard about the fact that she was using the Chicks against me. "I didn't mean—"

But Ada didn't let me finish. "The kiss last night was hot, but it didn't mean anything. I was bored, and you were there. It should've never happened." Okay, ouch. I didn't know why that hit me so hard, but this woman threw words like Gus threw punches.

She was right: It was just a kiss.

Even though it didn't feel like "just" anything. To me, anyway.

"And it's never going to happen again. This is strictly professional. Do you understand?" Ada's eyes were cold, and her voice was sharp. Compared to the laughs I got from her last night and today when I told her about the raccoon guy, this felt like a swift kick in the stomach.

But I wasn't about to tell her that.

She was right. She was here to work, and I needed her to do a good job.

So I nodded and said, "I understand."

And tried to ignore the sound of my heart cracking.

Chapter 9

Ada

My opinion on this had recently changed, but I was now convinced that it was much easier to hate your boss than it was to be attracted to him—especially when he literally looked like he'd just stepped out of every woman's cowboy fantasy.

For the past week, I'd successfully avoided being alone or having to interact with Weston beyond questions about the project. Luckily, he woke up earlier than me and did whatever it is that cowboys do for the first few hours of the day before stopping by the project site. Usually he'd find some way to be helpful, but other times he would just check in before going back to work.

Even though I was seeing less of him than I had during my first day in Meadowlark, I wasn't able to avoid him entirely. That was impossible.

And as the weeks went on, it would only get more impossible. At the beginning of a project, Evan took the lead. I basically became a part of his crew during this time—doing demo, framing, and construction—but it was also my crunch time for making sure we had the materials to put on top of the foundation that Evan and the crew were creating once it was ready.

I also had to worry about keeping up with my socials. I posted stories every day, three photo posts and one video post per week during projects. It could get overwhelming, but I didn't see it as a chore. My job as I knew it existed because of the community that I'd built around my page, and I loved sharing my work with them.

There were people out there who thought I wasn't a "real" interior designer because I didn't go to school for it. I wondered what those people would think about me if they knew I *did* go to school for it—I just didn't finish.

Like any space, the internet had its share of assholes, but I was grateful that they were minimal on Home Is Where the Hart Is. And my community seemed to like me. I ignored the little voice in my head that told me it was only because they didn't know me.

A few days ago, I'd posted a photo that had Wes in it. It was unintentional, and he was just in the background, staring up at the house with a smile, but it took less than five minutes for me to start getting comments that said things like "Save a horse" and "That cowboy is hitting different."

I tried not to be annoyed by it.

And right now, Weston was wearing a white T-shirt that might've been slightly too tight and swinging a sledgehammer into the wall between two of the bedrooms.

He was letting out these little grunts that were making me wonder if someone had accidentally jacked up the thermostat.

Being physically attracted to him was . . . weird. It wasn't something that happened to me often. I could look at someone and know that they were good-looking, but if any other man I'd been attracted to had been letting out mini porn grunts, I'd probably have wanted to punch him in the face.

Not Weston, though.

"Ada, you good?" Evan said next to me, and I realized I'd been staring at Weston.

"Yeah, sorry. What's up?" I asked. Evan and I had been working together for a little over a year, but I felt like I'd known him my whole life. He wasn't really my friend, but he was more than a co-worker.

He also knew more about me than anyone else, but not because I'd told him. Evan's husband, Carter, worked with my ex-husband, Chance. It's how we met, so when everything with Chance went down, Evan knew all about it.

We didn't talk about it, but I knew Evan would be there for me if I needed him, and his being in Wyoming was proof of that. This was my first job outside California, and most of my jobs had been in the San Francisco area. When I told Evan about Wyoming and the project timeline, I didn't know if he would come, but he did.

And I was grateful.

"Nothing," Evan said. "I just wanted to make you aware that your staring is about as subtle as a gunshot." His eyes moved to Weston and then back to me.

I rolled my eyes but was grateful he'd called me out on it. The last thing I needed was for Weston to catch me staring and get the wrong idea about what that meant.

Even though something told me he wasn't that kind of

guy. When I told him that nothing was going to happen and that this was just a job, I expected him to . . . push—at least a little.

But he didn't.

He respected my boundary, and even though that was the bare minimum, it was new for me. Something about the way he interacted with me, the crew, everybody, made me think he was a nice guy.

But I'd had bad experiences with a nice guy, and I wasn't about to go for two. Plus, I had no desire to be in a relationship. My life was finally mine, and I was still trying to figure out what that meant for me.

When I went back to the materials spreadsheet on my laptop—marking off what had been ordered and what hadn't, checking confirmations and updating my supplier contact logs—I heard a sound that I didn't normally hear on a construction site in this stage: heels.

I looked up and saw a woman coming through the front door. She was probably taller than me even without the heels, but with them, she was most likely closing in on six feet. She had dark curly hair that fell to her elbows. She was wearing the hell out of her long-sleeved-white-shirt-tucked-into-black-wide-leg-slacks ensemble and carrying a leather messenger bag. It looked like one of those bags that were simple but cost an insane amount of money.

Her eyes, which looked black from here, were scanning the space, looking for someone. When they locked on Wes, my heart dropped.

Shit. Shit. *Shit.* Did I accidently mack on a man with a girlfriend? A very hot, very powerful-looking girlfriend?

That's what you get for making out with a stranger in a bar and not asking any questions, Ada. But he'd kissed me back. So this was his fault too.

I fucking *knew* it. I knew that this man couldn't be as nice as he seemed.

Wes had stopped hammering and brought his T-shirt up to his face to wipe away some sweat.

Damn.

If I posted that on my page, I'd have a million followers within the week. And now that I was really mad at him, I got angry thinking about how all a man had to do was exist and be semi-attractive for people to flock to him.

He made eye contact with the woman and gave her a wave and a dimpled smile. When she got closer to him, he went in for a hug but she stopped him with a hand in front of her and gestured toward his sweaty form.

Glistening form might have been the more accurate term.

He laughed and then motioned toward the table that I was sitting at. Great. They were coming my way.

"Ada," Weston called as they approached the table. "I want you to meet someone." I stood up and thought about how I would tell her that her boyfriend actually sucked. I'd have to do it later—I couldn't drop that bomb in the middle of a construction site.

"This is Cam, or, uh, Camille," he said like he wasn't used to using her full name. Her name fit her. It felt . . . regal. "She's the attorney who's helping with the project."

"Lawyer, Wes," Camille corrected. "Lawyers have graduated from law school, and attorneys are lawyers who have passed the bar. I haven't done that yet."

"Yes, you have. You just don't have the results yet," he said. Huh. What would it be like to have someone be so sure of you and your abilities? She rolled her eyes, but she was clearly fighting a smile. Okay, so he did have that effect on everyone.

"Ada," I said as I reached out my hand. "Nice to meet you."

"Camille, but everyone around here calls me Cam." Because everyone around here, including Weston, was familiar to her. As I shook her hand, I noticed the absolutely massive diamond on her left ring finger, and my heart dropped again. Was he . . . *engaged*? God, I'd really fucked up. "I've never actually been in here before," she said as she looked around. "I can already tell it's going to be great."

"Ada's vision is incredible," Weston said immediately, and his eyes landed on me, bright and soft. "She's talented."

"Obviously," Cam replied, and she smiled at me warmly.

"So, uh," I said, trying to think of a way to ask about Weston and Cam's relationship. If they were engaged, I felt like she had a right to know about the kiss, but I didn't really have any friends who were women, or friends in general, so I didn't know for sure how I should handle this. But surely Weston would've mentioned a fiancée in the rundown about his family? "How long have you guys been together?"

Weston's eyes looked like they were going to bulge out of his head, and Cam guffawed. I didn't get it.

"We're not," Cam said at the same time Weston said, "She's family."

Oh god.

Did I just assume that he was engaged to his cousin or something? *Goddammit, Ada. You are on a roll.*

"Wes's brother is my daughter's dad." Well, that was a mouthful. So she was engaged to his brother? Cam must've seen my eyes dart to her ring because she said: "And no, I'm not engaged to his brother either. It's a whole thing," she said with a wave of her hand.

"I—I'm so sorry. I saw the ring, and I just assumed . . ." Foot, meet mouth.

"No, it's okay," Cam said with a laugh. "It's refreshing to meet someone who isn't aware of my entire romantic history." She seemed so genuine. I hadn't met anyone in Weston's family yet besides his dad, but if all of them were like this, I was going to need to work on the fact that I always assumed the worst.

Weston, who looked like he was still recovering from the fact that I'd assumed he was engaged to Cam, said, "Now that we've established the fact that I'm not engaged to my brother's baby mama"—he looked at Cam—"do you have those papers for me to sign?"

Cam laughed again. "Seriously, Ada. You made my day. It's fun to feel like a mystery," she said. "And yes. Just a few occupancy papers that I need to take to City Hall this week." She set her bag on the table, and I felt bad that it was going to be covered in dust within a millisecond, but she didn't seem to mind.

She flipped through a few files with her fingertips before pulling out a manila folder. She opened it and went through a few pages, quickly telling Weston where to sign, before she looked at me again.

"So, Ada, how are you liking Meadowlark?" Cam asked. When she smiled at me, it felt genuine.

"It's nice," I said truthfully. I would be lying if I said I wasn't totally smitten by the mountains and the big blue sky. "I haven't seen much of it, but the ranch is beautiful."

"I mean, you've been to the bar and the coffee shop, so you've seen half the town, basically," Cam said with a wave of her hand. I had no idea how she knew about either of those things, which must've been written all over my face. "Small town, remember?"

"The Hallmark movies aren't lying, are they?" I said, hoping my sarcasm landed the right way.

"No, but we definitely don't have as many hot inn owners."

"But you seem to have a monopoly on hot cowboys." I said it without thinking. It got Weston's attention, his head snapped up to look at me. Our eyes met for a fraction of a second and I immediately regretted it.

The air hummed, and I did my best to ignore it.

Cam laughed again. "You are definitely in the right place for those."

"Tell me more about these hot cowboys," Weston said, leaning on the workbench in an annoyingly cocky and attractive way. "Anyone specific?" He crossed his arms over his broad chest, and even out of the corner of my eye, I could see those godforsaken dimples on full display.

"Your dad," I quipped without meeting his gaze. I'd already made that mistake today, and I didn't want a repeat of what happened last time Weston and I had prolonged eye contact. Cam smacked her hand over her mouth and broke into a fit of giggles, but I was saved from Weston's response by a little human throwing herself into the back of Cam's legs.

"Mama!" the little one squealed. Cam was still recovering from her laughter but wrangled her kid up into her arms and gave her a squeeze.

"Hi, Sunshine," Cam said. Cam's daughter had her hair, but her eyes were green and she had two big dimples that looked familiar to me. She was wearing what looked like a pink soccer uniform.

"Riley," a gruff voice called from the door, "I literally just told you that you needed a hard hat before we went inside." I looked up to see who the voice belonged to and what do you know, I was met with yet another cowboy. This one I assumed was Gus.

It was obvious that Weston and Gus were related, but where Wes wore a smile, Gus wore a frown. His hair and eyes were also darker, and he was sporting a neatly trimmed mustache. It took a special kind of man to pull off a mustache, and Gus seemed to be doing it.

"I already have a hard head," the little human—Riley—called back to him. "You said that when I didn't want to put my jammies on."

"Not a hard head, a hard *hat,*" Gus said with a sigh. He was walking toward us now.

"I don't know what that is," Riley said, and Gus shook his head.

"She's got you there," Cam remarked. "Wonder where she gets that hard head from." Her daughter had her arms around Cam's neck and was looking at me as she nuzzled into her mom's shoulder.

"Who are you?" Riley asked, looking straight at me.

"I'm Ada. Who are you?"

"Riley Amos Ryder," she said. Cute.

"Nice to meet you, Riley Amos Ryder," I said with a smile I couldn't help.

"Do you have a middle name? What's your last name?"

"Sorry," Cam interjected. "This is one of her things right now. She needs to know everyone's full name." I nodded at her, letting her know it was okay.

"Ada Althea Hart," I said, sure that my mother would be thrilled that someone had asked my full name. Althea was my grandmother's name. The grandmother who gave my mom the money she needed to get to the United States from Greece when she was twenty-two.

Riley nodded in what looked like approval. "That's pretty," she said. "I like your drawings." She pointed at my arm that was covered in a tattoo sleeve.

"Thank you. I like your pink soccer uniform."

"My dad has drawings too, but you can only see them when we go swimming," Riley stated. I liked that about kids—they would just tell you things. No secrets, no filter, just vibes. "And Uncle Wes told me that Uncle Brooks has a drawing on his butt, but I've never seen it." *See what I mean?* "So I don't know for sure."

I heard Gus sigh, and Cam started laughing again.

I felt a laugh bubbling up too, and I didn't know how to react to it. It felt like when you eat a bunch of sour candy and wash it down with a soda and the back of your throat fizzes. It wasn't a bad feeling, but it was a feeling I didn't know how to handle.

"Riley," Gus said.

Riley looked at him. "What?"

"It's not polite to talk to someone about your uncle's butt when you've known them for less than five minutes."

"Oh." Riley looked confused. "Sorry."

"It's okay," I said. "Thank you for telling me about all the drawings."

"On that note," Cam said, "I need to get this little chatterbox to soccer practice"—she looked at Riley—"and we've gotta do something about this thing your dad calls a ponytail." Wes gathered up the papers he'd signed and placed them back in Cam's folder and then put the folder back into her messenger bag, since her hands were full.

"I did my best, Cam," Gus said with a shrug.

Riley groaned in a way that hit a little too close to home coming from someone who couldn't be older than five or six. "Can I be goalie today, Mom? I hate running."

"I'll think about it," Cam said with an amused smile. Gus took Cam's bag off the table and gently slung it over her shoulder.

"Kick ass, Sunshine," he said to Riley. "Love you." He kissed his daughter's forehead, and she kissed her palm and pressed it against his cheek.

"Love you."

"Can you pick her up tomorrow?" Cam asked.

"Yeah, I should be able to," Gus said. "If something comes up, I'll send Brooks or Emmy."

Cam nodded. "Thank you," she replied. "All right, Riles. Say bye." Riley waved her little hand, and Wes, Gus, and I all waved back.

"Love you, kid," Wes said. "Thanks, Cam. For helping out."

"No problem. I'll drop these off, and I'll text you with anything else. And, Ada, it was nice to meet you. Let me know if you ever want to grab coffee or something—we can really get those Meadowlark tongues wagging."

"Sure thing," I said, even though the chances of my joining her for coffee were slim. I wanted to—Cam seemed great—but I just didn't know how to have friends, really. I was afraid that if she talked to me for more than five minutes, she'd decide she didn't like me as much as she thought she did. I was best in small doses.

"See you all later," Cam called as she walked to the door, and Riley waved to us again, and I couldn't help but wave back.

I turned toward Wes, who was looking at me.

He was always looking at me, and I was always looking at him.

It was a problem.

A big fucking problem.

So I decided to look at Gus instead, but he was already looking at his brother with one eyebrow raised, and his brother was looking at me, so we were just in a big weird lookfest, and I needed it to stop.

"I'm Ada," I said, reaching my hand out toward Gus. He kept his eyes on his younger brother for a second longer before turning to me.

"Gus Ryder. Nice to finally meet you," he said as he shook my hand. Firmly. Ah, so he was one of those guys.

"Likewise. I like your kid."

Gus shook his head, but I could see a smile in his eyes. "She's a good one."

"All right." Wes clapped his hands together. "Now that we've all met, Gus, I'll give you the walk-through."

"It's okay," Gus responded as he folded his arms over his chest and leaned against the workbench. "I want to talk to Ada about the project."

I'd never seen Weston anything less than jovial until now. He looked . . . nervous. His throat was working and he was tapping one of his index fingers on the workbench repeatedly while he rubbed his chin with his other hand.

"I'm happy to walk you through," I said. "But Weston knows everything that I know."

I didn't know why I suddenly felt the need to do something that I thought would calm Weston down.

That wasn't like me.

Chapter 10

Wes

I learned a lot about myself this week. First, I apparently had a thing for tattooed women in overalls who ignored me most of the time. A really big thing. Second, apparently I gave off the energy that I would kiss said woman in a bar hallway while I was engaged to someone else.

That didn't make me feel good, and I hated that Ada had assumed that about me. But it also made me wonder if she knew someone who *would* do that.

And if that was the case, I hated that too.

It was so easy to forget that she didn't know me and I didn't know her—even though I desperately wanted to.

It was the end of the first week, and the project had been coming along without a hitch. I knew that wouldn't last forever, but damn, Ada was . . . impressive. She and Evan connected with the crew in a way that made them want to listen. Ada was quiet and professional—I'd heard crew members refer to her as "cool," or "aloof," but I didn't think that was the case. Especially because every once in a while she'd throw out a joke that got the whole crew hollering. Then she'd sink back into her work, which is where she seemed the most comfortable.

She was always tucking pens behind both of her ears. She was so immersed in her work that she didn't realize she already had one, so she ended up with these little pen horns.

It was fucking adorable.

I liked her a lot. But it was obvious that she was trying to have as little contact with me as possible, so I did my best to take the hint.

Even though all I wanted was to be near her.

I wanted to figure out what else made her laugh the way she did that night at the bar. I wanted to know what songs she listened to when she was having a bad day, or a good one, and what her favorite food was.

I wanted to know if her body reacted to mine the same way mine did to hers.

I wanted a chance.

But none of that was in the cards. Ada had drawn her line, and I didn't want to cross it. Well, I did want to cross it. But I wanted her to *want* me to cross it.

Our kiss was still running on a loop in my brain. Every time I saw her, I remembered how pliable her body felt under my hands and how responsive she was to my touch.

I remembered the way she bit my lip and how she moaned into my mouth when I pinned her hands to the door.

Goddamn.

I didn't get this way about women. I didn't *want* to get this way. Because of that, I sometimes wondered if there was something wrong with me. I mean, I knew there were some things wrong with me—there are some things wrong with everyone—but my neutrality toward many of the women who had ever shown interest in me made me the odd man out, especially because I grew up around Gus and Brooks.

Before Emmy, Brooks was a playboy, and Gus would deny it now, but before Riley, he wasn't exactly known for commitment because he never let any woman in. Except for Cam, but it wasn't because he was in love with her, it was because she was his friend and he respected her.

Now he wasn't a commitment-phobe, he was a dedicated father, and women liked that, too, but Gus still had the door closed on any sort of relationship.

As for me, it wasn't that I didn't want one—it was that I didn't want one with anyone who'd ever been interested in me. And now I wanted to get to know the girl who was decidedly not interested.

Great.

Speaking of that girl, I could see her in her ridiculous little car as I walked toward the front of the Big House. It was Saturday morning, so there was no work at Baby Blue today. I'd taken my horse, Ziggy, on one of the trails around the ranch early this morning and then popped over to the riding ring to see Emmy.

I looked down at my watch. It was a little past ten, which was later than I expected. Ada was banging on her steering wheel, and I wondered why until I heard her try to start the car and it wouldn't turn over.

The way that car was squealing and shaking when she drove it into Rebel Blue earlier last week, I'm surprised it got her to Wyoming, let alone lasted this long.

I walked up to her car and tapped on the window. She

jumped and flashed me a dirty look after the surprise wore off, but I just smiled at her. I'd take her dirty looks over anyone else's affectionate ones any day.

"Something wrong?" I asked as she opened her car door.

"This stupid piece of shit won't start," she said with a huff. She laid her head on the steering wheel, defeated.

"Where were you headed?" I asked, trying not to overstep.

"I just wanted to go buy a few hoodies and a few other things in town," she said, head still against the steering wheel.

"We have an extra truck you can use," I said. "It's in the garage."

Ada looked up at me. "Really? You'd let me use it?"

"Yeah," I said. "Why wouldn't I? No one else is using it."

"It's not the ugly blue one that's parked next to me, is it?" she asked, throwing a worried glance at Emmy's truck, and I chuckled.

"No, that's my sister's, but I'll be sure to let her know you think her pride and joy is ugly." Ada's eyes widened. Those big brown eyes did something to me.

She bit her bottom lip, and I was hit with the memory of her biting mine. "That's . . . really nice of you. That would be great. Thank you."

"Yeah, the keys are already in it. Follow me." I held her car door open as she got out before shutting it and heading toward the garage.

I walked us over to my old GMC Sierra pickup. It wasn't in the best shape, but it was drivable, and a hell of a lot more reliable than the car Ada'd rolled up in. Safer too. No collision could take this steel cage out.

It was at the back of the garage, so I'd have to move my truck to get it out. Ada looked at it, shook her head, and said, "I've never seen so many trucks in my life as I have at this ranch."

"Welcome to Wyoming," I said as I opened the driver's-side door.

"Maybe I won't get as many stares from the townspeople when I drive this bad boy," she said. "This'll help me fit in."

"I hate to break it to you," I said, "but a beautiful woman is always going to get stares. No matter what she's driving." As soon as I said it I regretted it. Not because I didn't think she was beautiful, but because I felt like I had just pushed on her boundary.

It was like I could see Ada's walls immediately going up. Shit.

She looked away from me and didn't say a thing. When she looked inside the cab of the truck, her shoulders fell.

"I can't drive this," she said. I'd never heard her voice sound like that—small, timid.

"I'm sorry," I said quickly. "I shouldn't have said that, but of course you can still drive the truck—"

"No, I literally can't drive it," she said. She was fiddling with the silver rings on a few of her fingers. "I don't know how to drive a manual."

I hadn't even thought about that. Honestly, I'd forgotten this truck was a stick shift too. But there was something about her response that felt off-kilter in my head and heavy in my heart. It seemed a lot deeper than just not knowing how to drive a stick shift—that was pretty common, even in Meadowlark.

"Shit, I'm sorry," I said, trying to think about a way to phrase my next suggestion that wouldn't send her running for the mountains. I didn't know much about Ada, but I knew she spooked as easy as a horse faced with a plastic bag. "I can drive you," I said quickly. "To town. I have to grab a few things anyway."

She bit her lip again. She did that when she was thinking. Her eyes were firmly on the ground—refusing to meet mine as usual. "I guess . . ." she started, then said, "that's fine."

"My truck is that one," I said, pointing at the brown pickup behind us. I walked to the passenger side with her, opened the door, and waited for her to get in.

She looked like she was thinking again, backpedaling, probably. "You know," she said, "I think I'm actually good. Thank you for offering, but it's not urgent. I don't want to derail your day."

Derail my day? I'd drive my truck off a cliff if it meant that I got a few moments alone with her, but she didn't need to know that.

"You're not. I need to go to town anyway and you need a ride." I tried to make it sound transactional—like it was strictly business. She didn't respond to me, but she responded to business.

"No, it's fine—"

Yeah, I was done with that. "Get in the truck, Ada." My voice was more demanding than I'd intended; Ada's spine went ramrod straight, her eyes finally met mine, and she was staring me down.

"You don't get to tell me what to do on Saturdays," she said matter-of-factly.

"I do when you're being ridiculous," I said. I didn't say things like that. I didn't act like this, but she was just so . . . frustrating. "It's a ride to town—not a marriage proposal."

She didn't like that response, but I wasn't backing down. We stared each other down for a few seconds longer. I liked her eyes on me—even if they were pissed off. It was better than the cool looks I'd been getting from her all week.

"Fine," she bit out before getting in the truck.

"Remind me to check the weather in hell," I muttered to myself as I shut the door.

"I heard that," Ada said.

"Good," I retorted.

I walked around the front of my truck, opened my door, and positioned myself in the driver's seat. It took less than a second for me to realize that Ada and I were alone—in a small and enclosed space.

She couldn't run away from me in here, so I did something that I probably shouldn't have done.

I grabbed her hand off the seat next to her and placed it on the gearshift knob—with mine on top of it. She tried to jerk it back, but I kept it there.

"What are you doing?" she asked, sounding both annoyed and confused.

"I'm teaching you how to drive a stick shift."

"I don't want to learn how to drive a stick shift."

"Yes, you do," I said. Ada let out an annoyed huff, but she didn't deny it. I knew it—I'd seen her face back there, and I knew it. This was something I could do for her. "All right, so right now, the gearshift is in neutral, but if you move it over"—I moved the stick using both of our hands—"and down, it's in reverse—did you feel how it kind of clicks into place?"

She nodded. She tried to look uninterested, but I could tell she was interested.

"I'm not going to be able to look at you while I'm driving, so answering in words would be good when I ask you a question."

"Yes, sir," Ada said with an exaggerated eye roll. Well, that shot straight to my dick. Maybe I hadn't thought this through, but it was too late to turn back now.

"Okay, so a manual has three pedals instead of two, and to make the truck move, you've gotta ships-in-the-night the gas and the clutch."

"I have no idea what that means."

"It means they have to pass each other, so you let off the clutch while pressing on the gas, and where they meet in the middle is the sweet spot."

"The spot that makes the truck move?" she asked.

"Yeah," I said, pushing the truck into motion and getting us out of the garage, basking in the sensation of my skin on hers again. I moved the gearshift back to neutral just before the truck stopped. "And when the truck stops, make sure it's not in gear or you'll kill it."

"Kill it?" she asked. I put the truck in first gear and let my foot off the clutch, and the engine sputtered and died.

"Kill it," I said. I took my hand off hers and immediately missed the way her skin felt, but I had to restart the truck. Then I put my hand back on hers. "We're in first gear right now, and that's where we need to be every time we start going forward. Once the truck gets moving," I said as the truck started down the drive, "we go to second." I pushed in the clutch and shifted. "And once you hit about fifteen miles an hour"—*clutch, shift*—"you go to third, and so on."

"And you push in the clutch every time you shift?" she asked.

"Yes. Push in the clutch, foot off the gas, and shift."

"That's a lot to remember," she said quietly.

"It's not as hard as it seems," I said. "I promise." After that, we were silent for a while. I could tell that Ada was focused on me, on our hands, on what I was doing—trying to take it all in—so I didn't push a conversation.

I let us be.

After a few minutes, Ada said, "I was married before." Her voice was small again—the way it was when she said she couldn't drive stick. I kept my hand on hers and tried not to react. I was surprised that she'd offered up anything about herself, and I wanted her to continue. "We had one car. It was a stick shift."

"But you couldn't drive it?" I asked, tightening my hand that was on the steering wheel.

"No, which meant I didn't leave the house unless I was going somewhere within walking distance or my ex drove me."

"He didn't try to teach you?"

"He said I didn't need to know how to drive it when he could take me anywhere I wanted to go." An image of Ada flashed through my mind—an image in which she looked like a bird in a cage. My head was reeling about what that meant—that she wasn't able to do things on her own—and it made me fucking angry.

Whoever this asshole was, I wanted to find him and kick

his ass off a cliff. "At the beginning, I thought it was sweet that he wanted to drive me everywhere—I thought he was taking care of me—but after a few weeks, I started to feel trapped."

"I'm sorry," I said, unsure how to make this better.

"It's okay. It's over now," she said simply. I kept my eyes on the road because I knew if I looked at her, I would stop the truck and pull her to me.

I downshifted from fifth gear as we came to the last stop sign before town and turned to her. Our hands were still atop each other, and I could feel her heartbeat in my fingertips. "I really can teach you how to drive stick, Ada, if you'll let me. You don't have to feel trapped like that again."

She looked away from me, and I had no choice but to start driving again. After a few minutes, a small "Thank you" came from the other side of the cab.

I stayed quiet, not sure how to care for her right now. Should I push the conversation along? Or should I stay quiet and let her be?

Luckily, I didn't have to decide because Ada spoke first. "So do you actually have things to pick up in town or were you just being nice?"

I smiled and answered honestly—well, semi-honestly. She didn't need to know how badly I wanted to spend time with her. "Both."

"I'm going to be nosy to distract from the fact that I just spilled my guts to you a few minutes ago. What do you need in town?" She used air quotes when she said "town."

I hesitated for a second. "Do you want the real answer? Or the easy one?"

"The real one," she said without hesitation. "I just told you about my ex-husband, and I don't think it gets more vulnerable than that."

"You showed me yours, so I have to show you mine?" I said, amused.

"Something like that," she responded. I thought she smiled a bit too.

"Well," I started. "I have to pick up my antidepressant from the pharmacy, and they close at noon on Saturday, so your car had perfect timing in biting the dust. I might not have made it." I didn't mind sharing this with Ada. I was open about it, and I wanted her to know me.

Whether I liked it or not, this was part of who I was.

Stupid sad brain.

Ada was quiet again, so I jumped in. "Now we both know something about the other," I said.

"Yeah," she finally said with a small smile. "Look at us, being open and shit."

"Feels kind of good, doesn't it?"

"Actually, yes," she responded. "I—um—" She hesitated for a second. "Thank you. For making me feel less weird about dumping all of that on you. It's nice to feel like I'm not the only one who has shit to deal with."

Yeah, it was.

Chapter 11

Ada

I don't know what possessed me to tell Weston about my ex-husband, and I don't know what I expected him to do when I told him. I thought he would stop looking at me like he thought I was better than I was or like he was still hungry for me, but neither of those things happened.

Instead, he brought his truck to a stop, looked me dead in the eye, and said the words I didn't even know that I needed—that I craved: *You don't have to feel trapped like that again.* They rang through me like a victory bell. When he said it, I believed him. Maybe it was the big blue Wyoming sky, but I didn't feel trapped here.

The rest of our drive was uneventful. I had a chance to think about what Wes told me and about how willing he was to make sure I didn't feel alone in my weird vulnerable state by telling me about his depression.

Honestly, I never would've guessed that was something he dealt with. Wes looked so happy. But I guess depression wasn't really about what you looked like or how you appeared but more about what you felt like.

After that, we talked a little bit. He asked me what my favorite food was, if I was having a good time with the project so far—surface-level stuff. He was easy to talk to. Before I knew it, we were rolling into downtown Meadowlark. I wanted to buy a few hoodies, a warmer coat, and some gloves. I thought I could just go to a clothing store, but when I told Weston what I needed, he pulled to the side of Main Street right in front of the tractor supply place.

"I don't think this place has what I need," I said as he put the truck in Park.

"Trust me, this place has everything you need and probably things you don't even know you need yet," he said. "And for half the price you'd pay anywhere else." He moved to get out of the truck and I followed.

"Are you going to be okay on your own?" he asked. Instead of responding out loud, I rolled my eyes before giving him a dirty look. I thought he would shrink back a little, but he didn't. He just flashed his dimpled smile at me and kept talking.

"I need to pick up a prescription, and I have a couple of pairs of boots at the cobbler." He tilted his head toward the small storefront across the street. Of course there was a fucking cobbler. "I'll meet you back here in thirty?"

I nodded, even though part of me wanted him to stay with me, not that I would ever admit that. I didn't know what it was about him, but when I was near him, I felt like I was floating. I felt okay. Those were two feelings I rarely felt anymore.

Still, the way that he constantly made a point of respecting my space and my boundaries also made me feel so grounded.

If I didn't know any better, I would think that Weston was a genuinely good and decent man all the way through. Too bad that was impossible.

"Sure," I said. He tipped his hat to me before turning and walking across the street. I tried to smother the butterflies that let themselves loose in my stomach. They were the same stupid bitches that had appeared when he ordered me into the truck earlier today.

I didn't believe that I was going to find what I needed in the tractor supply, but I walked in anyway. I was immediately proven wrong, because the first thing I saw was a rack of black, yellow, and green Carhartt hoodies on sale for thirty dollars each.

Damn.

They sold these same hoodies at a boutique by my parents' house in San Francisco for twice that.

If this was part of small-town living, I could get used to it. I flipped through the hoodies, picking out a black one and a green one before I started to wander the rest of the store.

There were definitely tractor supplies, or what I assumed were tractor supplies, but there was also a bunch of other shit—like those little dinosaur grabbers, a lot of clothes, home improvement stuff, which I made sure to make a mental note of, and a bulk candy section.

I spotted a dispenser with peach rings and couldn't help myself. I took one of the bags and filled it to the top. After I'd walked around for a while and grabbed a few other things— a beanie, gloves, and a coat, which was another discount item—I made my way to the register.

A blond man was there to ring me out. He was handsome—

not handsome like Weston, but handsome enough. That was something I noticed now—whether a man was good-looking in comparison to Wes.

"Did you find everything okay?" he asked. His eyes lingered on me a little longer than was comfortable.

"Yes, thank you," I said. He started ringing up my items.

"I haven't seen you in here before," he said. It was almost accusatory.

Between his saying that and the weird way he was looking at me, I was starting to get annoyed. "Was there supposed to be a question in there?" I asked, shooting the cashier my best "Try me" glare while sliding my card across the counter. He shied away from my aggressive stare, and I had a feeling he wasn't going to answer.

Good.

I watched the cashier run my card. After a few seconds, an aggressive and terrible noise came from the card reader, and I wanted to crawl under a rock. I knew what was coming next.

"Uh," he said, "I'm sorry, but this card is declined. Do you have another one we can try?" No, I didn't. This was the only credit card I had that wasn't in my ex-husband's name. Of course I didn't use those after the divorce, but I didn't qualify for any others, and my bank account was drained.

I did the mental math in my head of what I'd used the card for over the past couple of weeks against the limit.

Fuck.

"I—I—" I stammered. "Let me check." I pulled out my wallet, trying to figure out how I could get out of this situation.

Just as I was about to make a run for it, another card slid across the counter and Weston's voice said, "Use this." I didn't want him to save me. I didn't need him to take care of me. This is what I got for opening up to him in the truck— another man who thought he could swoop in. "Your credit card company probably thinks your card got stolen," he laughed. I knew that wasn't true, but the cashier laughed along with him. He was covering for me, eliminating my embarrassment.

"That wouldn't be the first time that happened," the blond employee said. "How's the project up at Rebel Blue going?"

"It's good, Kenny. Thanks for asking." Wes gestured toward me. "And you just met the woman in charge." The cashier—Kenny—looked at me again.

"Welcome to Meadowlark," Kenny said.

"See you later," Wes said as he grabbed the bag with all of my stuff off the counter and headed for the door.

Once we were outside, I stopped and looked at Weston, who came to a stop next to me. The expression on his face was expectant, like he knew what I was about to say.

Well, he had it coming. "You didn't have to do that. I don't need you to take care of me," I snapped.

"I know I didn't have to do that," he said. "But watching you shiver every morning is driving me fucking crazy, and you won't take any of the coats I offer." Yeah, because the one time I wore one of his coats I was so distracted by the smell I almost kissed him again.

"Because I was planning on buying my *own* coat," I retorted.

"That plan worked out great, didn't it?"

"I would've figured it out," I said, even though I really didn't think so. Worst case, I would've just had to leave without my haul. Best case, Kenny would've fallen for my "but I'm just a girl" shtick and extended me credit.

"Ada," Weston said, using one hand to rub at his temple like he was the one entitled to be annoyed, "I did what I would've done for anyone else." I ignored the way that made my stomach drop just a little bit. "If it's that big a deal, I will take it all back." Well, no. I didn't want that. "But you need a coat. Your card didn't work, and mine did. Pay me back later." He looked at me then. "You can even add interest if it makes you feel better."

It didn't, but the way one of his dimples was trying not to make an appearance did.

"Fine," I said.

"Fine," he responded.

The ride home was quiet, the only sound the soft rock playlist—Tom Petty, the Eagles, Fleetwood Mac, Steve Winwood—that flowed through the speakers.

And there were no stick-shift lessons.

But that didn't stop me from imagining how my skin would feel pressed against his.

Great.

Chapter 12

Ada

Every morning at Rebel Blue was beautiful, but when I woke up on Sunday morning, I knew those mornings were going to become my favorites.

I wasn't an early riser. Or a night owl. Really, I would just rather be sleeping. But there was something about waking up in a log cabin surrounded by evergreens and cool mountain air that made waking up early a hell of a lot easier.

I tried to remember whether I'd snoozed my alarm at any point in the last week and realized I hadn't. That was rare for me. I didn't set an alarm on Sundays, but that didn't matter at Rebel Blue because I rose with the sun.

I rolled out of bed and took my time washing my face and going through my morning skin care routine. I didn't have any big plans today—I tried not to work on Sundays. I didn't always succeed, but at least I tried. I pulled my new black Carhartt hoodie over my head, slid on a pair of leggings, and topped them with a thick pair of wool socks that someone had left outside my door a few days ago.

There was a note attached to them that had "For the cold floors" scribbled on it.

When I put them on the first time, I knew I never wanted to let these socks go.

I padded across the house to the kitchen, planning to just grab a yogurt from the fridge, and was immediately hit with the smell of butter and bacon. It wasn't often that I could actually feel myself start to salivate, but the smells coming from the Big House kitchen were delectable.

Amos was standing in front of the stove, wearing a worn-out pair of jeans and a plaid button-down. His salt-and-pepper hair was damp.

He gave me a warm smile when he saw me. Even though Wes looked more like his mom, at least from the pictures I'd seen scattered around the Big House, I thought he looked like Amos too.

"Good morning," he said. "Sleep okay?"

I nodded. "There hasn't been a night yet when I haven't slept like a rock." Again, rare for me. "Thank you for letting me stay here. It's been amazing being so close to the job site."

"We're happy to have you. Have you been able to settle in?" I thought about how my clothes were no longer in my suitcase but in the once-empty dresser of my guest room, how I had my own four-wheeler that I liked to ride to the job site, and how at the end of the day, coming back to the Big House felt like coming home.

"Yes, I have. I like it here," I said truthfully.

"Good. We like having you here—Weston especially." My heart jumped. Oh god. I hoped Amos didn't know anything.

"He's impressed by your work. He tells me every day that we made the right decision bringing you on."

He talks about . . . my work? To his dad? And he's impressed?

Well, that's . . . nice, which is how I responded to Amos. "Where is he?" I asked. Not that I was wondering.

"Weston wakes up earlier than any of us. Probably out on a trail somewhere with Waylon." Of course, wherever Weston went, that dog followed. "Could be cliff jumping into an ice-cold lake—you never know." Amos chuckled. The way he talked about his kids made me wonder how my parents talked about me.

After a few beats, Amos spoke again. "He's been waiting for this a long time. He loves that old house," he said with a small smile as he moved an obscene amount of scrambled eggs around in his frying pan.

"It's a beautiful house," I said. "Is that where you grew up?"

"It is."

"But you chose to build something new for your family?" I asked, curious about the history of Rebel Blue. I took a seat on one of the stools at the counter, settling in for a conversation with Amos.

"I did," Amos said. "My father and I had a"—he paused, and a deep line worried his forehead—"complicated relationship." I nodded. That was something I understood. "I wanted my marriage, my family, to be different. And I guess that started with a new house for me. We moved in here a few weeks before August was born." I thought about something Wes told me during my first day at Rebel Blue—how his dad used his and his siblings' full names. I assumed August was Gus.

I had more questions, but I didn't think it was polite to ask, so I changed the subject. "That's a lot of food," I said dumbly.

Amos's smile was big this time. "Breakfast is a family affair today." I could practically feel the pride rolling off him at the mention of his family. "Obviously, we'd love for you to join us. But I also know it's your day off, so I can make you a plate to enjoy somewhere that won't be as loud as this place is about to be."

I tend not to do very well in group settings. My resting bitch face and general energy don't usually lend well to these types of situations.

"It's okay," I said. "I can just grab something out of the fridge."

"You're not joining us?" Weston's voice came from behind me, and Waylon's head somehow ended up under the hand that was dangling at my side. I turned in my stool to face Wes, unable to help myself, and nothing could've prepared me for what I saw on this fine Sunday morning.

He had obviously been running, because his chest was still heaving slightly. His long-sleeved white T-shirt was wet with sweat in all the right places and clung to his body in a way that wouldn't be out of place in one of those hot-man calendars.

I made a mental note to google "cowboy calendars" later, and tried to convince myself that Rebel Blue Ranch had awakened in me a thing for cowboys in general, not just one specific cowboy.

My eyes tracked back up Weston's frame, and I was met with a smirk. I'd just been caught, and as if getting caught openly ogling my boss wasn't enough, he chose that moment to *wink* at me.

A really good wink. One of those winks that makes your jaw drop and sends a heat wave down your spine.

Damn him.

He was still waiting for my answer to his question.

"Not today" was what I settled on.

"And you're not joining us either unless you shower," Amos chimed in. Wes rolled his eyes. He looked at me again as he grabbed the hem of his T-shirt to wipe the sweat from his forehead. This man knew exactly what he was doing, and I had to consciously try not to keep staring. "You stink."

"I'm going, I'm going," Weston responded to his dad. He turned to walk out of the kitchen and called back, "But convince Ada to stay for breakfast."

I faced Amos again. He looked amused, but all he said was "I'll make you a plate." I responded with a look that I hoped he interpreted as grateful.

At that moment, I heard the front door open, and two voices carried through to the kitchen.

"I told you"—it was a man's voice, and it sounded weirdly familiar—"I would rather buy you a new truck than try to fix that ugly blue monster."

"Me and the truck are a package deal." A woman's voice now. "If she goes, I go." Two people appeared in the kitchen. The man I immediately recognized as the bartender—Brooks—which meant the brunette next to him was Weston's sister, Emmy.

Emmy was tall—probably a couple of inches taller than me. Her long brown hair was wild and windswept, like she'd ridden a horse here and let her hair fly behind her. Everything about her just looked so . . . free.

I'd felt locked in a cage of my own making my entire life. One look at this woman and the first thing I felt was envy.

"Hey, Spud," Amos called. "Luke, good morning." Emmy blew her dad a kiss and Brooks gave him a nod before turning back to Emmy.

"Fine," Brooks said. His eyes were on Emmy in a way that made me feel like I was intruding on something, even though they were the newcomers in the kitchen. "But you owe me, sugar."

Emmy's face lit up even more, and Brooks slung an arm around her shoulders, pulling her toward him so he could give her a quick kiss on the temple. As he did it, Emmy's eyes scanned the kitchen and landed on me.

She shirked out of Brooks's hold—he looked thoroughly disappointed at the loss—and stuck her hand out to me. "Hi," she said. "You must be Ada. I'm Emmy."

Brooks looked at me then, and his mouth stretched into a knowing smile. "Well, well, well," he said. "If it isn't the girl who ran out on her tab."

Emmy looked back at Brooks, confused, and then back at me. She studied me for a second, and I saw a light flash behind her eyes. "Wait, *you're* the girl who was making out with my brother at the bar?"

I'd never wished I was a hermit crab before, but there's a first time for everything. In that moment, I would have given anything to have a shell to retreat into.

Amos coughed behind me, and lighting myself on fire would probably have been more enjoyable than this moment.

"Sorry," Emmy said quickly. "I didn't know the mystery girl in the bar and the interior designer were the same person." The words were falling out of her mouth now.

"Me either," Brooks said, smirking.

"Shut *up,* Luke." Emmy shushed him. "I'm really sorry," she said, turning back to me. "Sometimes my brain doesn't move as fast as my mouth."

"It's okay," I said, even though all I wanted was to get out of there. Brooks was still smirking. "I'll pay the tab," I said to him, annoyed.

"No need." Brooks shook his head. "Wes covered it after you broke the world speed record for running out of the Devil's Boot."

Of course he had. Wes was Wyoming's Dudley Do-Right.

Emmy elbowed Brooks in the ribs, but he was unfazed. He just pulled her back to his chest and wrapped his arms around her. She resisted for half a second before melting back into him—as though in his arms was the only place she wanted to be.

Brooks kissed Emmy's head again.

I thought about what Wes had said—that when I met them, I'd get it.

I got it.

I've never felt like a very likable person. My ex confirmed that suspicion, especially at the end. For the most part, it didn't bother me. But looking at Brooks and Emmy, I felt a pang in my chest, and for the first time in a long time, I wondered what it might be like to be not just liked but loved.

I shook my head. That was too much for me to think about at seven-thirty on a Sunday morning.

The sound of a plate being pushed across the counter caught my attention—I turned back to Amos, who was giving me an apologetic but also vaguely knowing look. It was the same look he'd given me after Weston returned my tote bag on my first day at Rebel Blue.

The plate he'd built for me was more of a platter—stacked high with bacon, eggs, broiled tomatoes, two kinds of toast, hash browns, and what I assumed was a banana nut muffin. I'd eaten a few of these muffins since I'd been here—they were always in the pantry.

"Wait, are you not eating with us?" Emmy said. She sounded genuinely disappointed.

"It's her day off, Spud," Amos jumped in. "Let her have it."

Emmy's shoulders fell, but she nodded. "We should get coffee sometime," she said. The second woman in the Ryder family to invite me to do so. For someone who wasn't used to invitations, friendship or otherwise, it felt . . . good. "I know Teddy is dying to see you." Teddy had texted me a few times since I'd arrived. Her dad wasn't feeling well, and she was watching him closely, so she hadn't been able to come see me yet. "Maybe this Friday we can do something?"

"Yeah," I said noncommittally. "Let me see how this week goes." Emmy looked at me like she knew what that meant: Probably not. I knew that face. My whole life, I've been described as icy, bitchy, and rude. I know I'm not super warm or overly kind, but the truth is, I'm just shy. I don't think I'm a people person, certainly not in the way this entire family seems to be. They make being nice look so damn easy.

Whereas I don't seem to know how to talk to people in a way that makes them like me or keep coming back for more. I seem to always turn out to be a disappointment, so why bother?

Before Emmy could push more, I turned back to Amos. "Thank you so much for breakfast." And then back to Emmy and Brooks. "It was really nice to meet you, Emmy. And, Brooks, it was mildly okay to see you." Both Emmy and Amos laughed at that—thank god.

I pushed off my stool with my breakfast platter and headed back to my room. "I hope we'll see each other again soon!" Emmy called after me.

I walked past the upstairs hall bathroom that Wes was using for his shower. The running water brought all sorts of images to my brain that I would really rather not dwell on.

I sat down at the desk in my room to eat and scroll through my phone. Some of my best ideas have come from mindlessly spinning through Pinterest on my days off. But when I reached for my sweatshirt pocket, it wasn't there. Fuck. I must've left it on the kitchen counter.

Was going to get it worth it? I had all the confidence in the world in Emmy, Amos, and Weston's ability to get me to stay and eat breakfast with them, which might not be so bad after all. I liked the Ryders—one of them a little too much. Weighing my options, I decided that it was better to try to get my phone now than wait until later—who knew how long breakfast lasted for a family that actually *liked* one another?

Just as I passed the hall bathroom, the door opened with a billow of steam. I didn't have time to stop myself before I ran smack into Weston's broad chest.

"Whoa there," he said. Originally, I'd put my hands out as an involuntary reaction—my body's way of protecting me from collision. But now my hands were limp on his chest, and I stared at them—what they looked like while they were touching him. "Going somewhere?"

My mouth couldn't form words—I was too focused on what it was like to be touching him and for him to be touching me. Tiny lightning bolts shot up and down my arms from where his hands were on my elbows. "S-sorry," I stammered.

I dragged my eyes up and down his form—taking him in the same way I had in the kitchen. I'd seen the way his shirts clung to his body, and I'd seen glimpses of his stomach at the job site, but now he was in front of me in nothing but a towel.

It didn't take long for me to conclude that he actually should *not* be allowed to wear shirts. He should just always walk around like this—shirtless and glistening.

In that moment, I felt like a teenager with a crush. An intense and inescapable crush.

Except crushes aren't quite as fun if they're on your boss.

If anyone else had been standing in front of me, the fact that every logical thought basically ran out of my head wouldn't have been a big deal.

I wouldn't even have thought twice about wanting to touch him—everywhere.

"I'm not," he said. One of his hands moved to my waist, pulling me out of my cloudy head and back into the moment. My breath caught in my throat. I needed to get out of his grip, but I couldn't think straight when his hands were on me. All I could think was *more.* Almost involuntarily, I rubbed my hands up his chest to his shoulders, and his lips parted slightly. I still wasn't breathing. "Do that again," he whispered.

So I did, even though I knew I shouldn't, but I didn't stop there. I traced my palms back down the panes of his stomach and up again.

I finally let out a shaky breath. What was happening to me?

"Is this what you were thinking about? When you couldn't take your eyes off me in the kitchen, were you thinking about touching me?"

I swallowed and nodded, unsure when I decided to admit that to him—or to myself.

"I see you, Ada. I always see you, even when you won't look at me."

Everything felt so . . . charged when I was around him, I didn't know how to make it stop, but I didn't even know if I wanted it to.

Especially right now.

"I'm looking at you now," I said. It was like I was having an out-of-body experience, like my palms pressing against him had tilted the world on its axis. I moved closer to him, and the water that was dripping down his skin soaked through my hoodie.

"Why now?" he asked. *Because you're standing in front of me like some Wild West god in nothing but a towel,* I thought.

This feeling, this pull, was unheard of for me. I hadn't even known it existed until the night I met Weston in the bar. There was a part of me that wished I could go back to the version of me that didn't know what this felt like, but a much larger part of me felt like it could breathe for the first time.

Weston's hand trailed up and down my back, leaving sparks in its wake. "Why *now*, Ada?" he asked again, more forcefully this time.

"I—I don't know" is what I settled on.

He pressed his forehead to mine, and I could feel his breath on my face. The hand that was stroking my back slipped under my hoodie, tugging me to him. I could feel him getting hard against my stomach.

That was a lot to take in.

My breath was shaky, and I waited for him to go on. Instead, he said, "Let me know when you figure it out," and walked back to his room, his door shutting me out with a firm *click*.

Chapter 13

Wes

My post-shower run-in with Ada was all I could think about when I sat down at breakfast with my family, and the fact that Emmy wouldn't stop hounding me about her didn't help. She pelted me with questions: *Did you know she was the designer when you kissed her? Have you kissed her again? You better not harass her while she's working. Do you like her? Does she like you?*

Did I like her? Absolutely, without a doubt. The more time I spent with her, the more I liked her. Did she like me? I didn't know. I knew she was attracted to me—you couldn't fake the heat in her gaze—but that didn't mean she liked me. At least not the way I liked her.

Which was an all-consuming, daydreaming, slightly annoying way.

I didn't answer those last two questions from Emmy. It was bad enough that she was giving me the third degree under the watchful and frustratingly observant eye of Amos Ryder, and my siblings' commentary made it worse. Well, Emmy's commentary, Luke's amused face, and Gus's single comment that basically equated to "Don't fuck this project up."

Obviously, I didn't want to fuck anything up—not the project or whatever was happening with Ada.

I wanted both.

And I wanted her to want both too.

That's what I was thinking about on Wednesday morning when Ada walked into the small sitting area down the hall from her room. I hadn't seen her much since the shower debacle, and I had a feeling that was on purpose. On Monday, I didn't have time to go by the job site, and by the time I'd made it back to the Big House, Ada's bedroom door was shut and the lights were out. Yesterday, I watched her run out the back door of Baby Blue when I got there, and Evan said he was going to walk me through that day's progress.

She was doing a great job of avoiding me, so I wondered why she was approaching me now.

"Hey," she said, looking down at her feet.

"Hey," I responded, looking up from my sketchbook and taking her in. It was early, maybe around five—I didn't really know because I hadn't been sleeping well, so I'd come out here around three to sketch. She hadn't changed into her work clothes yet. She usually wore overalls with a long-sleeved shirt or a tank top under them. I liked it when she wore a tank top because I could see her tattoos. The sleeve of roses, vines, and thorns inked onto her right arm was all I could think about sometimes. But right now she was wearing black leggings and a black hoodie. In the weeks I'd known her, I'd seen her wear something other than black, white, or denim maybe twice. Three times, if we're being generous.

On her feet were the socks I'd left outside her door. She wore them all the time, and every time I saw them, I had to try not to smile.

Smiling would give it away and she would know for sure that it'd been me. Then she'd probably decide never to wear them again and let her toes freeze off just to spite me.

I liked that about her—her stubbornness—but it also drove me insane.

She drove me insane.

"I want to talk to you," she said, still not looking at me.

"New rule," I replied. "You have to look at me when you talk to me."

Her eyes shot up. That got her. "You don't get to make rules," she said.

"Really? Because you make them all the time," I said. What was it about her that got under my skin so badly and made me act so different than I would normally? "We can't look at each other, be near each other, breathe in each other's general direction. Unless, of course, you accost me after I get out of the shower. Then everything's fair game."

"That's not what happened," she said with a huff.

"That's not how I remember it." I tried not to remember it, actually—the way her hands felt on my back, her sharp breaths that I wanted to bottle, the way she looked at me like she was ready to let whatever was going to happen between us happen.

Because it was going to happen.

Feelings like this didn't exist to be forced into dormancy. I just had to wait for her to catch up.

"Well, that isn't what happened," she said as she folded her arms over her chest.

"Whatever helps you sleep at night, sweetheart." I looked back down at my sketchbook and started shading some parts of the leaves I was working on. She didn't go away. She just stood there. I let a minute or so pass before I said, "Did you need something?"

Ada looked annoyed. "Are there any updates on my car?"

Yeah, that piece of shit needed more work than it was worth, but I wasn't about to tell her that. "I need Brooks to look at it too. He's better with cars than I am," I explained. "But from what I can tell, it's misfiring"—I laughed a little because this next part was going to sound like I was making it up, especially if she knew anything about cars—"in every single cylinder." The odds that all parts of her engine had something wrong with it were low, but somehow, her car had managed it.

It was kind of impressive, actually.

Ada made a face. "Are you serious?" she said.

I put my hand on my heart. "I promise I am. You need a new battery too." *And who knows what else.*

"Okay, well, I need a car to do my job, so if you can't fix it, I need to find someone who can." Her speech felt rehearsed. I wondered how long she'd been thinking about this.

"When it comes to cars, you're not going to find anyone more capable than Brooks." Which was true. When we were thirteen, he found his old Chevy truck at the junkyard. The owner told Brooks that if he could get it running, he could have it.

He did. And proceeded to drive that truck for over a decade.

"I need a car, Wes," Ada asserted again.

"Then I'll get you a car," I said simply.

"You're not getting me a car," she scoffed. Her eyes fell to the floor again and she started tapping her foot.

"Well . . . do you have another idea?" I asked.

She took a deep breath and then sat on the other end of the couch that I was on. "I want you"—she paused, and I wished she could've ended her sentence right there—"to teach me to drive a stick. Like actually teach me. Not that flirty bullshit you did when you drove me to town." I smiled at the memory of my hand atop hers.

"That wasn't flirty bullshit," I said. Ada arched one of her black eyebrows at me. "Okay, fine," I conceded. "It was flirty, but it was also teaching. It's easier to do it on the driver's side once you know what it feels like."

"Whatever, cowboy." She shook her head. "So will you teach me or not?"

"I'll teach you," I said, trying not to make it obvious that I would've gotten down on my knees and begged her to let me. "On one condition," I added.

Ada rolled her eyes. "What's the condition?"

"You have to talk to me, Ada. You can't avoid me like you've been doing since you got here. You have this idea of me in your head—which I'm willing to bet isn't accurate—based on *that* night. I don't think that's fair, and in order for me to prove you wrong, you have to talk to me." Damn, I was on a roll. "That's my condition."

Ada bit her lip, and now my eyes were on her mouth. Goddammit, why did she have to be so . . . her. So everything.

After a moment, she said, "Fine." It wasn't exactly the enthusiastic response I was looking for, but for Ada, I'd take it. "When do we start?"

Chapter 14

Ada

"Of all the battles to fight, you're going to fight to keep the pink and yellow bathroom tile?" Evan asked. We were standing in the main powder room of the house, and Evan was looking at me with an expression that was somehow both amused and bored.

"Yes," I said simply. "And I'm going to fight for the powder-blue tile in the primary bedroom en suite too."

"Of course you are." Evan sighed.

"Of course I am." Since I started taking on actual design projects, I'd always done my best to restore rather than demolish when I could. When I started at Rebel Blue, I didn't know how much we could salvage, considering how long the house had been vacant, but thanks to the Ryders' maintenance schedule, the elements had largely been kept out of the house. Animals were a different story, even though I thought we had those managed at this point. Now the inside of the house, after our barebones demo, looked great.

I was bummed that we would have to do new floors. The current ones were in bad shape—probably more from having housed generations of a single family than from being abandoned for the last thirty years.

I made a mental note to see if there was any way that we could reuse them. I already knew I had enough wood from the old doors to create two large bookshelves for the living area.

"It's a miracle there aren't any leaks under this floor," Evan said. He was right. After inspection on both this level and the straight-out-of-a-horror-movie basement, we hadn't found leaks in any of the bathrooms—no mold, no water damage, nothing. There was water damage in the kitchen, though. We had already planned to rip that out completely anyway, so it didn't really matter.

"And who are we to question a miracle?" I asked.

Evan rolled his eyes. "Your boyfriend is here," he said. "You better ask him." I gave Evan the dirtiest look I could muster, which must've been a good one because he shrank back from my gaze.

Before I had time to revel in that, I caught a glimpse of Wes coming through the front door, leaving my favorite ball of white fluff outside.

"No dogs inside the active construction site" was a necessary rule, but every time I saw Waylon's pouty eyes, I wanted to break it.

I knew Wes hadn't been planning on coming by until the end of the day, so I wondered why he was here. He had his own uniform when he came to the job site, but today, since he wasn't coming to work, he was still in full cowboy mode, wearing a large work coat and leather chaps.

Damn.

I looked down at my watch. It was already half past four. How the hell did that happen? I needed to look at my notes. There were things that had needed to get done today that hadn't, and that was going to put us behind.

"Hey, Evan," Wes said as he made his way toward us. "Ada." It was annoying how much I liked the sound of my name when it fell from his lips. It always sounded . . . reverent somehow.

"Hey," Evan and I said at the same time.

"How was today? Everything go smoothly?" Wes asked. He was looking at me.

"Good," I responded. "I actually have some questions for you." I looked back at Evan. "Tell the crew they can head home, but that we need them here at seven instead of eight tomorrow." Evan nodded. He knew we needed to tear out the ceiling the next day. "Follow me," I said to Wes, leading him toward the powder room.

"Yes, ma'am," he said. Damn him and his stupid cowboy charm. Since when did the word "ma'am" make my cheeks heat? Nothing made my cheeks heat. I wasn't a blusher.

We walked, and he was a little too close to me, and I reveled in it.

After the whole shower incident and after he agreed to teach me to drive a stick shift, I figured I could stand to be marginally nicer to him. Which had nothing to do with the fact that I thought about him all the time, the fact that he was the best-looking man I'd ever laid eyes on, or the fact that he seemed to be a genuinely good person.

Obviously, it had nothing to do with any of that.

"So," I started, "I wanted to talk to you about a few of the bathrooms." We were outside the powder room now. Its door had been removed, so we could see inside. "What would you think about keeping the tile?" I asked. "We would obviously replace the toilet and the sink, and update the paint, but it's rare to see this type of tile work in such good shape, and I think the more elements we can preserve, the more cohesive our final product is going to be."

I was nervous while I waited for his answer. I didn't know why.

"I love it," he said after a few beats.

"Really?" I asked, kind of shocked. It was usually a fight for me to get someone to agree to keep something that felt dated. Everyone wanted all new, all sleek, all modern, all the time.

"Yeah. I love this tile, and the blue tile in the other bathroom too," he said, smiling. "As long as the appliances and pipes can be upgraded to handle the demands of guests, I'm all for it."

"Okay, excellent," I said. "That was easy."

"Were you expecting it to be hard?" A million inappropriate jokes came to my mind, but I pushed them down. This was my *boss*.

"Sometimes it can be," I said. "Most people prefer shiny new things."

"Not me," Weston said. "This place has history. I don't want it to feel like everyplace else." I knew that—it was one of the first things he'd said in his initial email to me—but now that I was here at Rebel Blue, and now that I knew the man behind the emails, I understood more deeply what he was looking for.

"While we're on that subject, I was thinking about furniture. We have enough old doors to make a few bookshelves, and there's probably a lot of salvageable wood here that we could repurpose. Is there a carpenter in Meadowlark?"

Weston's eyes were bright. He liked that idea too. "Several," he responded. "But I think you'll like Aggie."

"Can you reach out to her? Or do you want me to?"

"I'll do it," Wes said. "Aggie is an old family friend." Of course she was. "And Gus just convinced her son to come back to Meadowlark, so I don't think she'll tell us no."

"People leave Meadowlark?" I said jokingly, but immediately regretted it. I didn't want it to come off snobby, but Wes just smiled again.

"Dusty did," he said. "He's been a cowboy all around the world."

"That's a thing?" I asked. All of this was new to me.

"It's a thing," he said. "If anyone but Gus had asked him to come back, I don't think he would've."

"Why did he ask?" Everything seemed pretty well taken care of at Rebel Blue.

"Gus needs another number two since I've got this." He motioned around him, indicating the house.

"But this won't last forever," I said, not intending for my words to have a double meaning, but they did.

"Dusty likes temporary," Weston said. "He should be here this week. You'll like him."

"Oh, really?" I didn't think Weston knew me enough to know if I'd like the newcomer, or I guess oldcomer.

"He's like the man version of Teddy." He shrugged. "And everyone likes Teddy. Except Gus." *Interesting.* I pocketed that piece of information to ask Teddy about later. I still hadn't seen her. She'd sent a few more texts—she'd been busy with her dad but was going to come by on Friday.

"And his mom is the carpenter?" I asked.

"Yeah, she's cool. I'll talk to her and see if we can take materials to her this week, and we can talk to her then." There were a lot of "we's" being flung around today.

I nodded. "That's great."

Weston rubbed at the back of his neck, like he was suddenly nervous. "So," he said, "I drove my truck over here, and I thought you could drive it back to the Big House."

"Um, yeah," I said, also feeling suddenly nervous. "I guess we can try."

"Okay, great. I'll just meet you outside when you're ready."

After most of the crew had left, having agreed to tomorrow's earlier start, Evan and I came out of the house last. Evan was going back to San Francisco for the weekend, so tomorrow would be his last day on-site this week, and he wanted to brief me on what needed to happen before he came back. I was used to being solo on parts of a project, but not one this large. I was anxious, but I just needed to stick to my plan.

Evan got into his rental car, making sure to throw a pointed look my way as he said, "Have fun, you two." God, he was unbearable.

I turned to face Wes, remembering his rule. That I needed to look at him while I was talking to him. It was a stupid rule. I was perfectly happy looking anywhere but in his stupidly mesmerizing green eyes. But I was also perfectly happy looking straight into them.

An annoying predicament to be in, honestly.

I started toward the passenger side of Weston's truck, but

he lightly grabbed my elbow and pulled me back toward his chest.

"Driver's side, sweetheart," he said.

I blinked slowly, waiting for my brain to rewire itself. "Sorry?" I said.

"You get in the driver's side. You're driving us home, remember?" Weston's voice was amused.

"Right, sorry," I said, and went toward the driver's side this time. Weston opened the door for me, and I plopped myself in the driver's seat. The truck smelled like him.

"Okay, see that pedal on the left?" he asked. I looked down at the third pedal—the clutch, I guessed—and nodded. "Use your left foot to push it all the way down to the floor."

I did what he said, but I couldn't get it all the way down. I wasn't close enough to the pedals—the seat was pushed back for someone who was six foot something, not someone who was five six, maybe five seven on a good day.

"Keep your foot on the clutch," he said as he put his hand on a metal bar under the driver's seat—a metal bar he could reach only by putting his arm between my legs.

Was it hot in here?

He pulled the bar up and brought the seat forward a few inches. The fact that he did this with me still sitting there liquefied my insides, and if he kept this shit up, they'd be boiling within seconds. "Okay, now push it down again." I did, and it went all the way to the floor. "Good. Does that feel okay? Easy to go all the way?"

Keep your jokes to yourself, Ada.

"Y-yeah," I said, hoping he didn't notice that my voice sounded slightly breathy.

"And you can reach the stick okay?" At this point, I was really regretting not thinking about all the sex-related puns that could be thrown around when learning to drive a stick shift. I swallowed one and put my right hand on the gearshift knob, not answering but showing. That was easier. "Perfect," he said, smiling up at me. When I was sitting in the truck, we were nearly the same height, and he was so close, with one of his hands still on the bar under my seat.

I wondered if he realized how close we were—how a few more inches upward, and his hand would be between my legs. The way his tongue ran over his lips told me he did.

Shit, shit, shit. Get it together.

My foot slipped off the clutch, and the sound it made when it popped back up into its original position jolted both of us. Wes blinked a few times before pulling away.

"I'm just gonna . . ." he said as he used his thumb to motion back. I didn't know what he was trying to say until he walked around the front of the truck and opened the passenger-side door. Waylon jumped in ahead of him and went to the small back seat.

Right. Got it.

"Okay," he said. "You ready?"

Absolutely not. "Sure."

"Put your right foot on the brake. When you start the engine, the clutch needs to be pushed all the way to the floor"—I pushed it in with my left foot—"and the gearshift needs to be in neutral." He put his hand on top of mine, just as he had done when we drove to town, and moved the gearshift to neutral. "Good."

"Can we . . . um . . . turn some music on?" I asked. I didn't know if it was the stick shift or Weston that was making me nervous.

"Yes, but you have to turn the truck on first."

"Oh," I said sheepishly. I hadn't thought about that.

"Go ahead, then, turn the key," he said. "Keep your foot on the clutch, though." I did what he said, and the engine turned over. My nerves started to creep up my throat. "The steering wheel isn't going anywhere, Ada."

I looked at my hands and saw what he meant. The white-knuckle grip I had on the wheel was hard to miss. "Sorry," I said, and tried to loosen them.

"Why are you apologizing?" he asked. His voice was thoughtful. "It's okay to be scared when you're doing something new." I didn't answer. I didn't really feel like diving into my ex-husband at this point, but apparently that wasn't good enough for Weston.

"Are you still in neutral?" he asked. I nodded. "All right, take your foot off the clutch and the brake." I did what he said, unsure where he was going with this. "Look at me." I did. Weston's green eyes were soft. "You're probably going to fuck it up. A lot."

Well, that was reassuring.

"But everyone does. There's also no safer place to learn how to do this than right here. No one's around. There are no other cars for you to hit or anything."

"There are cattle, though," I said.

"You think I would let you hit a cow?" he asked. That pulled a laugh out of me, and I shook my head. I don't think either of us could handle the guilt of hitting a cow. "You're going to kick so much ass."

"Music?" I asked again now that the car was on. Wes opened the glove compartment and pulled out an aux cord.

"What do you like?"

I thought about it. "James Taylor," I said. There was nothing more calming than James Taylor, right?

Wes laughed lightly. "I like the way you think." I watched him scroll through a music app before he hit Shuffle on James Taylor's greatest hits. "Fire and Rain" started playing, so we were starting off strong.

"All right, James on the radio," he said, "left foot on the clutch, right foot on the brake, hand on the gearshift."

I assumed the position. "Remember what I said about the clutch and the gas?"

"Ships in the night," I said. I had to press on the gas and let off the clutch at the same time.

"All right, then, give it a go." I put the gearshift into first, and heard Wes murmur, "Good," and then started to let off the clutch and press the gas.

The truck shook and then went quiet.

"What just happened?" I asked.

"You killed it," he said. "Which isn't a good thing in this case. Put it in neutral again and start her back up." I did what he said. "Now let off the clutch—slowly—and you should be able to feel that sweet spot we talked about."

"The truck won't die?"

"Not while you're in neutral." Got it. I lifted my foot off the clutch slowly, and there was a point where it felt like there was more give on the clutch. "Did you feel that?"

"Yeah, I think so."

"So when you feel that sweet spot, you're going to give more on the gas," he said. "A little give and a little go."

"Are you"—I looked at him, knowing a smile was working its way up my cheeks—"quoting *How to Lose a Guy in 10 Days*?"

A blush crept up Wes's cheeks. "Yeah, I guess I am," he said. I laughed like I did that first night at the bar, and felt my shoulders drop a little. "Does quoting Matthew McConaughey help or hurt?"

"Helps," I said truthfully. *A little give and a little go.* I could do that.

"All right, all right, all right," Wes said with a weird drawl in his voice, and I laughed again.

"Is *that* your McConaughey?"

"Obviously," he responded, somewhat deflated.

"That is—quite literally—the worst McConaughey impression I've ever heard." I might have been exaggerating a little bit, but it really was bad. Weston's jaw dropped, and it was so fucking cute I couldn't help but laugh some more.

With every exhale, I felt lighter.

"All right, smartass," he said. "If it's so bad, I'd like to hear you do better."

I cleared my throat, not even having the chance to wonder when I became so comfortable with Weston, and wrestled up my best McConaughey: "All right, all right, all right."

Weston let out a laugh that felt like when you go out to bask in the sun after being in an air-conditioned space for too long. I could feel the warmth seeping into my fingers and toes.

And so I laughed too.

We laughed together, and the more we laughed, the harder it got to stop.

I kept trying to catch my breath, but I couldn't. It wasn't long before I felt tears pricking at the sides of my eyes and my stomach started to hurt. When Weston laughed hard, apparently he got one of those weird silent hiccup laughs. He had his head on the dashboard, and his upper body was heaving. He reminded me of a bug, and that made me laugh harder.

And when I snorted a little, Weston hit the dashboard with one of his hands and threw his head back and laughed some more.

This was so fucking stupid, but I couldn't stop. We couldn't stop.

I thought back to that night at the bar, how he made me smile, and how he'd made me smile every day since—even when I wasn't kind to him.

He was like the sun. No matter what, he would keep coming up.

I didn't think that my ears had ever been so far from my shoulders.

"That was so bad," Weston said, wiping a tear from the corner of his eye. "You are the worst impressionist that has ever lived. I am not kidding."

"No, you are," I said.

"At least I know how to drive a manual," he said with a wink. Christ. I thought the dimples were bad.

"Well, my teacher kind of sucks, so . . ." I shrugged.

Wes shook his head. "Start the truck, Ada." He was smiling, and so was I. I felt more relaxed than I had a few minutes ago—like I could actually do this and be okay.

"Neutral, clutch, gas?" I said out loud, looking at Wes.

"You got it." He nodded, and I started the truck. James Taylor started flowing through the speakers again. I put the truck in first gear and prepared myself to let off the clutch and press on the gas. *A little give and a little go.*

I started to let the clutch out, and when I got to the spot I'd felt earlier, I pushed on the gas pedal. Probably a little too hard, because the truck lurched forward, jolting all three of us.

But it went. It didn't die.

"Good," Weston said. "Get her going, and then we're going to shift gears, all right?" There was so much going on—so many things to focus on—but the truck was moving.

Holy shit. The truck was *moving.*

I just nodded.

"Okay, in a few seconds, you're going to take your foot off the gas, push the clutch in, and move the car into second gear."

"That's a lot of things." I gulped.

"You've got this, Ada. Now take your foot off the gas and push the clutch in." I did. The truck did something that felt like a hiccup. "Second gear, quick." I moved the gearshift to second and felt it lock. "Gas, sweetheart. Hit the gas now and let the clutch pedal up." *Sweetheart.* I didn't hate it, but I was trying to pretend I hated how much his voice calmed me down.

I did, and the truck lurched again. "Good, Ada. We're going to stay slow, okay? No faster than twenty-five miles an hour." I glanced down at the speedometer, which was currently sitting at ten. I felt like I was going at least fifty.

"Do you have it in you to shift again?" he asked, and I nod-ded. "All right, once we hit twenty miles an hour, I want you to show me what you can do."

God, he was so gentle—so comforting. He talked to me the way people talk to plants when they want them to grow.

Don't fuck this up now, Ada. Show him what you can do. I pushed on the gas lightly—glancing down at the speedom-eter a few times until it hit twenty.

Here we go. *Off the gas.* I lifted my foot. *Clutch.* I pushed it in. *Shift.* I moved the gearshift up to third. *Gas, sweetheart.* I heard Weston's voice in my head, since he was silent next to me.

I shifted into third gear, and the truck was still moving, and the Earth was still turning—as far as I could tell.

"What did I say?" Wes said.

"That I was going to kick so much ass?" I responded.

"And I was right," he said.

"What do I do now?" I asked. I felt like there was so much to do, and I wasn't currently doing any of it. Right now, driv-ing the truck felt easy?

"We cruise along at a nice and easy twenty miles an hour. We listen to James Taylor sing about a country road, and eventually, we come to a stop."

"That's it?" I asked.

"That's it. Don't get ahead of yourself." Weston started humming along to the music, and I kept driving, trying not to get distracted by the suns—the one in the sky and the one sitting next to me—bathing everything I could see in light.

Chapter 15

Ada

It was my third Friday at Rebel Blue, and things were going remarkably well. Besides another rodent incident—I wasn't sure if it was a good thing that they were deceased this time—vaulting the ceiling went off without a hitch.

When we removed the surfaces of the walls, we found a few areas with original red brick underneath. I was planning to keep those exposed. It looked like we were going to end up with a lot more color in the house than I'd originally planned, but I loved it. I was sick of people asking me to make things look chic, and clean, and . . . beige.

Listen, I had nothing against beige. Objectively, beige was great.

But this place deserved more than beige.

Since we were starting to make our way into the putting-things-back-together phase of renovation, my hands were itching to start making things, and since I wasn't skilled in carpentry and Aggie—who I had a lovely phone conversation with earlier in the week—was on that, I settled for curtains.

My car was still on the fritz, but I was able to order some plain white linen curtains online—a lot of them. And mallets.

I had a plan.

Even though I wouldn't classify the weather in Meadowlark, Wyoming, as "warm" just yet, wildflowers were starting to pop up around the ranch, and I'd been collecting little bouquets of them throughout the week. Tonight I was going to spend some time doing something with my hands, and my brain.

I wasn't good at drawing or painting or anything like that, but I could DIY the fuck out of anything, and that's exactly what I was going to do with these curtains.

It was near the end of the day, and the crew was starting to clear out, so I began setting up my work for the evening. I laid out three curtains to start, and grabbed the box that held all the wildflowers I'd been collecting.

Evan had just left for the day when I heard a familiar voice at the door. "Ada Hart, you are the only person whose ass looks that good in a pair of overalls," Teddy said.

I hadn't seen Teddy in real life since I was nineteen, but even though she looked different—of course she did, it had been seven years—she was unmistakable.

I wasn't sure if that was because of her looks or just her general presence—probably a little bit of both.

Her copper hair was pulled up in the same bouncy ponytail as the first time I met her. She was wearing black leggings, a white crop top, and a grin. She had a bottle of pink wine in her hands. Behind her, Emmy appeared. She was sporting a red matching sweat set that would've made me look like a clown, but somehow she looked cute and comfy, which felt unfair.

"It's good to see you, Teddy," I said, walking over to her. I didn't normally do hugs, but it felt appropriate to greet Teddy with one. I was surprised that Emmy pulled me into one too—but with just one hand, since she was holding a few boxes of pizza.

"I didn't even recognize it in here," Emmy said when she pulled away. "It's great."

"Thanks," I said awkwardly. Emmy intimidated me. I didn't really know why—she was kind to me when we met. Funny too. It wasn't that I didn't like her—I just didn't think that she'd like me.

"I'm literally so happy you said yes," Teddy said. "Wes told us you're keeping the colored tile in the bathrooms. He was like vibrating with excitement."

"I love that pink tile," Emmy said. "I'm trying to convince Luke that we need more pink in our home."

"I agree on that," Teddy chimed in. "Not nearly enough pink in the ClemenLuke household." She turned to me. "When you're done here, you should head there and convince Brooks to get rid of the flannel furniture."

"It's one flannel chair!" Emmy exclaimed. "He likes it!"

"When did you become a flannel apologist?" Teddy responded.

"Says the woman who I know for a fact has flannel sheets on her bed at this very moment."

Teddy held up her hand to stop Emmy. "We're not talking about me here." I felt a pang in my chest—it was a pang in the same family as the one I'd felt when I'd first seen Luke and Emmy at breakfast that Sunday.

I didn't have a lot of friends, and I especially didn't have a lot of friends who were women. I never felt like I knew how to connect, or speak the right language, always just to the left of the right social cue. My mom never seemed to have that problem; she had only sisters and a group of girlfriends she was close to with whom she'd go to dinners or events. But she was beautiful and vivacious. I'd never seen myself as being like my mom.

So I'd built walls around myself. I didn't prioritize cultivating female friendships. I employed a severe brand of "I'm not like other girls" and decided that disliking Taylor Swift, not wearing makeup, and listening to obscure indie bands would become my entire personality. All to distract from the fact that I actually wanted to be exactly like the other girls.

But by the time I realized that and got sick of thinking of the things I loved (pink! *Twilight*!) as guilty pleasures, it was too late. Everyone already had a best friend or a group that I didn't fit into, and that was even more apparent as I'd watched Emmy and Teddy basically finish each other's sentences.

"What are you guys doing here?" I said. It came off rude—like most things I said, and I shrank back a little.

"Wes told us you were staying down here for a while for a project; we came to see if you wanted company," Emmy said.

"Girls' night," Teddy said. "And you can't tell us no." This whole thing made me nervous. Teddy was great, but I hadn't spent time with her in years. What if it took less than five minutes for her to realize that I actually suck? "But you can tell us all about the fact that you got caught making out with Wes at the bar." I gulped.

"Teddy!" Emmy was giving Teddy an "Are you serious right now?" look, but Teddy wasn't looking at her. She was looking at me, and she was smiling like the Cheshire cat. I guess it would be kind of nice to talk about whatever was going on with Wes and me.

"I'm going to need some of that first," I said, pointing to the wine that Teddy was holding. "And that," I said, pointing to the pizza.

"We have a cheese, a veggie, and a double pepperoni," Emmy said. We walked over to the workbench and set everything down. Teddy pulled a stack of paper plates and red cups from her bag.

"Knock, knock," another woman's voice came from the doorway. We all looked up—it was Cam. She walked into the house, still giving off the same power she had when she was in slacks and heels, but now she was in an oversize Margaritaville sweatshirt, biker shorts, and a pair of white sneakers.

"Party's here," Teddy said as she gave Cam a hug. Emmy hugged her too, and then Cam came to hug me. I was really going to have to get used to all of this hugging. I didn't give or get a lot of human contact these days.

"I'm supposed to be picking up Riley," Cam said, "but it looks like she's not down here."

"Who told you she was down here?" Emmy asked.

"Amos. He said he was down here too."

Emmy thought about that for a second. "You should call him and tell him you're staying here with us."

Cam looked confused. "Why?"

"Because that's what he wanted to happen." Emmy shrugged. "Teddy and I went to the Big House first. He knew we were down here and that we would ask you to stay. He's probably already got Riley excited about s'mores or something."

"That man!" Cam shook her head.

"He worries that you work too much," Emmy said. "And you do. So, all in favor of Cam staying, say aye."

Teddy's, Emmy's, and my hands all shot up and we said "Aye" simultaneously. Cam rolled her eyes, but she was smiling as she pulled out her phone and dialed someone—Amos, I assumed. She put it on speaker.

"Hey," she said. "Are you okay if I stay down here for a bit?"

"Stay down there all night," Amos said cheerfully. "I've got you covered. Riley and I are doing s'mores."

"S'mores!" a child's voice said on the other end of the phone.

"Riley, be good for Papa, okay?"

"I'm always good at Papa's," Riley said matter-of-factly.

"Okay," Cam said. "Have fun, Sunshine. I love you."

"Love you, Mama."

"Thank you, Amos," Cam said.

"Have fun tonight, ladies," Amos responded—assuming correctly that he was on speaker. "Love you."

Teddy, Emmy, and Cam all responded "Love you" before hanging up the phone. It was weird, being around all of these people who seemed genuinely to like and care for one another.

"Now that that's settled," Teddy said as she twisted the cap off the bottle of rosé, "girls' night can officially begin."

Emmy grabbed a speaker out of Teddy's bag and connected it to her phone. "How does everyone feel about a little Taylor Swift this evening?" Both Teddy and Cam nodded enthusiastically. "Ada?" she said, waiting for me to answer.

"Sure," I said. In my "not like other girls" phase, I'd actively disliked Taylor Swift. Now I was just indifferent. After telling people that I didn't like her for so long, I never really got into her music after that point in my life had passed.

Emmy looked at me for a second before she said, "Even if you don't like her now, you will before you leave Rebel Blue."

"We'll crush that internalized misogyny, no problem," Teddy added, and I couldn't help but laugh, even though I kind of hated that both of them seemed able to read me like a book. "Show us what you're doing to those curtains." Teddy gestured to the large pieces of linen that I had laid out.

"Come see," I said. "But leave the drinks over here." All three of them dutifully set down their Solo cups and followed me to the middle of the room. I knelt, grabbed a purple wildflower out of my box, and positioned it on the bottom of the curtain. "I'm not sure if this is going to work, but we'll see." I put a piece of parchment paper over the flower and pressed it flat, then grabbed a mallet.

"I love hitting things," Teddy said, rubbing her palms together. "This is going to be great."

I hammered the parchment paper a few times, making sure I hit every point on the flower. "So ideally," I started, "when I pull this parchment paper away, the flower should stick to it, and"—I peeled the parchment paper off the curtain—"the pigment from the flower should stay behind."

An abstract image of the purple wildflower was indeed left behind. Emmy let out a delighted squeal. "This is so cool," she said. "How did you come up with it?"

"There's a lot of things swirling around up here," I said, gesturing to my head. "And I've just been trying to think of ways to bring Rebel Blue Ranch inside this house in different ways."

"I really love that. My dad is going to love it." Emmy smiled thoughtfully down at the curtain. "You can say no, but do you think we could do some roses on a few of them?"

"Are there roses at Rebel Blue?" I asked.

"Yeah, my mom's rosebushes are in front of the Big House. I think it would be cool if she was a part of this too." Oh. *Oh.* When I first arrived, I'd spent a lot of time looking at the pictures in the Ryders' living room. After Emmy was born, there were only a few with the woman that I figured was their mom. I correctly assumed that she'd passed away sometime around then.

"Yes, of course. I love that idea," I said genuinely. Emmy smiled at me, and even though she and Wes didn't look as much alike as she and Gus did, I could see their similarities.

"This is badass, Ada," Teddy said. She rubbed her hands together. "Let's do it."

"Can we do some for my house too?" Cam joked. When they all complimented my idea, I started to feel . . . shy, like I had done something wrong somehow or like I didn't deserve their praise. "Should we tear a bunch of parchment paper first? For prep?"

"That is the most Cam thing I've ever heard," Teddy said.

"I already tore it all. I didn't know if we could do it with one or if we would need multiples," I chimed in.

Teddy looked between Cam and me. "Oh my god, there's another one," she said.

"Some of us like to be prepared," Cam responded with a laugh. "Not all of us can get away with flying by the seat of our pants."

"What can I say, I'm gifted." Teddy flipped her ponytail. "But since the parchment paper situation has been covered, I say we start with pizza and then get hammering."

So that's what we did.

I didn't know if I'd ever been a part of any sort of girls' night—maybe a sleepover or two in middle school or something—but it had always been more one of those things I saw in movies or on TV. This night made me miss something that I'd never experienced, and now I knew that I was right to miss it.

Emmy and Teddy were sitting on the floor, clutching each other's faces and screaming to a Taylor Swift song about begging someone not to be in love with someone else; Cam was double-fisting slices of pizza; and I was soaking it all in. Cam set down one of her pizza slices and picked up her cup. Out of nowhere, she dropped her Solo cup full of rosé on the floor before she could take a drink. We all looked at her. She was staring out the front window and she looked like she'd seen a ghost.

"Cam, are you okay?" I asked.

She shook her head, but not like she was shaking it no—like she was trying to shake something out of it. "Yeah, sorry," she said softly. "I just . . . I thought I saw someone." She had barely finished speaking when there was a knock on the front door.

All of our heads turned toward the sound as a man wearing a black cowboy hat walked into the living room. He had wavy blond hair that fell to his chin. His hair reminded me of a beach in Southern California. His face was angular, and a silver ring pierced one of his nostrils. He was tall, tan, and tattooed. I could see an *A* tattooed in an Old English font at the base of his throat on the right side.

Teddy let out a squeal and was immediately off the floor and running toward him. He caught her with ease, and she laughed. "Dusty Tucker, what the hell are you doing here?" she cried. "Last time I heard, you were wrangling cattle in Australia." Ah, so this was who Wes was telling me about.

Emmy had gotten off the floor too, and she went to give Dusty a hug. "Hey, Dusty," she said. She shot a quick glance back at Cam. It was concerned, so I looked back at Cam, who looked even more uneasy than she had after she'd dropped her cup. She saw me looking and quickly shook it off. I saw Cam's mask go up. I could tell when it happened because I did that too and knew exactly what it looked like.

"What are you doing here?" Emmy asked Dusty.

"Emmy, good to see you too," he responded.

"It's girls' night, no boys allowed."

"Not even me?"

"Not even you," Teddy chimed in. "But it is good to see you. Welcome home." Dusty's eyes scanned the room, resting on me for a second before landing on Cam. I watched his eyes widen, then go back to normal. When his eyes landed on her, it was like someone sucked the oxygen out of the room.

"Ash," he said, still looking at Cam.

"Dusty," she responded. Did her voice . . . shake?

"So, Emmy," he said, but he was still looking at Cam—I could've sworn he glanced at her left hand too. "I heard you and Brooks are a thing now." There was a hint of something in his tone. Sarcasm, maybe? Surprise?

"What about it?" Emmy said, crossing her arms over her chest. When I looked at her, the first thing I thought was *Damn, that woman can shoot some dirty looks.* I made a mental note never to say anything bad about Brooks in front of Emmy.

"I think it's great," Dusty said, finally looking away from Cam and holding his arms up in surrender. "I'm just shocked because I think the last time I saw the two of you together, you were ripping him a new one at a bonfire."

"Things change," Emmy responded.

Dusty looked at Cam again. "Yeah, they do."

"I'm Ada," I said, feeling I needed to protect Cam for some reason—like I needed to get his eyes off her. Dusty looked at me.

"Nice to meet you. I've heard great things." He reached out, and I shook his hand.

"Seriously, though," Emmy said, "it's girls' night, so you gotta get out."

"Weirdly, enough," Dusty said, "it's also guys' night, but apparently I'm in the wrong place."

"They're at Gus's," Emmy said, and Teddy made a gagging noise. "Why would they be here?"

"I don't know," Dusty responded. "That's just what your dad said when I stopped at the Big House." Interesting that Amos Ryder had sent *two* people down here today.

"All right, well, time to go," Emmy said. She put her hands on Dusty's elbows and turned him around so he was facing the door.

"I'm going, I'm going," he said, but before he went out the door, he turned back to Cam and said, "You look good, Ash." Then he was gone.

I looked at Cam. "Ash?"

She swallowed and shrugged. "Old nickname. My last name is Ashwood."

Chapter 16

Wes

I heard Dusty's old black Ford Bronco before I saw it. That thing was fucking loud, and it always had been. As it rolled up to Gus's house, I could hear Led Zeppelin over the sound of the engine.

Gus's house was a white two-story at the west end of Rebel Blue. He built it right before Emmy left for college, so about ten years ago. He's got a good setup—the house has four bedrooms and is far enough away from everything else on the ranch that it really feels like his.

Brooks, Gus, and I were sitting in Gus's front yard shooting the shit when Dusty walked over. He looked the same as when I last saw him—just a little older.

All three of us stood up to give him a "Hey, man" and a handshake.

"What the hell took you so long?" I asked.

"Your dad sent me down to the old Big House," Dusty said with a shrug.

"What? Why?" That was weird.

"He said you guys were down there," Dusty said, and then turned to Gus. "Riley's getting big."

Gus ran a hand through his hair, which for once wasn't covered by a hat. "Yeah, she is. I'm trying not to think about it, though." Gus shook his head. "But when did you see her? Cam should've picked her up already."

Something flashed across Dusty's eyes. "Cam was down at the old Big House. It's girls' night down there, apparently."

Gus nodded. "That's good, she needs a break." Gus grabbed a beer out of the cooler and threw it to Dusty, who caught it easily. "Drink up, we're jousting tonight."

Cowboy joust was Gus and Luke's favorite thing to do when we were hanging out—probably because they were really fucking good at it. As soon as the ropes were out, they turned into teenagers—extremely competitive teenagers.

The rules were simple. Each person was given a lasso rope. You face off with another person, run toward each other, and try to rope your opponent's legs. The harder they biff it, the better.

Tonight, it was Dusty and me against Brooks and Gus, as usual. I think Dusty and I had won maybe four times in our entire lives against that duo. It wasn't because they were better ropers—it was because they talked so much shit that they got into our heads.

We played for points. If you successfully roped your opponent's legs but they didn't fall, you got one point. If they stumbled and then fell, two points. If it was a clean lasso and you were able to pull their feet out from under them, you got three.

First team to thirty points won.

To start, it would be me against Gus. We stood about fifteen feet apart, not far enough apart that I couldn't see his stupid cocky smile.

I swear, the only things that could make Gus smile were Riley and the chance to kick my ass at something.

"You ready to lose, little brother?" he asked. His eyes were glinting.

In true middle-child fashion, the only response I could think of was "Shut up," which made Gus laugh.

"Loser chugs the rest of their beer?" he asked.

"Done."

Luke gave us the go-ahead, and we started running toward each other. I whipped my lasso above my head and immediately aimed for Gus's feet. When I threw the lasso, he jumped over it and threw his right as we passed each other. I tried to jump over it, but I ended up jumping into it. He pulled it tight, and I stumbled, fell, and hit the dirt.

"Two points!" Brooks called.

"No shit," I called back, still on the ground, looking up at the sky that was changing from blue to pink. I sat up and unwrapped Gus's rope from around my feet. Gus reached his hand out to me, and I took it.

I walked back over to Brooks, who handed me my beer, reminding me that losers chug.

Brooks and Dusty were next, and even though Dusty got his rope around one of Brooks's ankles, Brooks was too damn fast and pulled his rope right around both of Dusty's legs, and he went down immediately.

At least Dusty and I got a point.

When it was time for me to go against Brooks, he said, "If I win, you have to tell us what's going on with you and Ada."

"The designer?" Dusty asked.

"Nothing is going on," I started, but Brooks cut me off.

"I've been there before. I said that too, and I was full of shit, so." Brooks shrugged. "I don't believe you."

Really, nothing was going on. Well, something was going on, but I didn't know what it was, and whether it would ever be what I wanted it to be.

So there wouldn't be much to tell him, anyway.

"Fine," I said.

The difference between Brooks and Gus when it came to their competitive edge was that Gus wanted to win at any cost and wanted to win big, while Brooks wanted to win but was willing to give up a few points along the way, which always lured me into a false sense of security. When I got my lasso around his feet, I relaxed, and that was a big mistake. I got so focused on making him fall that I didn't notice that he hadn't thrown yet. He didn't try to lasso my feet. Instead, he threw his lasso right where I was running, and as soon as I stepped in, he pulled it tight, and I went down.

Again.

It was his signature move, and it got me every fucking time.

To be fair, he went down after I did, but he still got more points.

Both of us were on the ground and Brooks was laughing—a big, hearty laugh that had started appearing more often after he and Emmy got together. We got up and made our way over to the chairs on Gus's front lawn for a break.

"All right, then, Wes," he said. "Start talking." We were sitting around Gus's fire pit, but there was no fire going. We'd probably start one after the sun had set.

"I don't know, guys." I ran my hands through my hair. "I like her."

"Obviously," Gus said.

"Does she like you back?" Dusty asked.

I said, "I think so," at the same time Brooks said, "Yes." Dusty looked at us in turn.

"I caught them making out at the bar," Brooks said. *Jesus Christ.* People thought that the older women in Meadowlark were the biggest gossips. Well, them and Teddy's dad, Hank, but Luke Brooks and his big fucking mouth had all of them beat. It was a miracle that he'd been able to keep his and Emmy's relationship a secret for so long.

"I didn't even know her then," I said. "But now that I do, I like her a lot. She's whip-smart and funny and she works so fucking hard. And I think she likes me too, but I don't think she wants to, and that's what sucks."

"Woof" is all Dusty said.

I looked at Brooks. "What did you do?"

Brooks looked confused. "What do you mean? About what?"

"With Emmy. I mean, you two used to hate each other. What changed?" Brooks smiled, and his face took on that dopey look that it got whenever someone talked about Emmy.

"Everything," he said. "Everything changed the day Emmy came home, but I think, without really knowing it, both of us just started giving each other pieces of ourselves, and then we realized we wanted to keep them. Forever."

Gus was looking at Brooks thoughtfully. When it first came out that Brooks and Emmy were together, Gus didn't take it well. I don't think it was really because he didn't want them to be together, but because two of the people he loved the most felt like they had to lie and hide their relationship from him.

But the reason didn't change the fact that Gus didn't handle it well. Brooks walked away with a black eye and Gus walked away with a whole lot of guilt that I don't think he was over quite yet.

"I think the turning point was when I took her to my secret place," Brooks said. "Maybe you could do something like that?"

"Wait," Gus interrupted. "You have a secret place? What secret place?"

"Well, if I told you about it, it wouldn't be a secret, would it!" Brooks countered.

"But Emmy knows about it." Gus sounded genuinely offended.

"Yeah, so?"

"So why don't I know about it?"

"Because it's a secret, Gus."

"But I'm your best friend." My brother folded his arms over his chest. *Jesus Christ, these two.*

"And Emmy is the love of my life!" Brooks exclaimed, shooting Gus an exasperated look.

That point was hard for Gus to argue with, but he muttered, "I still think I should know about the secret place," under his breath.

"Okay, I hate to break up the lovers' quarrel," Dusty interjected, "but we're talking about Wes here." He nodded at me, and Brooks and Gus suddenly seemed to remember that I was there.

"Yeah, we're talking about me here," I said.

"Do you want my advice?" Dusty asked. Dusty was a good guy—noncommittal, but a good guy—so I nodded.

"At the end of the day, if she doesn't like you, she doesn't like you, and you should respect that." I was ninety-nine percent sure she did like me, but I understood what he was saying. "But if she does like you," he continued, "try doing things that let her know you've been thinking about her— that she's been on your mind. Keep it simple."

I constantly thought about her. The way she smelled— like a fucking sugar cookie. The way she bit the inside of her lip when she was thinking, or the way she always sat cross-legged whether she was on the floor or on a chair or the couch. It didn't matter.

Ada wasn't just "on my mind," she was *in* it—in every nook and cranny.

Chapter 17

Ada

After Dusty left, girls' night went off without a hitch. We ate, we drank, we were merry. And we got all of the curtains done. I promised Emmy that we would add some roses to them this week. Teddy gave me a full history of Taylor Swift's discography, explained to me the relationship between *Twilight* and My Chemical Romance, and offered to take me shopping at the boutique she worked at. Cam, who probably kicks ass at trivia, told us all about Wyoming's weirdest laws—don't even think about taking a photo of a rabbit between January and April.

And I had a nice time.

Usually I feel out of place in situations like that, and by the time the night was over, I would've convinced myself that everyone there hated me and that all of us would be better off if they never saw me again.

But I didn't feel that way about that night. I felt good.

The best part about the night? I was back at the Big House by nine-thirty.

Cam drove me back, since she had to pick up Riley anyway. I learned that she and Gus were never actually together, but they'd decided to co-parent Riley. "I'm lucky that my daughter's dad is also my friend," she'd said. "And he's really great at both."

The dynamics of this group of people were so interesting to me. Maybe it was the wine, but I didn't think before I asked, "Are they all as . . . good as they seem? The Ryders?"

Cam let out a little laugh that told me she understood what I was saying. "Yeah, honestly, they are," she said. "They have their flaws—except Amos," she joked. "Gus is entirely too stubborn and rigid, Wes is too accommodating and has a bad case of middle-child syndrome, and Emmy bottles everything up and has issues with control, but at the end of the day, all three of them would put everything on the line for each other and the people they love, and I feel lucky that my daughter and I are a part of that."

"What do you mean," I asked, "about Wes?"

"The accommodating thing or the middle-child thing?" she responded. I couldn't tell for sure in the dark, but I thought she was smiling.

"Both."

"Honestly, they're probably related. Ever since I've known him, Wes has just been so fucking nice—even if it meant being so at his own expense. His friend wants to ask the girl Wes likes to the prom? Oh, that's okay. They'll have a nice time. You have a flat tire? He'll change it for you even if it means he can't get to where he's going." I understood what she was saying, but it confused me because I didn't understand why this nice guy seemed to be into . . . me. "He does the same thing for his siblings and for his dad—he takes care of them, and sometimes I think he thinks that's all he's good for."

"But it isn't," I said, feeling the need to defend him.

"I know it. His family knows it, but I don't think he does. I think this guest ranch was his way of proving it to everyone else, but we already know. I hope he proves it to himself."

It's funny. Wes and I were so different but had found ourselves in the same situation—both of us felt we had something to prove.

After Cam dropped me off, I didn't feel quite ready for bed, so I decided to do something I hadn't done since I got to Meadowlark: take *the* shower. Wash my hair, deep condition, exfoliate, shave my legs—the works.

Honestly, my bathroom at the Big House had the best shower stall I'd ever been in, and I felt I needed to take advantage of that.

After I was clean, smooth, and warm, I stepped out of the shower into the cloud of steam that I'd created and went through my full skin care routine—complete with one of those peel-off gel facial masks. I even decided to pull out the cute pajamas—a black silk tank top with white lace trim and matching shorts.

Between the shower and the lack of self-loathing I was feeling after girls' night, I felt like a new woman.

I snuggled down under my bedcovers, rubbing my legs together and basking in the smoothness. I pulled out my laptop and went to a streaming app—the one with *How to Lose a Guy in 10 Days*.

Nothing could've made my night better. Except maybe

popcorn. I fucking loved popcorn, and now that the thought had crossed my mind, I couldn't get it out.

I had no doubt that the giant Rebel Blue pantry had microwave popcorn. I looked at my phone. It was just past midnight. The house would be quiet, and I would just pull the popcorn out before the microwave beeped.

I padded out of my bedroom, down the hall, and out to the kitchen. The pantry was at the back of the kitchen, and its shelves were stocked like a grocery store. I switched on the light and started looking for popcorn.

I found it on a high shelf near the front. Movie theater butter. *Excellent.* I was about to reach for it, but then I heard the front door close. I flipped the light off and waited. A few seconds later, Wes appeared in the kitchen.

Huh. I thought he was already home. He nearly walked by without noticing me, but at the last second before he made it to the hallway that led to our rooms, he stopped and looked over at me and did a double take.

Even in the dark kitchen, lit only by moonlight, I could see his bright eyes track up and down my body. I was suddenly very self-conscious about my choice of pajamas. Of course this would happen the one time I wore something other than a giant T-shirt and sweatpants to bed.

His throat worked as he looked at me, and his hands were balled into fists at his sides. "Hey," he said. His voice was gruff.

"Hey."

"Did you have a good night?" he asked.

"Yeah." I really had. "Did you?"

"I got my ass kicked, but yeah, I did." I just nodded, not sure when the kitchen had gotten so small. "Were you looking for something?"

"Popcorn," I said, pointing to it on the shelf behind me. "But I don't think I can reach it." I watched Wes swallow again and tried to tamp down the urge I had to lick the same trail on his throat.

He walked toward where I was standing in the pantry, and with every step he took, I felt goose bumps rising on my skin. When he stopped in front of me and leaned in, I let my eyelids flutter closed.

I told myself I didn't know what I was waiting for, but that was a lie. I was an expert at lying to myself, but what I was waiting for never came.

I heard something slide off a shelf behind me and Wes's voice saying "Your popcorn." I opened my eyes to see him right in front of me. There was heat in his gaze and a smile on his face.

"Th-thank you," I stammered. He nodded and took a step back, and that step felt like someone ripping a warm blanket off me. We stared at each other for a second, but he didn't come closer.

Fine.

I walked past him, and I swear when my arm brushed his, there was an electric shock.

After I tore open the popcorn package, I unfolded it, tossed it into the microwave, and pressed the Popcorn button.

Wes was still in the kitchen—I could feel him—so I stayed facing the counter instead of turning back to look at him.

After a few seconds, I heard his boots make their way toward me, and then I felt his hand trail over my shoulder and move my hair to one side of my neck, and a shiver rocked my spine.

Then I felt his lips on my shoulder. "Is this okay?" he murmured. It was actually a miracle that I could hear him, considering how loudly my heartbeat was echoing in my ears.

"Yes," I breathed. He kissed my shoulder again, and then my neck. I heard him take a deep breath.

"Why do you always smell so fucking good?" he asked. I didn't think he was looking for an actual answer, so I stayed quiet. "My truck smells like you," he said. "And now I take my life into my hands every time I drive because you are all I can think about. This"—he brought his arm around me and pulled me to him, leaving no space between us—"is all I can think about."

He moved my hair again so he could give the other side of my neck some attention, and when I felt his lips on my throat, I dropped my head back onto his shoulder and couldn't help but let out a small moan.

"I like you, Ada." His hand was under my shirt now, pressed against my stomach, and I ached for it to go lower, but my insecurities were starting to shout at me. Wes was a good guy. He was kind and thoughtful, and I had no clue why he would be interested in a woman like me. I'd spent my entire marriage basically begging my husband to notice me, see me, love me—to *do something.*

He never did.

When you're treated a certain way for so long, you start to believe that's how you *should* be treated. It left me feeling like there wasn't anything about me that someone *could* love.

And now, there was Wes. He was all these wonderful things that sometimes I wished I could be: chatty, charismatic, and deeply thoughtful.

I was cynical, shy, and I didn't really *like* that many people. Wes seemed to like everyone, and everyone seemed to like him—including me. I didn't understand how we could fit.

I lifted my head from his shoulder and looked down at the floor. "I don't know why you keep doing this, Wes," I said quietly, still looking down at the floor. "I don't know why you want me. I'm not . . . nice."

"Ada," he breathed. He used the hand that was on my stomach to turn me around to face him. The familiar buzz of electricity that appeared when he came near me hummed. I felt his finger under my chin, forcing me to look up at him. "You are earnest and talented, tenacious and funny." I couldn't have looked away from him if I'd tried. His green eyes gripped me and wouldn't let go. "I would never insult you by calling you something as generic as *nice*."

It wasn't his words that got me—it was his eyes. From the first time he looked at me until now, I felt Weston Ryder saw me, no matter how hard I tried to hide.

"Kiss me," I whispered. "Ple—" I didn't get to finish asking, because his mouth was on mine in an instant.

Kissing Wes was the closest thing I'd ever had to a religious experience. It felt like the sky opened up and stars started falling around us, like lightning struck every place where our skin touched and like my heartbeat had turned into a thunderstorm.

One of his hands cupped the back of my head and the other was around my waist, holding me to him, but I couldn't get close enough. I put my hands under his shirt and he sucked in a breath. "Your hands are fucking freezing," he said against my mouth. I giggled like an idiot and brought them around to his back, clutching him to me.

He used the arm that was around my waist to lift me onto the counter. I wrapped my legs around him, and his hips rolled. I could feel his hardness pressed against my center, and I wanted more. I started tearing at his flannel shirt, pulling it down his arms, and he threw it to the floor.

One of his hands skated up my bare thigh until he reached the hem of my shorts, where he stopped, but only for a second. He moved his hand up to cup my ass, and I moaned into his mouth.

When was the last time I'd done this? I couldn't remember.

When was the last time I'd felt anything near what I was feeling right now? Never. I knew that for sure.

I bit his lower lip and he moaned too, rolling his hips into mine again. "More," I pleaded, but it didn't work. He pulled back, and I wanted to scream.

A smirk was playing at his lips. "More?" he asked. His voice had taken on a playful tone. I nodded. He brushed the hand that was in my hair across my collarbone—his feather-light touch driving me to the brink.

"These are the silliest straps I've ever seen," he said, snaking one of his fingers under the spaghetti strap of my tank top before gently pushing it off my shoulder. He leaned in and put his mouth where my strap used to be, and I clutched at his hair. I moved my other hand between us, being more bold than usual, and cupped him through his jeans.

He groaned against my neck, and I felt it all the way through my body. "Christ, Ada." I loved the way he said my name. He pulled back again, and since my other hand was no longer holding him to me, I brought it to his belt so I could start undoing it, but before I could get very far, one of his big hands covered mine.

"Slow down, sweetheart," he breathed. "Do you like seeing what you do to me?" I looked down at his dick straining inside his jeans. I nodded, and he put pressure on my hands and groaned again. "I want to feel what I do to you," he said, touching his forehead to mine.

Oh. *Oh.*

"Touch me," I whispered. I normally didn't like this part. I always got embarrassed. Was I too wet? Not wet enough? It was usually the second one. Sometimes my body didn't like to cooperate. But still, I wanted this. I wanted him to touch me. His fingers were drawing circles on my thigh—inching closer and closer to where he wanted to be—where I wanted him to be. I opened my legs wider, inviting him in.

Our foreheads pressed together, both of us watched as his hand slipped under my shorts and between my legs. I gasped at the sensation of his finger sinking inside me.

"Fuck, Ada," he growled. I watched his finger slide in and out of me, slowly. "Still want more?" he asked. His voice was lower.

"Yes," I moaned, and he added a second finger.

"So needy," he said. "Those city boys don't know how to fuck you right, do they?" I shook my head. Pressure was building inside me, and it felt so foreign. I couldn't take it anymore—I brought my hands up to Wes's face and pulled his lips to mine.

He kissed me hard and steady, his tongue dipping into my mouth as his fingers pushed inside me. My breath started to come faster, and my hips started to roll of their own accord. His thumb brushed my clit, and I moaned, a breathy "Yes" falling from my lips.

"Help me make you come like this, Ada. Tell me what you need to come with my fingers buried inside of you." I didn't know. I'd never come like this—never during foreplay and never during sex. The heat making its way down my spine was unfamiliar to me, and all I wanted him to do was just keep going. I was desperate to see where this would go.

I was about to tell him as much when we were both jolted out of our lust trance by the sound of the microwave going off.

My life was a joke.

Wes, who reacted a lot faster than me, reached up and opened the microwave to make the beeping stop. Then he slumped over, laying his head against my shoulder.

Both of us were breathing heavily, but we could still hear footsteps coming down the hallway opposite ours. Wes turned, and he was broad enough to block me from view—at least that's what I hoped as I pushed the strap of my tank top back onto my shoulder—especially in the dark.

"Weston?" Amos's groggy voice came from the hall. "Is that you?"

"Yeah, Dad," he said. He was trying to mask his heavy breathing but wasn't doing a great job. "Sorry if I woke you."

"It's fine. Everything okay?" Amos yawned.

"Yep," Wes said. "Needed a snack, so just making some popcorn."

"All right, well, keep it down." Amos's voice was getting farther away as he walked back down his hall. "You don't want to wake Ada."

"No, we definitely wouldn't want that," Wes said under his breath, and I stifled a giggle. This was the second time Wes and I had been interrupted. I didn't know what it was about him that made me revert to a horny teenager who threw all caution to the wind, but I liked it. I liked feeling the rush of joy that came from being around him. "Good night, Dad," he said a little louder.

"Night," Amos said.

When he was sure his dad was gone, Wes turned back to me. He was smiling, and my heart thundered in my chest again. He leaned in and kissed my temple, and I reveled in how intimate it felt.

"C'mon," he said. "Let me walk you to bed." I was about to tell Wes that I wasn't tired, but instead of those words coming out of my mouth, a yawn escaped.

It looked like I had been successfully cockblocked by Amos Ryder.

Damn.

Wes grabbed my popcorn out of the microwave and helped me off the counter. My legs were wobbly, which made Wes laugh softly. "Shut up," I said as I elbowed him in the ribs.

He walked me to my room, and we stopped outside my door.

"Do you"—I couldn't believe I was saying this, I had to look down at the floor to get it out—"want to come in?" I peeked up at him. He looked conflicted.

"Not tonight," he said finally.

"But another night?" I asked hopefully.

"Yes," he said immediately. Another kiss on my temple. "Another night."

I nodded—that was probably best. "Good night, Wes."

"Good night, Ada."

Chapter 18

Wes

Before last night, I had a leash on my attraction to Ada. I could walk past her in her overalls and not have the urge to push her against the nearest wall and show her exactly what she did to me.

Not anymore.

All I could think about was the way her bare skin felt under my hands. Now that I knew what she felt like, nothing would ever be enough.

She wanted me. She was the one who'd asked me to kiss her—who'd demanded that I touch her. And now I was ruined.

Totally fucking ruined.

That's what was going through my head as I assembled a bunch of ingredients to make one of her favorite foods—the spinach pie thing that she'd told me about in the truck when I took her to town.

I was taking Dusty's advice and doing something that showed her that I was thinking about her. All the time.

There was only a small problem. I wasn't a very good cook. I could cook, and I did cook, but I wouldn't say everything was always one hundred percent edible. My dad made sure all of us knew cooking basics, especially Gus and me. From the time we were little, he told us that someday we might have to share a home with someone, and when that happened, it would be important to split labor—whether that was cooking, cleaning, or whatever.

Gus was like my dad. He loved to cook, and he was good at it. It was another thing he was better at than me. Which was a good thing, because now he had to keep a small human alive.

I could do the basics—eggs, grilled chicken, pasta, and I could toss the hell out of a salad—but spanakopita—that spinach pie—was a little out of my wheelhouse. Especially because it started with homemade pastry, which felt like it could go very wrong very quickly.

Whatever.

I was a capable guy, and I was going to do this—maybe not well, but I was going to do it.

Ada had gone down to Aggie's to talk about the stuff she wanted her to build. Teddy came and picked her up—apparently they were going shopping too—so I figured I had at least four hours to make this happen.

So far I'd been at it for a little over an hour, and all I had to show for it was a kitchen covered in flour.

When the front door opened, I heard Gus call out, "Anyone home?"

"In here," I called back.

"What the fuck are you doing?" Gus asked when he came into the kitchen. His eyes widened at the sight of me and all of the flour.

"I'm baking, obviously."

"You sure as fuck are not baking."

"Okay, well, I'm trying," I said. And no, it wasn't going great. "Ada mentioned that she liked this spinach pie thing that her mom makes, and now I'm trying to make it for her."

Gus came closer, and he took stock of all the ingredients on the counter and the pieces of pastry that I couldn't get to stick together. "No offense," he said, "but I don't think you're doing a very good job."

"That's really helpful, Gus, thank you," I snapped. His eyes widened again. I didn't get snappy very often.

"Tell me the breakdown," he said. "Maybe I can help." Gus walked over to the kitchen sink and started washing his hands. He was serious.

"In theory, it's easy," I said, running a floured hand down my face. I didn't even want to know what I looked like. "Like a spinach mixture and phyllo pastry?"

"Okay," he nodded. "Where's the phyllo?"

"That's what I'm making?" I said, unsure. It's what I was trying to make, anyway.

Gus looked a little too concerned for a conversation about pastry, but he said, "You're trying to make phyllo pastry? Have you never seen *The Great British Baking Show*?"

"What? No. Why are you watching *The Great British Baking Show*?" If there was one thing I could not imagine my older brother doing, it was sitting down and choosing to watch a TV show about baking.

"Riley likes it, and their accents are soothing." He shrugged. I looked at him with my mouth agape. "Whatever," he said, brushing me off. "That's not the point. The point is that store-bought phyllo dough is your friend because you're never going to be able to roll it thin enough." *Or roll it at all,* I thought, considering that it was in pieces all around me.

"Well, I don't have store-bought phyllo dough."

"I'll call Emmy."

"Why are we calling Emmy?" I was confused about how my sister got brought up in this situation. Was she a phyllo expert? Did she have a skill set I didn't know about?

"Because she's at the store." I rolled my eyes. Of course he knew that. Last month, Emmy was doing a solo cattle drive, and she didn't have a radio. We couldn't get hold of her, so I'd done what any normal person would do: I checked her location on her phone.

Apparently Gus hadn't known that was a thing. Now he was checking our locations constantly. I swear, every time I left the house, I got a text from him asking what I was doing.

"You need to stop checking our locations all the time. It's creepy," I said. Gus was already dialing Emmy. As he brought his phone up to his ear, he said, "I don't have to check yours anymore. You're always following Ada around."

Asshole.

I heard Emmy pick up. "Hey, are you still at the store?" Gus asked. Pause. "Can you pick up a package of phyllo dough—maybe two—and bring them to the house? Wes is trying to make his own." I heard Emmy's muffled voice on the other end of the phone. "Yeah," Gus said. "That's what I said. He doesn't watch it."

Jesus Christ.

"All right, see you soon." Gus hung up the phone. "Emmy will be here in twenty minutes. Let's start on this filling."

Gus started chopping scallions, garlic, and onions, and I started wilting some spinach in the biggest pan I could find. As much as I hated to admit it, Gus was a good person to have around in the kitchen. He read the recipe and took charge, and things started going a lot more smoothly.

Before long, Emmy came into the kitchen with a few grocery bags in tow.

"All right," she said. "I got five boxes of phyllo dough, because the situation sounded dire." Okay, well, that felt a little dramatic. "I also got a loaf of sourdough bread and a bag of Sour Patch Watermelons."

"Why?" I asked.

"Because Ada and I bonded over our love of both of those things last night, so I figured it would be good for you to have a backup in case whatever you're making isn't edible."

I wanted to argue, but she had a point, so instead I just said, "Thank you."

"You're welcome, and I also got you some mini Reese's." Those were my favorite. They had the perfect ratio of chocolate to peanut butter.

"Emmy," Gus said, "can you start prepping the phyllo? I got some olive oil and a brush out for you." She gave Gus a salute. Before she got started, she connected her phone to the kitchen speaker and started playing the country station. Emmy liked to have background sound—music, TV, whatever—while she was doing things. She said it helped her focus.

"Yes, Captain."

The three of us worked together on the dish. I think it was the first time since Emmy came home that we were together—just the three of us. It was really nice.

I recognized that when it came to the sibling department, I was a lucky guy. If I had to live in anyone's shadow, I was glad that it was theirs.

"So, Gus," Emmy said, "did you give Cam any sort of warning that Dusty was coming back to Meadowlark?"

"What?" Gus said, confused. "Why would she need a warning about that?"

"You're an idiot" was all Emmy said, with a shake of her head. I hadn't thought of giving Cam a warning either. Cam and Dusty had dated in high school. As far as I knew, Cam was the last woman Dusty had actually dated. It didn't end well, but I didn't know if that meant she needed a warning that he was coming home.

Together, the three of us layered the spinach filling and phyllo dough. Once we got to our last layer, Emmy brushed olive oil over the top of it, and we put it in the oven. I set a timer for twenty-five minutes.

Of course, it was nice that my siblings showed up to help, but I was more grateful that they stayed to help me clean up. I had made a giant fucking mess.

"So," Emmy said as we were cleaning up the last of the flour, "what inspired this bout of baking? Did something happen with Ada? Besides the initial makeout, obviously." I stayed quiet a second too long, because Emmy's eyes got big and bright as she shouted, "I knew it! I fucking knew it!"

She didn't have a chance to say anything more because the front door opened. Shit, that couldn't be Ada, could it? I looked at the clock on the microwave—the cockblock of the century—it had been a few hours since I started. *Shit.*

But it wasn't her voice I heard first—it was Teddy's. "That corset top is going to look so fucking good on you," she said as she came into the kitchen. Ada was right behind her, and my heart felt like a kick drum at the sight of her. Her oversize black sweater had fallen off one of her shoulders. I thought about putting my mouth there last night.

Fuck. My jeans tightened.

Her hair was pulled up in a bun, but since it was short, the bottom layers were falling out. She was wearing jeans that were tight on her hips but loose everywhere else. When she saw my eyes on her, she smiled.

God, she was beautiful.

"What am I smelling?" Teddy asked, looking around the kitchen. Once she saw Gus, she said, "Shit. That's what I'm smelling."

Gus rolled his eyes. "Is that all you've got today, Theodora?"

"No," Teddy said. "But lucky for you, I'm not really in the mood to watch a grown man cry today." Ada was looking from Gus to Teddy and back, like she was watching a tennis match.

"Okay." Emmy clapped. "What you're smelling is actually none of our business, and all of us are leaving now." She started pushing Gus toward the door. "Except for you, Ada. You get to stay." Emmy winked at her.

Subtle.

"Why do I have to leave?" Gus asked.

"Because you have things to do," Emmy hedged.

"No, I don't," Gus said—the only one who wasn't getting it.

"Oh my god," Teddy groaned. "You are literally so stupid. C'mon, Top Gun, let's go shave off that mustache."

"Oh, fuck off," Gus snapped. Emmy started to push him out, and Teddy helped.

"See you guys later!" Emmy called.

When I heard the door shut, it was just Ada and me. Whenever it was just the two of us, wherever we were felt smaller.

"Hey," I said.

"Hi," she responded, tucking some of her loose black hair behind her ear. I wanted to go to her and fold her into my arms, but I didn't want to come on too strong. I didn't know how to do this. Not after last night.

"How was your day? You met Aggie?"

Ada's face lit up. "Yeah, it was great. She is great. We're getting two credenzas, a kitchen table, and a coffee table, and she's doing custom leather pulls for some of the drawers."

"That sounds amazing," I said truthfully. I loved the way Ada brightened when she talked about Baby Blue. "I'm glad you got to catch up with Teddy too."

"Speaking of that." Ada sat down at the kitchen counter. She was directly across from me now. "What is going on between her and your brother?"

I had never been more confused in my entire life. "What do you mean?"

Ada raised her eyebrows. "There's obviously something going on there. Did they date or something?"

I laughed. "Teddy and Gus? You think something is going on between Theodora Andersen and August Ryder?"

Ada nodded excitedly. "Obviously. Can't you see the tension?"

"Yeah, because they hate each other," I said, confused. "Like actually hate each other."

Ada didn't seem convinced by what I was saying. "I would bet my life savings that something has happened or will happen between those two." She seemed very sure. I liked it.

"Maybe when hell freezes over," I countered.

"Fancy a wager?" Her smile was playful.

"You're on," I said, and I reached out my hand to shake on it. She looked down at my hand, studying it for a second before she put hers in it. We looked at each other, and I saw her chest heave slightly.

I wondered if she was thinking about last night.

I sure as fuck was.

"So," she said, pulling her hand away far too soon. "What am I smelling in here, though? It smells amazing." As if on cue, the timer on my phone went off, and I quickly grabbed some oven mitts and pulled the dish out of the oven. I set it on the hot pads that were right in front of Ada.

"Spanakopita," I said, suddenly nervous about . . . everything.

Ada looked down at the golden pastry and then back up at me. "Seriously?" she asked with the biggest smile I'd seen her sport since the bar. Her smile took all the words out of my head, so I just nodded. She looked back at the dish. "Did you do this for me?" Her voice was quieter now.

"Yeah," I said.

She bit the inside of her lip. "Why?"

That felt like a loaded question. Because I couldn't stop thinking about her, because I wanted her to be happy at Rebel Blue, because I wanted her to think about me the way I thought about her. "Because you told me it was your favorite food" is the answer I settled on, which was also true.

"Can I try it?" She sounded kind of excited.

"Hell yeah," I said, pulling a knife out of one of the drawers and bringing it over to her, along with a plate and two forks. "Do the honors?"

"My mom would kill me for not letting it sit for a minute, but . . ." She sliced a square and put it on the plate between us. The filling was steaming. Ada picked up a fork and motioned for me to do the same.

Both of us picked up a bite and blew on it to cool it down. I waited for her to taste hers. I wanted to see her reaction. She smiled as she chewed. She brought her hand over her mouth as she said, "It's good," with a nod.

I took my bite, and I wasn't expecting to like it, but I did. It was warm, and salty, and flaky, and . . . good.

"Do you like it?"

"Yeah, actually," I said with a chuckle, "I do."

"I think even my mom would say this is passable," she said, shaking her head in what looked like disbelief.

"Passable! What a compliment," I said with an exaggerated eye roll.

"I promise you, coming from Thalia Hart, passable is equivalent to a Nobel Peace Prize."

"Will you tell me about her?" I asked, not sure where that had come from. Ada paused midbite. She looked down at the spanakopita for a minute.

"My mom is . . . fierce and forthright," she said quietly. "She's a good mom—in her own way. She isn't affectionate like your family, but she's always there—even if she doesn't want to be.

"Her expectations for me have always been high," Ada continued, "and most of the time, I feel like I let her down." Hearing her say that sent a knife to my heart. Ada was magnificent, and I wanted everyone to see it—to see her. "She left her whole life behind when she came to the U.S. Everything she has, she built herself. She had dreams for me growing up—dreams that I would never have to work for as hard as she did. I think that I'll always feel a little bit guilty for following my own dreams instead of hers."

"What did she say about coming to Wyoming?" I asked.

"Waste of time. She has been keeping up on my social media pages, though—sending a few messages when she likes something and a lot more when she doesn't."

She sighed and was earnest when she said, "But she's a good mom. And my dad is a good dad."

"Tell me about him?" I asked.

Ada seemed to think on that for a moment. "He's quiet, doesn't really love people, but he's a dedicated provider. He worked a lot while I was growing up, so he wasn't a hands-on parent, but I know he would do anything for my mom."

I nodded and reached across the table to grab her hand. I

liked that she'd told me all of that. I loved feeling like I knew her.

She didn't pull away. Instead, she said, "Now I get to ask you a question."

"Shoot," I said.

A smile stretched her lips. "Why do you have flour all over your face?"

Chapter 19

Ada

Things were changing between Wes and me. When we were at the job site, there were these little touches—our arms brushing when we passed each other, a hand on my elbow or my lower back to steer me out of someone else's path—stuff like that.

When we were at the Big House, we normally ate dinner together. Earlier this week, we watched a movie on the couch, and he put his arm around me.

And I didn't hate it.

I didn't know what this thing with him was, but I loved the way it felt. For the first time in my life, I think I had a big ol' crush. It was new and exciting, but it also felt stable and natural—like it was the start of something that would last.

That's what I was thinking about when he came up to me—without Waylon, I noticed—at the end of our workday and asked, "Can I take you out?" My head snapped up from my phone, where I was posting some updates on the vaulted ceiling and bathrooms on my stories. Wes was wearing what I'd started to refer to in my head as his uniform—white

T-shirt and blue jeans. These blue jeans looked like they were on their last legs, but he made them look perfect—like that Bruce Springsteen album cover.

"Take me out? Isn't it a faux pas to ask someone for permission to kill them?"

Wes's cheeks turned crimson, and all the butterflies in my stomach erupted from their cocoons. "Probably," he said. "But I don't want to kill you. I want to take you out like on a date."

"Oh," I said, surprised. "Um . . ." I wanted to say yes, but I didn't know what that would mean for whatever this thing was. What if we went on a date and everything changed? What if he spent enough time with me that he actually started to dislike me like everyone else?

Like my ex-husband.

He liked me until he didn't.

And for some reason, I had a feeling that if Wes decided he didn't like me, it would hurt a lot worse than Chance deciding he didn't like me—even though his decision ended with his leaving for work and never coming back, and my getting divorce papers in the mail.

Thinking about Chance and my marriage was still an unwelcome thing. Not because of him, necessarily, or the fact that I had been married, but because I wasn't proud of the person I was during that time. It took about a month after we got married for me to realize all of the small things he was doing that were ways of controlling me.

Even though it was a bad situation, I wouldn't undo it. But I wish I could go back and tell myself not to fight so hard to stifle myself and push myself into a box that I would never fit into. I cut off so many pieces of myself trying to fit into his box, and I was just starting to get all of them back.

"You can think about it," Wes said after I was quiet for too long.

"No," I said, and I watched his face fall. "I mean, yes to the date and no, I don't have to think about it." Wes wasn't Chance, and I wasn't the same Ada that I was a few years ago.

His face brightened again—like the sun coming out from behind the clouds. "Saturday?"

"Saturday," I responded. I said it quietly—like a wish. Wes's dimples appeared as he smiled at me, and I had the urge to plant one on him. Right here in the middle of the job site. I knew if I did it, he would start blushing.

Blushing Wes was my favorite Wes.

"Ada." Evan's voice drew a cloud across the sun that was Weston Ryder. He was walking toward us, looking worried.

"What's up?" I asked.

"There's a storm warning," he said. "Everyone just got an alert on their phone. It's supposed to hit within the next hour. They're saying to get to a spot where you can shelter in place."

I looked down at my phone and saw the same notification. I must've been distracted by Wes's dimples when it came through.

"All right," I said. "Let's make sure that anything that needs to be is tarped over, and then we'll send everyone home."

Both Wes and Evan sprang into action, working at lightning speed to secure the house. Wes even had the crew cover the windows in case the wind got bad. We hadn't replaced those yet—they were supposed to get replaced tomorrow—so the chances that a storm could knock them out was higher than it would be with new windows. And I had plans for the old windows, and to make those plans happen, I needed them to be intact.

In less than twenty minutes, the crew was heading home for the day, and the sky was already darkening. A lot.

"Do you want to stay here?" Wes asked Evan, who was the last one in the house with us. "You're welcome at the Big House. It looks like it's getting bad out there fast."

Evan shook his head. "I've become really partial to my little inn room. I'll be okay. Thank you, though."

I leaned in to give him a hug—something I didn't do very often, which Evan noticed, because it took him a second to awkwardly hug me back. "Text me when you get there, okay?"

"I will," Evan said. "Be safe, you two." Evan untangled himself from my arms and shook Weston's hand before heading out the door.

"Is it okay if I drive us back today?" Wes asked. I'd been driving us back to the Big House a few times a week, still learning how to drive stick. I was getting better, but I didn't have the confidence to drive in a storm, that was for sure, so I nodded, grateful he'd offered. "Are you ready to go?"

I looked around the house, making sure everything looked okay and that I wasn't missing anything. Not that I really knew that much about prepping for a storm. I was just guessing, so I was glad Wes was here. "Yeah, let's go," I said.

Wes opened the brand-new front door—I was pretty sure it would hold—and guided me out with a hand at my back before locking the door behind us. He grabbed my hand, intertwining our fingers, and I let him.

Even though it had started to rain, Wes still opened the passenger door for me and made sure I was inside before shutting it and heading to the driver's side. We were outside for less than ten seconds, and I was already soaked. Water was dripping off Wes's cowboy hat.

"Let's go home," Wes said as he shut his door. As if to emphasize his point, thunder clapped in the distance. He started driving back to the Big House, and the rain hit the windshield harder and harder the farther we got from the job site.

Thunder clapped again—closer this time—and it made me jump. Wes reached his hand across the bench seat and held mine again.

I let him.

He used his thumb to draw soothing circles on my hand, and when he needed to change gears, he brought both of our hands to the gearshift, just like that first day in the truck.

But so much had changed since then.

I watched the rain pelt the windshield. I watched the trees get jerked around by the wind and saw lightning on the horizon.

The truck's windshield wipers couldn't keep up with the rain, so I almost didn't see it when a small brown figure bolted in front of the truck, but Wes did. He swerved, and my head almost hit the window.

He brought the truck to a halt, undid his seatbelt, and slid across the bench seat to me. Before I registered what was going on, his hands were on my face. "I'm so sorry, sweetheart." His hands moved from my face to my neck to my shoulders, down my arms and back up. "Are you okay?" I nodded. I was fine—I just got jerked around a bit, but no more than I would during rush hour traffic in San Francisco. "I had to swerve. I think that was a calf." His hands were on my face again. It's like he was searching me for any sort of injury.

"I'm fine," I said. "Seriously." His hands were still searching, so I didn't think he believed me. "Wes," I said firmly before I leaned in and kissed his cheek. He froze. "I'm okay. Everything is okay." I kissed his other cheek. "You said that was a calf that ran out in front of us?"

"I—I think so. I don't know for sure. I need to check."

"Okay," I said. Our noses were almost touching. "Let's check, then." At the suggestion of our going back out into the rain together, Wes snapped out of whatever trance he'd been in when he thought I might be hurt.

"Stay here," he said. "I'll be right back." Before I could protest, he'd pushed open the driver's-side door and gone out into the storm.

"Oh, like hell," I said—to no one, since I was now the only one in the truck—and went after him.

The rain was fucking freezing—within a few steps, I was chilled to the bone. Wes was headed toward a small group of trees, and I ran to catch up.

I grabbed his hand—unsure of when I became such a big fan of hand holding—and he immediately turned to me. "I told you to stay in the truck," he said. His eyes were pleading with me.

"I want to help," I said, sticking my chin out. "I'm already out here." I could hear Wes's sigh over the rain—which was saying something.

"Fine," he said. He walked into the trees. Wes was right, it was a calf, and we found it after a few minutes. The small brown calf was huddled against the trunk of a tree. Wes approached it slowly and leaned down.

The poor thing was so much smaller than I expected it to be—and it looked so scared. It looked like it was hurt, too, and my heart broke.

"Hey, baby girl," Wes said softly. "What did you get into here?" It was then that I noticed something—some sort of metal maybe—around the calf's neck and down its chest.

Barbed wire, maybe?

Wes turned away from the calf and stalked back toward the truck. What the fuck was he doing?

I ran after him. He was not about to turn his back on this baby cow on my watch. Absolutely fucking not.

"What are you doing?" I shouted. I didn't know if he could hear me over the sound of the storm. He kept walking. "Weston!" God, had his legs always been this long? How was he walking so fast?

Why was he leaving?

When I reached him, I grabbed his arm and turned him toward me. "You can't leave her there!" I shouted. "She needs you!" I didn't know where they came from, but there were tears pricking at the corners of my eyes, pushing against them, desperate to fall. "You can't leave her alone. She can't be alone. Not in this storm. Couldn't she die out here?" I didn't wait for him to answer. "Please," I begged. "Don't leave her alone."

Wes's green eyes were soft as they studied me.

I was crying now—my warm tears mixed with the cold rain as both of them rolled down my face. I couldn't remember the last time I'd cried, but the thought crossed my mind that I might have been crying for more reasons than just a calf in the storm.

"Please," I said again.

Wes pulled me to him and held me tight. "I'm not going to leave her, sweetheart. I would never leave her," he murmured in my ear.

I pulled back and looked up at him. "Then why did you walk away?" I sniffed.

"I came to get the wire cutters. Then we're going to get her in the truck and take her home." *Oh.* Wire cutters.

"We-we're bringing her home?" I asked.

"Yeah, where else would we take her?" Huh. Good question. Wes kissed my temple. "There's a blanket under the jump seat. Get that out for her, okay?" He let me go and got a small pair of wire cutters from a toolbox under the front seat. "I'll be right back."

I stood in the rain and watched Wes walk back toward the trees. Once he was out of sight, I climbed into the truck and felt around in the back for the blanket Wes was talking about. I found it and pulled it out.

Less than five minutes later, I saw Wes coming back through the trees, and this time he had the calf in his arms.

When I saw him through the rain, I imagined that this is how some people might feel when they saw a man carrying a baby. I wasn't a big fan of babies, but apparently I was a big fan of baby cows, because Weston Ryder had never looked better.

A cowboy, with his white shirt clinging to his body, his brown cowboy hat, and a calf in his arms that he'd just rescued from a storm?

Damn.

Damn.

He made it to the truck and I opened the passenger door for him. I hopped out but left the blanket inside. I wanted it to stay dry.

"I need you to climb in the back, sweetheart," Wes said.

Well, this was definitely *not* the context in which I thought this cowboy would say those words to me, but I did what he said. I was not graceful about it—it was less of a climb and more of a flail and fall.

He gently set the calf on the blanket and then wrapped it up and around her body. The calf was looking up at him the way Waylon did—with complete adoration.

He quickly shut the door and ran around to his side and got in. It was then that I noticed a growing crimson stain on his shirt.

"What happened?" I asked. I didn't even try to mask the concern in my voice.

"What?" he responded.

"Your ribs," I said. "You're bleeding."

Wes looked down and let out a heavy exhale. "Must've had a run-in with the barbed wire. I didn't feel it. I'll look at it when we get home." With that, he started the engine and got us back to the Big House. I spent the drive alternating between looking at the baby calf, who was probably the cutest thing I'd ever seen, and the cowboy, who was absolutely the greatest person I'd ever met.

When we pulled in to the garage, the thunder was getting louder, and I noticed that Amos's truck wasn't there. I hoped he was somewhere safe.

Wes got out of the truck and opened the door to the house, then he came back and got the calf and I got out behind them. Waylon came running out of the house and into the garage.

I was glad he'd stayed home today. I knelt and gave him a good rubdown.

Wes set the calf down on a dog bed near the door to the house. He walked to the back of the garage and returned with a space heater and a stack of blankets. He turned on the space heater and arranged a nest of blankets around the calf.

"Sweetheart," he called. That was me. "There's a heating pad in the hall closet. Can you go grab it for me? You should see it right when you open the door." I nodded and ran inside to the hall closet, grabbed the heating pad, and got back out to the garage as fast as I could.

Both Wes and Waylon had settled in next to the calf. It looked like Wes had cleaned her cuts—there was no more blood sticking to her chocolate fur. I quickly pulled my phone out of my pocket and snapped a picture before Wes noticed.

I wanted to remember this moment.

"Thank you," Wes said when he saw me with the heating pad. I handed it to him, and he turned it on low. He put it down next to the calf, whose eyes were starting to droop.

"What do we do now?" I asked.

"We give her a name," he said. That was the last thing I expected to come out of his mouth. He must've seen my confusion because he said, "When calves get left behind, we bring them home. We name them and they're ours. Growing up, we had Dolly, Tammy, Patsy, and Reba."

I wasn't a country music fan, but I could pick up on the theme in the names Wes just shared. So I said the first name that came to my mind: "What about Loretta?"

Wes smiled. "Loretta is perfect." He reached out and gave one of Loretta's ears a good rub. She nuzzled into his other hand.

"Tonight, we feed her. We make sure she stays warm and sleeps." As if on cue, the calf closed her eyes. "Tomorrow, I'll have the vet check her out."

I nodded. That sounded good. "Is she okay for right now?" I asked.

"Yeah," he said. "Waylon will keep an eye on her. He'll come get us if something's wrong. I put some feed behind the bed for her, and I'll give her a bottle later."

"But she's good?" I asked again. "All taken care of?"

"Yeah, why?"

I grabbed Wes's hand and pulled him toward the door. "Because someone needs to take care of you now."

Chapter 20

Ada

"Take off your shirt," I demanded. Wes and I were standing in the hallway bathroom because that's where the first aid kit was. He'd told me about it on my first day here. I wasn't really a caretaker. I didn't know how to be one, but I would do my best for Wes.

For the first time ever, I *wanted* to take care of someone. In the past, I was mostly concerned with myself, which I needed to be at the time. I had to focus on taking care of me or I would've faded away. But right now, I felt like Rebel Blue had helped heal me enough that I could care for someone else.

"Ada, I can clean this up," he said, gesturing to the blood-stain on his shirt, which looked a lot bigger than it did in the truck. "You have to be freezing. Do you want to take a bath? I bet there's bath stuff in your bathroom. I can start it for y—"

I didn't let him finish that sentence, even though a bath sounded lovely. "Weston I-don't-know-your-middle-name Ryder. Take off your goddamn shirt. Now."

He let out an annoyed sigh and pulled his wet T-shirt over his head. I took in his form in front of me but tried not to make it obvious. I didn't know how long I would've stared at him if I hadn't had other matters to attend to, but it was probably an alarming amount of time. His chest was broad and muscular and bore a smattering of dark hair. The panes of his stomach were defined but not exaggerated.

The cut didn't look too bad, thank god. I reached out to touch the skin near it and Wes hissed. "Your hands are fucking freezing!" he said between clenched teeth.

"Sorry," I murmured. "Does it hurt?"

Wes shook his head. "Not really."

"Good," I responded. "So, I should probably clean it first, right?"

Wes's mouth cracked into a smile. "Yeah, you should clean it first, or I can, and you can go take a bath and warm up your icicle hands."

"No can do," I said. I found a clean washcloth under the sink and wet it under the hot water. I took a deep breath before I dabbed the cut, which was a couple of inches long. Wes jerked away the first time I dabbed it, but then was able to stay still. I looked in the first aid kit and saw a bottle that said ANTISEPTIC SPRAY, which sounded promising. I figured Wes would tell me if I was doing something wrong, but he stayed quiet after I grabbed it, so I continued, trying not to notice the way the air was thickening around us.

I sprayed the liquid on the cut, and Wes flinched. Next, I went for the familiar-looking yellow antibiotic ointment and used a cotton swab to apply some along the length of the cut.

"Is that good?" I asked.

"It's good," Wes breathed. So I found the biggest Band-

Aid in the kit. I tore it open and thought about the best way to get it on the cut. I went with the tried-and-true stick-and-peel—starting with the pad on the cut, then slowly pulling the paper off and sticking the adhesive part to the skin at the same time. Once it was in place, I gave it one more firm press.

And then the lights went out.

The darkness charged the air around us with an electric current that I could feel in my bones. I heard Wes swallow before he murmured, "Rhodes."

"What?" I whispered, not moving my hands from his body.

"My middle name is Rhodes," he said. Weston Rhodes Ryder. *That's a good name,* I thought. It was the last thing I remember thinking before he kissed me.

It was a short kiss. He pulled away after a few seconds, and I immediately missed his mouth on mine. I didn't have to miss it for long, because he kissed me again, and again, and again. The space between the kisses got shorter, and the kisses themselves got longer, more languid.

This wasn't like the bar or the kitchen. There was no frenzy. It was just us and these kisses. Slow and deliberate.

I skated my hands up his chest and onto his shoulders. I loved the way his warm skin felt under my hands.

He knotted his fingers in my damp hair and pulled my head back slightly, using his extra leverage to tangle our tongues together. I was desperate for him. I wanted to be closer. I pushed up on my tiptoes, and Wes dragged one of his hands down my body and over my ass. I lifted my leg, and he grabbed behind my thigh and hitched it up over his waist.

"Take me to your room," I said against his mouth.

His hand tightened in my hair and his hips rolled. "Are you sure?" he breathed.

"Yes." I don't think I'd ever been more sure of anything. I tried to bring down the leg that he was holding, but instead, Wes hoisted me up, and my legs instinctively wrapped around him.

He carried me out of the bathroom and down the hall. I kissed and sucked at his neck as he walked. I heard him open a door, and even though it was dark and I'd never been in here before, I knew we were in his room.

It smelled like him. Like cedar.

Instead of taking me to his bed, which is where I was desperate to be, he set me down and stepped back a bit. He put his hand to my face, then moved it to my neck, then down over my breasts and stomach. His touch was so light that it made me want to scream.

He stopped at the hem of my shirt. "Can I?" he asked.

"Please," I breathed. He gripped the bottom of my shirt with both hands and gently pulled it over my head. I was grateful that I'd put on one of my not-trashed black bras today. His nostrils flared as he took in the sight of me.

I didn't even want to know what I looked like—probably a drowned rat—but I didn't care, and apparently he didn't either.

Wes tossed my shirt aside and knelt. He put his hands on my hips and kissed my stomach as he started to pull my leggings—torturously slowly—down. I was less lucky with the underwear—there were definitely a few holes in the ratty black thong—but he didn't seem to care about that either.

I put my hands on Wes's shoulders for balance as he

helped me step out of my leggings. He tossed them on top of my shirt and looked up at me. This man was on his knees and looking up at me like I was the most precious thing in the world. He was touching me that way too—dragging his fingers up and down my thighs, over my hips, and under my thong. "You're beautiful," he said, then kissed each of my hip bones and got to his feet.

His words hit me just right. It's not like I thought I wasn't pretty, but I would be lying if I said my self-esteem hadn't taken a hit after everything with Chance—especially in the bedroom. Chance and I had been together—a term I'm using loosely—for two years, then married for three and a half months. We had sex maybe ten times during that two-and-a-half-year period. When we were just dating, that didn't really bother me, but after we got married, it started to take a toll on my self-esteem. I felt like I grossed him out, like he didn't want me, and whenever I tried to tell him that I wanted to feel like he wanted me, he shrugged it off.

There was no doubt in my mind that Wes wanted me as much as I wanted him, and it made me feel free and bold and excited.

So I kissed him again. I wrapped my arms around him, wanting as much of our skin touching as possible. He held me tight, lifted me off the ground, and took me to his bed. When he laid me down, he did it gently. No one had handled me with such care before—not just during sex, but ever.

"I haven't stopped thinking about this since the night at the bar," Wes whispered. He was hovering above me. "Do you ever think about what would've happened if we hadn't got caught?"

I nodded. I'd played that fantasy in my head over and over again the past few months.

"I wanted to fuck you against that wall." Wes bit my neck softly. "When we got caught, I was just about to tell you my name because I wanted to hear you moan it over and over again while I was inside you." He licked up my neck, and I drew a sharp breath. "And then you showed up here, and for the first time in my life, I felt lucky."

I let out a breathy laugh. "I'm sorry I was so mean to you."

"Don't be," Wes said as he rolled his hips into mine, and that made us both groan. "It weirdly turned me on."

"Wes . . ." I said, suddenly nervous. "Before we do this, I—I—" I stumbled over my words, trying to get them out as quickly as possible because I didn't know how he was going to react. "Sometimes it takes a while for me to get wet, and it's not because I don't want this or because I'm not attracted to you, because I do and I am—it's just my body." He didn't respond right away, he kept biting and sucking at my neck.

Then he whispered against my skin, "Sometimes it takes a while for me to get hard because of my antidepressant, and it's not because I don't want you. Honestly, I don't think I've ever wanted anything more."

This moment felt raw and vulnerable and important. I wanted to see him. I knotted my fingers in his hair and pulled his mouth away from my neck, forcing him to look at me. "So," I said, "we'll get there together, then?" He swallowed and nodded.

"Tell me what you like," he said.

I thought about it for a second, because what I'd liked in the past really didn't matter—only Wes did now. Everything was different with him. "I like kissing," I said, which won me one of his big-dimpled smiles and, of course, a kiss.

"Noted," he said.

"And I like it when you talk to me," I continued. "And when you bite me."

Wes dragged one of his hands down my body—over my breasts, down my stomach, until his pinky skated under my thong. Heat followed his trail. "Should I tell you about how I almost came in my jeans in the kitchen? Just from touching you?" He brought his mouth down on mine and forced mine open so his tongue could make its way in. "Should I tell you about how I had to get in the shower and fuck my fist to the thought of you writhing on the counter?" Wes started to pull my underwear down. "Or should I tell you that your pussy felt so good on my fingers that I would literally die to know what it feels like wrapped around my cock?" He rolled half-way off me so he could drag my thong all the way down my legs and throw it across the room. Then he pulled me on top of him. "Should I tell you that I felt like I could taste you on my fingers for days?"

Jesus Christ. Not only did Wes ask me what I liked in bed, but he also followed through. This man was something else. I leaned down and kissed him. Hard. My hips started to roll of their own accord. Wes's large hands were kneading my ass, guiding me to grind on his jeans. The pressure felt so good. He felt so good.

I could feel my body reacting to him—like lava rolling down my spine and pooling between my legs. "That's it, sweetheart," he said against my mouth. "Take what you need."

Him. I needed him.

I sat up and brought him with me so we were upright and tangled in each other. I scraped my nails over his back and knotted my fingers in his hair. He kept one hand on my ass and unclasped my bra with the other. The sensation of the straps falling down my arms made me want to scream.

He made everything feel like too much. Or just enough. I didn't know.

I was naked now, and getting wet, but Wes wasn't in any hurry. He kept kissing me and touching me and letting me roll my hips on his jeans. After a few minutes, he flipped me onto my back again. He stood up, and I reached for him. "One second, sweetheart," he said. "It's time for these to go." He unbuttoned his jeans, and I could see the veins in his forearms as he pulled them down and stepped out. I could see his dick straining against his briefs. It looked like the foreplay makeout session had worked for both of us.

"Briefs too," I breathed. He flashed me a roguish smile and I might have been able to orgasm from that alone. It shot heat all the way through me. But he did what I said. He stood at the edge of the bed and pumped his length a few times as he looked at me lying naked before him. My mouth watered.

"You're magnificent," he whispered reverently. Normally, that would make me want to cover up and run away, but not with Wes. Instead, I preened under his praise, I basked in his sunlight.

He was back on top of me now, kissing me harder and with more urgency. His cock slid against my pussy and both of us gasped. He started moving his hips, and I met each of his thrusts. "Fuck, Ada," he breathed. "You have no idea what you do to me."

"Show me," I said. With that, he brought one of my hands to his dick. I wrapped it around his length and pumped. He moaned. I did it a few more times and the arms that were holding him steady above me started to shake. I loved watching the effect that I had on him. It made me confident. It turned me on.

"Fuck, fuck, fuck," he said as he pulled my hand away. "Can I touch you now? Please, god, let me touch you." Underneath him, I spread my legs more, inviting him to do exactly what he wanted. "Tell me I can," he breathed.

"You can touch me," I said. Wes wasted no time in sinking one of his fingers into me and I gasped. I could feel how wet I was—I could hear it, too, as he pumped his finger in and out of me—adding a second one after a few thrusts.

"You're so perfect, Ada. You feel so perfect," he said. "I want to make you come on my fingers, like I would've in the kitchen." His thumb rubbed against my clit as his fingers moved, and I jerked. He smiled, knowing he was on the right track. His fingers curled inside me, and I jerked again. "Be good," he said as he brought his other hand to my hips, holding me down.

His long fingers were hitting a spot inside me that my small ones couldn't reach, and holy fuck, this man was going to do exactly what he said and make me come on them. He kept going, not slowing down, not speeding up, he kept a steady pace and I felt my orgasm starting to build. It felt foreign and overwhelming and wonderful.

I started to pant. "Wes," I moaned.

"Fuck," he said. "That's right, sweetheart. Let go. Let me see you come apart." My body started to thrash, but Wes held my hips in place. His fingers hit that spot inside me one more time, thunder boomed, and I fell over the edge.

"Oh my god," I moaned as the orgasm rocked my body. Wes didn't let up, he kept doing exactly what he'd done to bring me to the edge. My hips bucked, and I grabbed on to a pillow behind me—needing something to hold on to or else I felt my body would float away.

As I came down, Wes's fingers slowed. He leaned over me to kiss me, and I could feel his cock against my thigh. Long, thick, and rock fucking hard. When he pulled away, he brought his fingers to his mouth and closed his eyes, as if savoring the taste, and I felt myself blush.

Fuck.

"I want you," I said, clutching at his shoulders. "I want to feel your cock inside of me, please. I need more." Wes brought his mouth down to mine again and kissed me firmly. I could taste myself.

"I haven't done this since my last physical," he said. "I don't have any STIs, but I do have condoms."

"I'm all clear too," I said. I got tested right after the divorce. "But I would feel more comfortable if we used a condom this time," I said honestly. I'd never had sex without one—even when I was married.

Wes kissed my temple and nodded. "You got it. Don't move," he said as he got up and crossed the room to his dresser. I saw him pull out a box and then a foil package be-fore he walked back and knelt on the edge of the bed. I watched him hungrily as he tore the package open with his teeth and started to roll the condom down his length.

He was watching me watch him. Everything with him felt so charged. Once the condom was in place, he crawled back up my body slowly, deliberately, kissing, licking, and sucking along the way. When he slotted his dick at my entrance, I was already panting again.

Everything about him did it for me.

"Is like this okay?" he asked, and I nodded eagerly. I didn't want to wait another second. When he slid the head of his cock inside me, it was like all of my bones melted. "Ada," he said as he slowly worked himself in, "I think you were made for me." It was a tight fit, so he worked slowly, pulling out and then sliding back in a little farther each time.

I was shaking beneath him, and I could see sweat on his forehead. When he was all the way in, he collapsed against my neck. "Fuck," he groaned, kissing me there, "just give me a second."

I could feel his heartbeat, and I knew he could feel mine—it was kicking so hard against my ribs I thought they might break.

Finally Wes started to move, and the world stopped. He started slow, thrusting in and out of me at an easy pace. It felt so good. "I've imagined what it would feel like to be inside you a million times," he moaned. "My dreams don't even come close."

He started to pick up the pace. I clutched at his back, his hair, his ass—anywhere I could get my hands on. I wanted to touch all of him.

"Wes," I moaned. "This is so good." My voice was almost unrecognizable to my own ears.

"Say my name again," he demanded.

"Wes," I said. I chanted it over and over as he drove his hips against me harder and faster. I closed my eyes, nearly ready to fall over the edge again. But his hand gripped my jaw firmly.

"Open your eyes, Ada. There's no one coming, no one to catch us. You can't run away from me here. I want you to look at me when we come together." I did what he said, and when I looked at Wes, he looked crazed—like he was possessed, but in the best way. I'd never seen him wild and undone, but this might have been my favorite version of him.

I felt the pressure build at the base of my spine. Wes kept his pace, knowing I was getting close. "I can feel you getting close," he said. "Fuck, I can feel it."

My moans were getting louder and so were his. Both of us were careening toward the edge of a cliff and we were desperate to fall. Wes kissed me sloppily and roughly, and when he bit down on my lower lip, I came. My whole body clenched and my toes curled. My moans turned into screams, and Wes started pounding into me harder and faster, racing toward the finish line, wanting to be there with me.

"Fuck, Ada" was the last thing he said before his body went still and he jerked haphazardly into me a few more times, then collapsed on top of me.

I felt his lips on my neck. "I didn't know it could be like that," he whispered.

"Me, either," I breathed. I didn't move. I wanted to cling to him and this moment for as long as I possibly could.

Chapter 21

Wes

I was halfway in love with Ada Hart, and I had no clue what to do about it. I'd known it for a while, but today I passed the point of no return. We were still in bed, tangled up in my sheets and in each other, and I would've stayed there for the rest of the night if I hadn't felt her shiver against me.

Shit.

Neither of us had had a chance to shower yet. We'd been too busy getting busy, I guess. It was only a matter of time before the cold caused by the rain caught up to us.

I pulled Ada closer to me and brought my comforter up around her shoulders. I wanted to soak in as much time with her here as I could. I didn't know when she'd let me do this again.

"Are you cold?" I asked.

"I usually am," she said. "But yes." Dammit. I couldn't let her freeze to death on me.

"Ready for that bath?" I asked as I kissed her hair.

"Only if you get in with me." Her voice was playful, and I'd only ever heard her use that voice with me. It made my heart swell. It put ideas in my head—ideas about what we were and where we were going—that would surely send her running in an instant.

To be fair, they scared me too. It was weird to feel something that you'd convinced yourself you never would.

"That can be arranged," I said. I kissed her one more time—soft and slow—before I peeled myself out of the bed. "Stay here. I'll get everything ready."

Ada rolled to her side to look at me. She had her head propped on her hand, and the sheets were covering most of her body, but not all of it.

I couldn't have dreamed her better.

The top drawer of my dresser was open, so I grabbed a pair of boxers and slid them on. I took one last look at Ada, who was smiling at me in a way that made my heart feel like wild horses in my chest before making my way to my bathroom.

The power was still out. My phone was where I'd left it on the bathroom counter, so I checked it. It was a little past eight and almost fully dark out.

I had a bunch of texts from my family. The first one was from my dad.

> Dad: Came to help Hank and Teddy prep for the storm. Staying here for the time being. Be safe.

Then there were several in a group chat with my siblings.

> Emmy: roll call.
> Gus: Riley and I are home and safe.

Luke: Here, sugar.

Emmy: Luke, you are literally right next to me.

Luke: Come closer.

Gus: Yuck.

Teddy: Me and the dads are all good!

Gus: Double yuck.

Teddy: 🖕 🖕 🖕

Gus: What is she even doing in this message thread.

Teddy Andersen has removed Gus Ryder from the chat

Emmy Ryder has added Gus Ryder to the chat

Emmy: Wes? You good?

Emmy: Paging Weston. Hello?

Gus: I'm sure he's fine. Wes, tell our baby sister your fine.

Teddy: *you're*

Gus: WHY ARE YOU IN HERE

Luke: Seriously, Wes. Text us back. Emmy is freaking out.

The last message was from a few minutes ago.

Emmy: Wes, if you don't respond in the next ten minutes, I'm calling the National Guard.

I didn't need that, so I quickly typed out a response.

Wes: All good over here.

Teddy: HE LIVES.

Teddy: Is Ada with you?

Teddy: 😑😑😑
Wes: Yeah, she's fine too.
Emmy: Well, I guess everything makes sense now.
Teddy: Use protection! Have fun! Light some
candles!
Luke: Nice.

I put my phone down and tried to wipe the smile off my face. I was just so fucking happy about today. I started running the bath, then went into Ada's bathroom. I knew Emmy had some bath salts. I liked to use them after a long day—they were good for muscle soreness.

I grabbed the bubble bath that was the same scent too—eucalyptus or some shit—and went back to my bathroom and started pouring the salts and the bubble bath into the tub.

Teddy'd actually given me a good idea about the candles—the power was out, after all. I knew we had tea lights in the emergency kit—I checked to make sure the bath wasn't in danger of overflowing before I headed out to the hall to find them.

First thing I saw when I opened the hall closet: a massive bag of tea lights and a lighter.

Jackpot.

A few minutes and a number of flaming candles that would probably give a firefighter an aneurysm later, I went back to Ada.

She was right where I'd left her—looking like a fucking goddess in my bed.

I knelt on the bed and started crawling up her body, placing kisses and playful bites wherever I could. I gave her waist a squeeze, and she giggled.

Ada wasn't a giggly woman, but she giggled for me, and it made me feel like I could run through a wall. In a good way.

"That tickled," she said, and I had no choice but to squeeze her waist again. She kicked and laughed. "You're such an asshole," she said with a smile. I stopped tickling her and planted a kiss on her mouth.

"We'll see if that's what you think after you see the setup I've got going for us in the bathroom." I got off the bed and scooped her up, sheets and all. I was rewarded with another laugh, and I couldn't believe my luck.

When we reached the bathroom, I set Ada down on her feet. She let the sheets fall as she took in the scene—the bubble bath, the candles. If I'd had rose petals, I would've sprinkled those, too, but I couldn't win them all.

"Damn," she said. "I'm going to need the power to go out more often." *Same,* I thought. She linked her fingers through mine and pulled me behind her to the bathtub. It was big, so there was plenty of room for the two of us.

She was about to step in, but I stopped her. I bent down and touched the water first to make sure it wasn't too hot. An expression I hadn't seen before flashed across her face when I did it, but I didn't know what it meant and it wasn't there long enough for me to try to figure it out.

"All good," I said, and she stepped in and lowered herself into the water. I shed my boxers and got in behind her. I pulled her back against my chest and both of us relaxed into the water.

She let out a soft moan, and it was like music to my ears. "This is perfect."

So are you, I thought.

Ada and I stayed in the bath until the water started to cool, and then I made her get out because I wasn't about to let her get chilled again on my watch.

I left her to get dressed in her room, even though it was the last thing I wanted to do, but while we were drying off, Waylon had come to get me, so I needed to check on Loretta.

Loretta.

The woman who told me she didn't like country music named a calf after Loretta Lynn today.

Waylon led me back to the garage, where Loretta was still in her bed but wide awake now. When the calf saw me, she stood on wobbly legs. That was good. She wasn't lethargic and she had good reflexes.

"Hey, baby girl," I said as I approached. "You hungry?" Loretta was young. Really young. She would probably need a milk replacement before she transitioned all the way to solid feed. It tugged at my chest when a calf got separated from her dam, but it was a fact of ranch life. There were a million reasons that it happened—especially in first-time heifers, and there wasn't really anything we could do to prevent it.

But we could take care of the calf. Bottle calves weren't uncommon at Rebel Blue, and I secretly loved having them. I liked having something to take care of. I went to the back of the garage, which was stocked with a fair amount of farm supplies—not as much as our stables, but enough.

I set up one of the camp stoves and boiled some water in a kettle. I let it sit until I could touch it to my wrist comfortably before mixing in the milk replacement and shaking it up. I settled back in with Loretta and started trying to get her to take the bottle. This could be an adjustment for calves, so it took a little finessing and a lot of patience.

As Loretta finally latched on to the bottle, I heard the door from the house to the garage open. My heart kicked in my chest because there was only one person it could be.

Ada had changed into a hoodie and sweatpants and was still the most beautiful woman I'd ever seen. She paused for a second when she saw me with Loretta on my lap. "The way you look right now is enough for me to want to drag you back upstairs and have my way with you," she said. "Are you seriously shirtless and bottle-feeding a baby cow right now?"

I winked at her and she groaned, "You've got to be kidding me."

"Come sit with me," I said. She sat down with her back against the wall. Waylon made his way over to her and set his head on her lap and she started stroking his head.

"Is that just milk in there?" Ada asked, gesturing to the bottle.

I shook my head. "It's a milk replacement—it's like human baby formula but for calves."

"Every day is a school day," she murmured, and then was quiet.

"You okay?" I asked, starting to worry that she had already started running from me in her head.

She nodded. "Can I ask you something?"

"Anything," I said truthfully.

"It's about . . ." She hesitated. "Depression," she said after a minute. Ah. That explained the hesitation. People felt weird talking about it, but I didn't. It was just as much a part of my life as my family, my hobbies, my dreams, and I tried to talk about it the way I would talk about any of those things—with respect and care.

"Go on," I said, trying to make sure my voice was gentle.

"Do you"—she paused again, and I could see her chewing her words before they came out—"feel that way all the time?" It was a good question.

"No," I said. "It hasn't been as bad the past couple of years. I found a routine that works for me—medication, therapy, work—all of that makes me feel better. Waylon does too. I need him." I thought back to when I was at my lowest. I used to have a hard time with change. It made me unsteady. I also like having things to take care of, and for my entire life up until Emmy went to college, it was her. I think both Gus and I felt a specific sort of pressure to look out for Emmy, more than we would've felt if our mom was around. Gus protected her—in a very literal sense of the word—and I was just *there* for her.

Growing up, Emmy didn't want to stay in Meadowlark any longer than she had to. It wasn't a surprise when she picked an out-of-state college, but I missed her while she was gone. It was like Gus and I didn't really know what to do when she wasn't around. My identity has always been who I am in relation to my siblings, so when one of them was gone, my entire being was thrown out of whack.

Plus, I've always had big feelings, so when I felt sad, lonely, or hopeless, it was substantial and . . . scary. "It was really bad after Emmy left for college, but my dad and Gus were here. That was before I really knew what depression was. I had felt milder versions of it before, but I couldn't put a name to it. I just felt bad.

"It was my dad who suggested I see someone, and I'm happy he did. That's also when I got Waylon." I went to the pound to volunteer and came home with a tiny ball of white fluff. He'd been abandoned at the fire station. As soon as I saw him, I knew he was mine. I'll be grateful to that dog for the rest of my life. He is my tether. It doesn't matter what is going on, when Waylon's big head finds its way under my hand, I feel better—at least for a minute.

"I feel stupid saying it now, but I honestly didn't expect feeling better to be so . . . hard, I guess. And right now, I'm okay," I said. "Right now, what I'm doing works, but I expect that there will come a day when I feel the ache in my bones—like the kind my dad feels before a storm—and what I'm doing now won't work, and I'll have to start over. It terrifies me."

Ada laid her head on my shoulder. She didn't say anything—she didn't have to. For years, I had desperately wanted someone to just . . . be . . . with me. To sit next to me while the power was out and weather the storm together.

Chapter 22

Ada

Emmy and Teddy were sitting on the bed behind me, watching me try on yet another outfit in front of the full-length mirror on the closet door. I'd stopped counting after the tenth. Apparently, Wes had let it slip that we were going out tonight, and apparently, that meant that Emmy and Teddy had to help me get ready. At least, that's what they told me when they showed up with Diet Cokes and extra outfit choices in hand.

I just went with it—I didn't know the friendship rules, but I was happy they were here. I missed Cam, though. She and I talked pretty regularly now, and I was starting to feel I could call her my friend.

"I think you should wear the skirt we bought last week-end," Teddy said. It was a long black suede skirt covered in layers of fringe—very Western, but maybe too on the nose.

"You haven't tried that on yet, have you?" Emmy asked.

I shook my head. "No, but I don't know if that's the vibe for tonight."

"Fringe is always the vibe," Teddy said. She stood up and

went for the shopping bag on the floor. Even though I wasn't living out of my suitcase, putting away my purchases with my other clothes made things feel too permanent. I wasn't quite ready for that.

Teddy pulled out the skirt, and Emmy made an "oooh" noise. "That's good," she said. "You have to wear that."

Teddy thrust the skirt at me. "Go." She shooed me with her hand. "Just try it on. What have you got to lose?"

"Fine," I agreed, and went into the bathroom. I slid off the jeans I was wearing and replaced them with the skirt. I didn't bother to look in the mirror before opening the bathroom door and walking back into the room. Emmy and Teddy paused their conversation, stood up from the bed, and started to hoot and holler. The two of them could get jobs as professional hype women. They felt so genuine.

"Ada, you are hot, hot, hot," Emmy said. She fanned herself for good measure.

"Never take that skirt off," Teddy said. "I'm not kidding. It literally looks like it was made for you, and coming from someone who actually makes clothes, that's saying something." Teddy turned me to look in the mirror.

It was perfect.

The skirt hugged my wide hips without being too tight. The fringe followed my every movement, even the smallest ones. It was like a slight breeze was blowing on me at all times.

It made me feel confident.

"It looks awesome," Emmy said with a smile. She was standing behind me, but Teddy had gone back to the bed.

"Now we just need the right top," she said, sorting through

a pile of shirts she'd brought. "If you had to pick your favorite feature from the waist up, what would it be?"

I had to think about that for a second. No one had ever asked me that before, and I'd never thought about it before. "Honestly," I started, "my boobs." As far as boobs went, I thought they were nice. "And my tattoos."

"Excellent choices," Teddy said. "And you feel most comfortable wearing black?" I nodded, not sure how I felt about her noticing that. Teddy pulled a top out of the pile and tossed it to me. "This one."

I went back into the bathroom and put it on over the lacy pink bra—bold for me—that I was wearing tonight. With matching panties.

You know, just in case.

This time I looked in the mirror before I went back out to Emmy and Teddy. The shirt Teddy had chosen was a tight black short-sleeved shirt. There was a seam down the middle of the front that cinched the top, making the neckline lower than it looked when it was hanging up. It was simple—the skirt remained the statement piece.

I opened the bathroom door and was met with applause. I couldn't help but smile. I didn't know if Emmy and Teddy treated everyone this way, but that didn't matter, it made me feel special anyway.

"I wore these here, and I'm taking this as a sign," Emmy said, holding out a pair of black cowboy boots. "Try them on."

I grabbed a pair of socks from the top drawer of the dresser and slid them on, and the boots right after.

I'd never worn cowboy boots before, not even the ones made for fashion over function like these, but I loved them.

"This is our best work," Teddy said to Emmy before looking at me. "You look amazing. Seriously, Wes better keep you close tonight because you're going to attract every cowboy within a thirty-mile radius."

I took in the entire outfit in the full-length mirror. The last time I'd really looked at myself in a mirror was in that motel on my first full day in Meadowlark. I didn't look very different than I did then—a few freckles had appeared because I was spending more time in the sun, my bangs had grown out more, my cheeks looked fuller—a sign of life—but I felt like an entirely different woman.

The woman I saw in the mirror was comfortable. She still enjoyed solitude, but she didn't feel lonely anymore, and for someone who'd felt lonely her entire life, that was worth everything. It wasn't that I grew up feeling like I didn't belong, but like I didn't belong where I was but might belong elsewhere.

Maybe I could belong here.

With Wes.

And Emmy, and Teddy, and Cam. With Amos too.

There was a knock at my door. "Ada," Wes's voice filtered through. "Are you almost ready?"

Before I could answer, Teddy and Emmy shouted "Go away!" in unison, which Emmy followed up with "She'll meet you in the entryway."

"And she looks fucking hot, so prepare yourself!" Teddy called.

I could hear the smile in Wes's voice when he said, "Can't wait." Then I heard his steps depart from the door.

"Jacket. Bag." Teddy handed me my worn leather jacket and my purse. I took both. Suddenly I felt nervous. I couldn't remember the last time I'd gone on an actual date.

"Deep breath," Emmy said, sensing my nervousness. She made a show of breathing in loudly, and I followed her lead, exhaling at the same time too. "Tonight is going to be great."

With that, I walked out of the bedroom and down the hall. Wes was waiting for me in the entry. He didn't hear me approach at first. I saw him run his hands through his hair and adjust the flannel shirt he was wearing over his T-shirt. His jeans looked new, and he was wearing a pair of boots I hadn't seen before.

Weston Ryder was the most beautiful man I'd ever known—inside and out.

When he saw me, his dimples appeared with a big smile, and he made a show of bringing his fist up to his mouth and biting his index finger, as if looking at me frustrated him— not in a bad way, but in a way that showed me how much he wanted me. "God, you're pretty," he said. He leaned in and kissed my neck. "How am I supposed to keep my hands off of you?" he growled, and it sent heat through me.

"Who said you had to keep your hands off me?" I said.

"Good point," he said with a kiss at my jaw. Then he tilted my chin up and kissed me hard and hot until we heard an "Ahem" from the hallway.

It was Emmy. She was beaming. Teddy gave us a wave and said, "Have fun, kids. Don't do anything I wouldn't do."

Good thing for Wes and me, that left things pretty open.

✪

"What are we supposed to do with twenty pieces of pie?" I asked as Wes and I walked back to his truck. He was carrying a bag full of to-go boxes that literally had twenty pieces of pie in them. Wes had ordered a slice of all twenty flavors of pie from the Meadowlark Diner.

"Eat them, obviously."

"That's a lot of pie, Wes," I countered.

"I have faith in us," he said simply. "Are you okay to hold them while I drive? If that coconut cream pie touches the cherry, I can't lie to you, I might cry."

"Not a fan of foods touching?" I asked.

"Not a fan of anything ruining the perfect flavor of my coconut cream pie," he said. Huh, I didn't have him pegged as a coconut guy. I was going to store that information for later.

"I'll do my best to keep these boxes stable," I said, and gave him a mock salute. He opened the truck door for me and I slid in. He put the boxes of pie on my lap and placed a quick kiss on my temple before shutting the door.

"So, where are we headed?"

"You'll see," he said with a small smile. "Tell me about the rest of your week." I assumed he meant tell him about my week since Wednesday, which was the day of the storm and the power outage and the day that we . . . you know . . . banged.

We hadn't seen much of each other, but we'd seen enough of each other for me to know that he was busy on the ranch with the aftermath of the storm, but I didn't know the specifics.

Honestly, the last few days had been the most eventful of

the renovation. Before that, everything had gone mostly smoothly. That meant there was some overdue chaos, and it started after the storm.

"The storm blew off a shit ton of shingles and revealed some damage on the roof that we hadn't noticed, so a new roof is on the agenda, but luckily the roofers can come next week. The cabinets for the kitchen came, but they're the wrong color, so that's also on the docket." I shook my head. "Oh, and we also ran out of flooring because the measurements were off, and I dropped and broke an entire box of tile."

After I'd finished giving him the rundown of the week from hell, I wondered if I should've downplayed it. For a second, I worried that I was too comfortable with Wes, that I'd crossed the line even more than I had already. I wanted so badly to tell him about my week that I'd forgotten what we were: an employee and her boss.

A new roof—even a partial one—was a big deal. So was openly admitting that a measurement was off. I'd taken care of all of it, of course. I'd expected to replace the roof before I got here, so it was covered by the budget, but I did have to make sure I didn't put that money anywhere else in the meantime. The additional wood flooring would be there Friday, cabinets were semi-easily painted, and the box of tile was an extra I was taking down to the basement. Plus, I had my two-week buffer, and at this point, I knew I was going to have to use at least some of it—mostly for the cabinet painting.

I held my breath as I waited for Wes to respond.

Wes let out a low whistle. "One of those weeks, huh?"

Yeah, definitely one of those weeks. And the weird thing about it was that shit like this only seemed to happen at the site when Wes wasn't around.

He was a good luck charm.

"Are you worried at all?" I asked, trying to gauge whether or not he was as calm as he seemed.

"Are you?" he responded.

"No, I'm not," I said, and I meant it. I could do this.

"Okay, then. I trust you to do your job, Ada. If you're not worried, I'm not worried." Wes shrugged his shoulders. "And if you were worried, we'd figure it out together. This project is both of ours."

I let out a small sigh of relief, which he must've noticed because he reached his hand across the bench seat to where mine was resting, grabbed it, and gave it a reassuring squeeze.

"Where have you been this week?" I really hadn't seen him since Thursday morning. After we'd spent the night in his bed, we made breakfast early when the power came back on. Amos came home while we were cooking, and the three of us ate together before both of them left to assess any damage that the storm had done on the ranch. He still came by the site at the end of the day so I could drive his truck back to the Big House, but later than normal, and he left again once we got back to the Big House.

"The storm did a lot of damage," he said with a sigh. I knew that already. "We already had some weather damage from the winter"—I remembered how he had talked about cabins flooding on my first day, which is why I was staying at the Big House—"and we haven't gotten around to fixing all of it, so some of it got worse. Plus, storms like that can spook cattle, and they can end up in places they shouldn't, so we've been having to drive a bunch of them back. We have to clear fallen trees and stuff too. There's always a lot to do after a weather event like that."

"Is that why Emmy's and Brooks's trucks have been at the Big House every morning when I leave for the job site?"

"Yeah. Emmy is still on the ranch at least four days a week because she does horse training in addition to lessons, but both she and Brooks have had to pitch in on other ranch work this week too. Brooks has always been our handyman—he can fix almost anything—but this week he's had his work cut out for him."

I thought back to when I first met Emmy—I wondered if he'd fixed her truck up yet. I'd have to ask.

Even though I'd been at Rebel Blue for a few months, I still had no idea what it took to run a ranch day-to-day. One thing was for sure, I was in awe of the Ryders. All four of them were different, but one thing they had in common was that they loved their ranch, and they all worked fucking hard to take care of it and everything that that encompassed—cattle, sheep, horses, stables, ranch hands, everything.

I admired them. I thought it was a special thing to love something that much.

Wes turned onto a winding dirt road that led us up a mountain. It got steep enough that he had to downshift a couple of times. "Seriously, where are you taking me?"

"We're almost there," he said, "I promise." The road was surrounded by dense trees, almost like a tunnel. I'd never seen anything like it before. "In about thirty seconds, we're going to break out of these trees," he said. "And you're going to see the best view that Meadowlark—maybe even all of Wyoming—has to offer." Wes's thumbs were tapping on the steering wheel—like he couldn't contain his excitement— and it honestly looked like he was holding his breath.

Just as he'd said, we soon broke through the trees, and even though we were much closer to the edge of a cliff than I ever wanted to be, he was right. I was utterly wonderstruck by the view. I think my mouth literally dropped open. I didn't think I'd ever been this high up before. I felt like I could see the whole state of Wyoming laid out before me. The sun was setting, and the sky was painted purple and pink above the tree-covered mountains. I saw a few doll-size houses amid big patches of land and bodies of water. Wildflowers dotted the meadows like paint splatters.

Before I could take it all in, Wes flipped the truck around. He put his arm on the seat behind me, looked over his shoulder, and started backing toward the cliff edge. If I hadn't been terrified that we were going to drive right off it, I would've thought a million inappropriate thoughts about the way he looked backing up the truck so smoothly.

"What the hell are you doing?" I demanded just as the truck came to a stop.

"C'mon," he said. "I'll show you." He took the pie boxes off my lap and got out of the truck, and I had no choice but to follow.

When I got out, I realized the truck wasn't as close to the edge as I thought, which was a relief, but it was still pretty close. Wes hadn't outright told me this, but I felt like he had a thing for triggering his own fight-or-flight.

I wasn't afraid of heights, but I had *some* sense of self-preservation, so looking over the cliff made my stomach flip a little.

Wes popped the tailgate and set the pie boxes on it. He hopped into the bed effortlessly (I was going to be playing that little jump on a loop in my mind for the foreseeable future), lifted the lid of the silver storage box behind the cab, and started pulling out blankets and pillows and lining the truck bed with them. He'd gotten all of this ready . . . for me?

I was reeling over that when he offered me his hand. "Use the tire to step up, and I've got you the rest of the way," he said with one of his soft smiles.

At his core, Weston Ryder was gentle, and I thought that was the best thing that a man could be.

I grabbed his hand and stepped up onto the truck tire as gracefully as I could, which wasn't graceful at all, and then he pulled me the rest of the way up and I was in his arms. We stood together in the truck bed for a minute, and I looked up at this man, this cowboy who had been a stranger to me just months ago.

Now I was wondering if I could ever live a life that he wasn't a part of.

The thought petrified me, so I pushed it out of my head. I didn't want to think about that. Not tonight.

We settled onto the blankets, and Wes started popping open pie boxes. There were three of them, eight pieces in two and four in one.

"So," he said, "you might not know this, but Meadowlark is the pie capital of the western United States."

"Really?"

"No," Wes laughed. "But should be." He handed me a fork

and took me through the options. I couldn't remember them all, but there were, among others, strawberry, blueberry, peach, banana cream, pistachio cream, sweet potato, pumpkin, pecan, key lime, cherry, and Wes's favorite, coconut cream. "Which one are you going to try first?" His excitement was rubbing off on me. I wouldn't say I was a fan of pie—I didn't hate it by any means, but it wasn't something I ate or thought about eating often—but Wes's energy for the things he loved was contagious.

So the possibility that I would become a pie enthusiast after tonight was quite high.

I studied the slices for a minute before settling on the key lime. I scooped some up with my fork and slid it in my mouth.

Holy shit. I felt my eyes widen, and Wes beamed at me. "I told you so," he said.

"That is seriously the best pie I've ever had in my life." And so the pie eating began. Wes even pulled one of his small sketchbooks out of the truck so he could draw up a pie bracket for us.

As he flipped through the pages, I could see some of his drawings. He was good. Really good, actually.

We ate, we laughed, and we talked.

"Do people come up here a lot?" I asked.

"They used to. In high school, this place was known as Makeout Point," he said with a waggle of his eyebrows and a mischievous grin that made my heart flutter. "But I don't think it is anymore—or we'd be surrounded by foggy-windowed trucks right now."

That made me laugh. "Were you a frequent flyer up here?"

Wes shook his head. "Not really, but when I turned sixteen, Gus and I shared a truck for a while. One night, I was lying in the truck bed just outside the Big House, looking at the moon and the stars, when I heard Gus sneak out of the house. I was curious about what he was doing, so I stayed down and quiet. Then he got in the truck and started driving."

"With you still in the back?" I asked, giggling.

"Yes! And then he stops to pick up this girl—Mandy Miller—and at that point, I'm like shitting myself, but I felt like it was too late to say anything. He drives her up here, and instead of making out inside the truck like a normal person, they get out and pull the tailgate down."

A laugh bubbled out of me—the kind that comes from your belly—at the image of a teenage Wes ruining his brother's night because he got stuck in the back of a truck.

"And when Gus sees me, there's practically smoke coming out of his ears."

"What did you do?" I asked, still laughing.

"I waved." Wes shrugged. "What about you?" he asked. "Any embarrassing stories?"

"Plenty, I'm sure," I said. "But not as good as that."

Wes reached up and tucked a lock of hair behind my ear. "Then tell me something else," he said.

"What do you want to know?"

"You," he said simply. "Tell me something no one else knows."

I took a bite of pecan pie and thought about it.

Honestly, I thought there were a lot of things that no one

else knew because I didn't know if anyone actually knew me, or if anyone ever actually wanted to.

And if that was true, I was happy that Wes would be the first.

"When I was little, I wanted to be a *Price Is Right* model," I blurted. Of course that's what I went with. "I loved the idea of getting to drop a Plinko ball, show off a new blender, and drag my fingers across a brand-new Volvo."

Wes was smiling so wide that his cheeks had to hurt. "Ada Hart," he said earnestly, "you would've made one *hell* of a *Price Is Right* model."

I laughed and shoved his shoulder. "Shut up."

And that's how it went for the next couple of hours. We traded stories and anecdotes, and I carefully added new pieces of Wes to my growing collection of things about him that I was holding close to my heart.

Chapter 23

Wes

On Thursday, I had come back to the Big House to feed Loretta before heading back out to the ranch when my phone rang.

It was Ada.

"Hey, sweetheart," I said in greeting.

"Hi, cowboy." The sound of her voice made my heart do a backflip. If I was half in love with Ada a couple of weeks ago, I was all the way in love with her now.

But she didn't need to know that. Not yet.

"What's up? Everything okay?" I asked.

"Yeah, do you think you'll be able to stop by the site today? There are a few things I want to run by you before we start moving furniture in next week." I couldn't believe it was already that time. There was about a month left to go on the project, and Ada was *busy*. She'd been leaving Baby Blue later and later each day. I knew she was tired, and I wished there was something I could do for her.

But lately, she'd started crawling into bed with me a few nights a week when she was really beat, and I'd hold her in my arms and trace my fingers up and down her back until she fell asleep.

"I can come by Baby Blue now," I said.

Ada was quiet on the other end of the phone. Shit. What did I do? "Weston?" she said. "Did you just refer to the job site as Baby Blue?" *Shit*. I was only supposed to call it that in my head.

"Um, yeah," I said.

"Have you been calling it that in your head this whole time?"

I swallowed. "Yeah."

She was quiet again for a few seconds before she said, "That is without a doubt the most perfect thing I have ever heard. I can't believe you were keeping that all to yourself!"

"I'm sorry?"

"You should be! Now get your leather-chap-wearing ass over to Baby Blue so I can be mad at you in person." She hung up before I could answer. I'd ridden Ziggy back to the Big House today, so instead of driving down to Baby Blue, I took Ziggy along the trails, and Waylon ran alongside us. I hadn't been riding as much as I normally did while the renovation was happening. It was easier to drive.

Plus, driving meant guaranteed time with Ada in the evenings.

I wondered if Ada had ever been on a horse—something told me no. I thought about riding with her, having my thighs bracket her hips and having her pressed up against me.

I was going to have to make that happen now.

When Ziggy and I arrived, six members of the crew were

carefully carrying a giant rectangle into the house. I assumed it was the island countertop—Ada had decided on emerald-green marble, and I could see it peeking through the cloth that covered the slab to protect it.

With Ziggy secured to a post outside, I followed them in. Evan was directing them, shouting "Easy does it" and "Slow down," and finally "Good" as the crew lowered the marble to its forever home.

I hadn't been here in a few days, and I was amazed at how quickly things were moving. Especially after all the hiccups last week.

The floors were in—even though they were covered right now—and the drywall was up and ready for paint. The right cabinets were supposed to be here tomorrow, and Evan had finished installing the built-ins around the living room. The beams were in on the vaulted ceiling and the exposed brick wall had been power washed.

My favorite feature, though, was the fireplace. It used to have just a wooden mantel, but I showed Ada a photo of it that I'd found in the attic last year in which it looked like stone. She had painstakingly disassembled the wooden mantel after seeing that photo. Now the stone fireplace, with its vintage marble border and gold inlay, was beautifully restored and a focal point of the room.

Everything had that "almost finished" feeling, and it made my heart swell. I was proud of what this house had become, but I was even more proud of the woman who'd led the charge. I was more than happy to be an accessory to her greatness.

Speaking of that woman, she was standing in the corner,

with a pen behind each ear and her stylus in her mouth, looking at something on her iPad.

As if she could sense that I was looking at her, she glanced up from her iPad. When she saw me, she hit me with the quiet smile that had become my favorite. When she smiled at me that way, it was like sharing a secret that only the two of us knew.

I walked over to her and, without thinking, leaned in and gave her a kiss on the temple. She didn't seem to mind.

"What are you so caught up in over here?" I asked.

She flipped her iPad around to show me a digital rendering of the space we were standing in. "We're doing the wainscoting tomorrow," she explained, pointing across the room to where two men were applying blue-and-white floral wallpaper to the top half of the wall. The blue was light, subtle. I liked it. "I think I want it tall," she said. "Maybe two-thirds up the wall. What do you think?"

"Is it going to be that same blue that's in the wallpaper?" I asked.

"A little darker," she said. "But not by much."

"Then I think two-thirds up the wall is perfect," I responded. "The counter looks amazing," I said, gesturing at the marble. "All of the colors in here make it feel so"—I tried to think of the right word—"homey."

Ada smiled. "That's the point, cowboy. Let me show you the bedrooms," she said, and started walking toward the back of the house. "I wanted to stick with a vintage color palette, so there's lots of powder blue—obviously—some greens, and some pinks to pay homage to that bathroom tile we love."

I liked the way she said "we." Ada led me through all six of the bedrooms. They weren't furnished yet, but they were finished otherwise. They had a mix of paint, wallpaper, and wainscoting. One of them shared the exposed-brick living room wall. They all felt unique and different—something you would expect in an antiquey bed-and-breakfast—but still fresh and clean, not cluttered or fussy.

The primary suite had French doors that opened onto a small patio that had been refinished. I knew landscaping was on the docket for next week and the week after, but it already looked great.

The French doors were bracketed by white linen curtains that looked like they had a field of wildflowers painted on them. Roses too. "Where did you get those?" I asked, pointing to the curtains. "I like them."

Ada's cheeks turned pink—something that didn't happen very often. "We made them. Emmy, Teddy, Cam, and I. That's what we did that night a few weeks ago. They're wildflowers from around the ranch and roses from the bushes outside the Big House."

My mom's rosebushes. "They're amazing," I said, loving them even more now.

"I saved the wildflowers we used and dried them. I poured resin coasters with them and modpodged them onto candles, jars, glasses, and tea lights. It could come off kitschy, but I'm hopeful. And that brings up the other thing I wanted to talk to you about," she said. "Are there any specific decor items—art, trinkets, books, anything—that you want to incorporate down here? Pieces of Rebel Blue that might need a new life at a new home?"

"We can search the attic at the Big House," I said. "That's where most of the original stuff from this place ended up. But..." I paused, feeling a lump form in my throat over what I was about to say.

"But what?" Ada asked softly.

"There are a few things for sure that I know I want in here," I said. Ada nodded, waiting. "My mom was a painter. A brilliant painter, really. We have stacks of her paintings in the attic. They've been covered for so long, and I think"— I tried to swallow the lump in my throat, but that fucker wouldn't budge—"I think she would be happy to have them here."

Ada wrapped her arms around my waist and laid her head on my chest. "I think that sounds perfect, Wes."

Chapter 24

Ada

I had been severely neglecting my social media, which was a bad call on my part, considering that it was the foundation of my entire career.

I didn't have a degree to back me up, or any formal training—all I had was my portfolio, and that was housed on my social pages.

It was Friday. I told Evan I needed to catch up on content, emails, and some admin work this morning, and he was happy to handle everything at the job site for the day. *Baby Blue,* I thought. I couldn't believe Wes had been sitting on that for months—maybe even years.

It just fit the house. I loved it.

I was sitting at the kitchen table at the Big House with my phone, laptop, and iPad, firing on all cylinders. So far, I'd caught up on stories for the past week and edited three videos to post. I'd also edited a few photos and written some captions. Honestly, I hadn't captured as much as I normally did, but luckily, Evan had been working with me long enough that he had known to snap some photos and film some videos that I could use.

It was coming easily right now. That's what happened when I was in the middle of a project. Content got so much easier because my creativity was flowing freely. I felt like I couldn't be stopped.

When I didn't have a project, content was tedious—a chore that I loathed—so I made sure to soak in how I was feeling about it right now.

It was also a great way for me to avoid looking at my email inbox. The way I saw it, I was still working, still being productive, so it didn't count as procrastination.

Sound logic, in my opinion.

It took me another two hours to set up enough content for the next two weeks, but once it was done, I felt lighter than I had this morning. That was the good news.

The bad news was that now that it was done, I didn't have an excuse to neglect my email. I looked at the clock on the oven. It was just past ten. I poured myself another cup of coffee, took a deep breath, and opened my email on my laptop.

I had a few from Evan, who just forwarded expenses or other information. Easy—I sorted those into their proper folder. There were a lot from brands who were interested in my using their products in the homes I designed, which was exciting, but then I saw an email with the subject "Job Inquiry—Tucson, Arizona." I opened it tentatively.

Hi Ada,

My name is Irie Fox, and I'm writing to you from sunny Tucson, Arizona. First, I want to say that I'm a huge fan of your work! I've been following your Instagram since the beginning, and it's been so cool to watch you evolve. I am especially impressed with the scope of the project you've recently taken on at Rebel Blue Ranch in Wyoming. I've never been to Wyoming, but following along with your reno has made me feel like that's a mistake I need to remedy immediately.

Anyway, long story short, I've recently come into ownership of a small bed-and-breakfast. It's got charm and good bones. I really believe it could be something great, but I need someone to help me get there. I think you would be a perfect fit!

Are you open to jobs right now? I'm hoping to get started at the beginning of August. If you are interested, please let me know a good time for us to set up a call.

Warmly,

Irie

This email should've made me happy. It was the exact result I was hoping for when I took the job at Rebel Blue.

So why did I feel like someone had just doused me with a bucket of ice water?

I closed my laptop immediately. I didn't want to deal with that right now. I still had a few weeks left at Rebel Blue. A few weeks left to figure out what was next.

A few weeks left with Wes.

That thought turned my heart into broken glass, and the

shards started poking at my chest. *Don't think about it, Ada. Don't think about what it's going to feel like to leave him.*

God, I was so stupid.

I drew a line with him when I got here. I had a plan. I had dreams, and I didn't want to derail them for anyone. Wes respected that, he gave me my space, he didn't try to make a move until I stepped up to the line.

And now that line was obliterated. The boundary was crossed, and we couldn't take it back. And I didn't want to.

I had no idea where that left me or my dreams when this was all over.

Fuck, I needed some fresh air. I slid on some beat-up boots that were sitting by the back door. They fit me, so they had to be an old pair of Emmy's. I walked out the back door of the Big House, which I'd done only a few times before, and started walking the path that led from the back porch.

My head was spinning, and I kept walking, with no idea of where I was going, but I couldn't be still right now. Being still would make me feel stuck, and feeling stuck was something I never wanted to feel again.

I came to a fork in the path. I looked down the path to the right and saw a small cabin at the end, so I took the one to the left.

As I walked, my head started to feel fuller and fuller and I felt off-balance. I had to stop. I squatted, wrapped my arms around my knees, and tucked my head between them.

I stayed like that until I heard a voice.

"Ada?" It was Emmy. "Are you okay?" I could hear her boots getting closer to me on the dirt.

"I'm fine," I said, but I didn't lift my head. I felt Emmy

crouch next to me. She put her hand on my hair and started to smooth it. I didn't stop her or move away.

"You look fine," she said sarcastically, but worry laced her tone too. "Totally normal for someone to be curled into a ball on the path down to the stables on a Friday morning." Emmy's hand on my hair was more soothing than I thought it would be. Emmy was nurturing. It wasn't a strength that I had, but it was one I was starting to admire in other people.

For the past year, I'd been so focused on being strong. That's what everyone told me I needed to be. "Be strong and you'll get through this," they said. It wasn't until I came to Rebel Blue and spent time with other women that I realized that softness was a strength too—one that Emmy had in spades.

Being around Emmy, Teddy, and Cam made me wonder why I'd spent my life thinking that I could be only one thing.

I stayed quiet and let Emmy stroke my hair. I needed to be weak—just for a minute.

When I lifted my head, Emmy was looking at me with concern. "Do you want to talk about it?" she asked.

I shook my head. "Not really," I said.

Emmy nodded. "Luke and I started this thing after we moved in together last year. Both of us were dealing with a lot of shit that we needed to sit with. So we said if there's something that's bothering one of us, and we're not ready to talk about it, it's okay to not want to talk about it right now, but we pinky-swear to talk about it eventually." Emmy held up her pinky. "Pinky-swear you'll talk about it eventually," she said.

We locked pinkies.

"We usually seal it with a kiss, but I won't make you do that." That made me smile.

"Do you want to be alone?" Emmy asked.

"I don't know," I said honestly.

Emmy looked at me thoughtfully, like she understood what I was saying even though I didn't even understand what I was saying. "Well, I'm headed down to the stables. Fancy a ride?"

"Like on a horse?"

"Yeah, like on a horse," she laughed.

"I—I've never been on a horse," I said—not even a pony at the fair or anything.

"Don't worry, I've got just the horse for you," Emmy said. "And I promise, it's much harder for your worries to fill up your head when you're riding through a place like Rebel Blue." She looked up at the sky—big and blue—and smiled. "How about it?"

I chewed the inside of my lip. "Sure," I said. This felt like as good a way as any to get my mind off Tucson.

"Excellent," Emmy said. She stood, and so did I. We walked side by side down to what Emmy called the stables, but my mental image of stables and where I was standing now were very different. This felt like the five-star hotel of stables. I felt like *I* could live in here. Emmy walked down the row of stalls and opened one. She went inside and reappeared a moment later with a horse behind her.

"This is Maple," she said. She brought the horse over by me and secured her to ties that were hanging from the wall. "She's my angel." Maple nuzzled Emmy's neck and then went for Emmy's pocket. "Oh, I get it," Emmy said to her.

"You want to butter me up with affection so I'll give you a treat." Emmy pulled something out of her pocket and fed it to Maple.

Maple was chestnut-colored. Her coat was very shiny. I didn't know much about horses, I found them terrifying, but I did love animals and knew that a shiny coat was generally a good sign of a healthy one. "And I'm going to get Moonshine. You'll ride her today." Emmy walked into another stall, and Maple stared at me.

I stared back.

Emmy returned another minute later with Moonshine. She was light and speckled. When I saw her, the first thing I thought was that she looked wise. Her nose was kind of gray, like a dog's muzzle when they get older, but what struck me most about Moonshine was her eyes. They were soft and kind and knowing.

"Moonshine is a good horse for beginners," Emmy said. "She likes to take care of people." She scratched behind Moonshine's ears. "Do you want to pet her?" Emmy asked, and surprisingly, I nodded without a second thought.

I approached Moonshine slowly. I was about to reach my hand out but stopped to look at Emmy, who nodded, giving me the go-ahead to continue. I put my hand on Moonshine's snout. It was surprisingly soft. "Here," Emmy said, handing me one of the treats she had in the pocket of her jeans. "Lay your hand flat when you give it to her."

I did as she said, and Moonshine ate the treat off my palm. Her tongue was the weirdest thing I'd ever come in contact with. The sensation made me laugh.

Then Emmy handed me a brush and said, "Follow my

lead." I watched how she brushed Maple and tried to do the same with Moonshine.

"Wes said you give riding lessons?" I asked. "And do horse training?"

Emmy nodded. "Yeah. I haven't been doing it very long here. I moved home from Denver last July. I told myself it was temporary, but obviously it wasn't." She smiled to herself as she brushed Maple's coat. "I started doing the lessons in November and just took on some horse training clients from my dad at the beginning of the year."

I didn't know Emmy had come back to Meadowlark—I'd assumed that she had always been here. I couldn't imagine Rebel Blue without Emmy, and I didn't even know her that well.

"And you and Brooks?" I had noticed that only Emmy called him Luke. "How long have you guys been together?"

Emmy smiled. "Since I moved home, I guess," she said.

"You didn't date before?" I asked, confused. The way those two interacted, I would've thought they'd been together forever—even though I vaguely remembered Dusty being surprised that they were an item.

She shook her head. "No, Luke and I didn't get along very well growing up. When I moved back here, I hadn't seen him for more than five minutes in nearly ten years." She started cleaning out Maple's hooves with a stick thing as she spoke. "I came home under less-than-ideal circumstances, but I'd do it all over again to be with him."

"Is it weird?" I asked. "To look back and know that you were so close to your soulmate your entire life without knowing it?"

Emmy moved over to Moonshine and started cleaning her hooves, but she looked at me with a big smile as she said, "Luke Brooks is without a doubt the love of my life, but my soulmate has always been Teddy Andersen."

"That's fair," I laughed, despite the pang of jealousy in my chest. I didn't have a friend that I could say that about.

Emmy straightened and went for the saddles hanging on the wall. I had no idea it took this much effort to saddle a horse. I thought it was just a throw-it-on-and-go situation. Emmy worked in silence for a few minutes, and after she got the saddles on, she unhooked each horse from the ties that were holding them and said, "We'll mount outside. You can take Moonshine's reins. She'll follow you."

Emmy picked up a large block in one hand and grabbed Maple's reins with the other and started walking Maple toward the stable door. I followed with Moonshine.

Once we were outside, Emmy set the block on the ground, and Moonshine walked toward it. "This is a mounting block," Emmy said. "It just makes it easier to get in the saddle—gives you a little more height than being on the ground."

"Do I just like . . . stand on it? Or use it as a step?"

"You'll stand on it." I did as she said. "Now put your left foot in the stirrup—nice boots, by the way—good, put one hand on the horn—that's that little knob—and one on the back of the saddle—yep—and then you'll push off your right foot and swing it over the saddle."

"I feel like that sounds easier in theory," I said shakily.

"If you can get on a bike, you can get on a horse," Emmy said. "I promise." I tried to think of the last time I'd been on a bike but was coming up blank.

"You've totally got this," Emmy said. "Do you want a countdown? Sometimes that helps." I nodded. I would take anything at this point. "Remember, just push off your right foot and swing your leg over." I nodded again. "Okay, three . . . two . . . one . . . go!" On Emmy's mark, I pushed off the block with my right and swung.

A little too hard.

I made my way over the saddle but had so much momentum that I started going over the other side. I thought I was going down, but Emmy ran around and pushed me back upright.

And now I was on a horse.

"Good," Emmy said with a laugh. "That was quite the leg swing!"

"Sorry," I said sheepishly.

"No, it was good, honestly. I would've felt bad if you'd fallen, but I like the zeal." *Zeal,* I thought. *That feels like a compliment.*

"Any advice?" I asked.

Emmy smiled wide and said, "Keep a foot on each side and your mind in the middle." I didn't know if that was helpful or not.

Emmy went over to Maple and put my mount to shame. Everything she did around the horses was so effortless. The first time I saw Emmy, I thought she looked free, and she did, but out here, with the horses, she didn't just look free, she *was* free.

"Moonshine will follow Maple, but she's neck-rein, so if you need to steer her, just pull her reins in the direction you want to go," Emmy said. I nodded.

Maple started walking, and Moonshine followed. Holy shit, this giant animal was moving. And I was moving with her.

Holy *shit*.

Moonshine kept her head and neck beside Maple's haunches, so she was neither behind her nor beside her—just near her.

"So," Emmy called back to me after we'd been walking for a bit. "How much longer do you have on the renovation?"

"A few weeks," I said. "Everything is starting to come together, but the last few weeks are always the hardest. There's a punch list of a million little things."

"That makes sense," Emmy said. "This is your first project on this scale, right?"

Ugh. "Yeah, it is. In San Francisco, I mostly did houses, or rooms in houses, but I did do a coffee shop once."

"Do you think you'll go back to San Francisco?" Emmy asked. It was an innocent question. It was natural to the conversation, but it still made my throat tighten.

"No," I said honestly. Emmy was quiet, probably waiting for me to elaborate. "I took this job for a new start. I just wanted a chance to chase my dreams." It felt like I was chasing so much more than that now. "I have some debt on an apartment, but I'll be able to pay it after this, and that's the last tie I need to sever."

"It's funny," Emmy said. "I get what you're saying. I came to Meadowlark for a fresh start too." The difference between Emmy and me, though, was that she could stay.

"Wes said Meadowlark was known for the pie, but maybe it should be known for the fresh starts," I joked, trying to avoid getting deeper into this conversation. Our horses were walking along a trail that led into some trees up ahead.

"He is very fond of the pie." Emmy nodded ahead of me. "He's very fond of you, too, you know."

I stayed quiet for a minute before I whispered, "I'm very fond of him too."

At first, I didn't even know if Emmy could hear me, but then she said, "Is that why you were curled up like a dead bug earlier today?"

"How did you know?" I sighed.

"Lucky guess," she said.

"I don't know," I said. "I hope this isn't weird for me to talk to you about because he's your brother, but I think he's great—really fucking great—but I don't know where we can go."

"Is there a reason it has to be about where you can go instead of where you are?" Emmy asked.

"I can't feel stuck again," I said. "I've been married, I tried the love thing, I was desperate for it. I still dream about it, but I made myself so small that I didn't know who I was anymore." Once I started talking, I couldn't stop. "And now that I've kind of figured it out, I've realized that I'm not the type of person everyone likes. I'm the type of person everyone tolerates." I let out a deep breath. "And I'm fine with that, I like who I am, but if I figured that out, it's only a matter of time before Wes does."

I hated how scared I sounded.

Emmy looked back at me. "If you like who you are, why is it so hard to believe that other people do too?" She turned forward again, leaving me to think about what she'd said.

I didn't have an answer.

The silence that stretched between Emmy and me wasn't awkward. It was contemplative. Was this what it was like to have a friend? To have someone you could talk to, who could push you and make you think? To have someone who cared about you enough to do that?

I looked around at the scenery we were passing. When I got to Rebel Blue, it wasn't winter, but there were patches of snow. Now Rebel Blue was lush and green. I loved the way the pine trees looked pressed up against the sky.

Being on a horse wasn't as scary as I thought it would be—probably because Moonshine and Emmy were doing all the work. I just had to sit here, but I didn't think that I would mind learning how to do it on my own at some point.

"Ada," Emmy said after a while, "I don't want you to take this the wrong way, but I need to ask you for a favor."

"Okay," I said tentatively.

"I don't want this to come off the wrong way, because you and Wes are grown-ups, and I am desperately trying not to meddle, but . . ." I heard her take a deep breath. "Don't treat him like your final destination if he's just a pit stop. I don't think he'd recover from that." She didn't look back at me, so she couldn't see me when I nodded.

I didn't think I'd recover from that either.

Chapter 25

Wes

Ada fell asleep in my bed last night. She wasn't a big cuddler when she fell asleep—she liked her space— but she always migrated closer to me during the night, and by the time I woke up, she had ahold of me like a baby koala.

She didn't come back to the Big House until after ten last night, and I didn't see her until she crawled into my bed around eleven-thirty. For a while, Ada had been staying in her room more than she stayed in mine, but this past week she'd slept in my bed every night.

And I couldn't get enough.

I could feel her starting to stir. She was an early riser, but not as early a riser as me—growing up on a ranch did that to you. I'd been awake since half past four, so I'd been waiting for her to wake up for almost an hour.

At this point, I was pretty sure I'd been waiting for her my whole life, so an hour was easy.

I pulled her tighter to me and started kissing her neck, her tattoos, her forehead—basically everywhere. She kept her eyes closed, but I could tell she was trying not to smile.

"I know you're awake," I said with another kiss on her neck.

"No, you don't," she groaned. "I want to be asleep."

"Sweetheart, it's a good day to be awake. It's Ryder Day." Ryder Day was a family tradition. We did it every year. As holidays went, it was up there with the major ones on the Rebel Blue Ranch calendar.

Ada's eyes popped open. "What the hell is Ryder Day?"

"It's the day my parents met," I said. "The day my mom rolled into town in a beat-to-hell Volkswagen Cabriolet and my dad came to her rescue and she told him to fuck off."

I watched Ada's eyes glint at the last part. "Is that really how they met?" she asked.

"Yep. They got married that same day the next year—right under the oak tree that's just out the back door."

"That sounds like a movie," Ada said as she curled into me. "So, what does Ryder Day entail?"

"A lot of food, mostly," I said. "On big holidays like Christmas and Thanksgiving, my dad always gives the ranch hands the day off, so we work the ranch on our own those days. Ryder Day is our day."

"And is Ryder day just for Ryders?" she asked.

I shook my head. "Ryder Day is for our family, but our family is more than just the one we're born with," I said, quoting my dad. "So Teddy and Hank—that's her dad—will be here. Cam might come—her fiancé has yet to show up, though. Since Dusty is home, he and Aggie might join us at some point."

"And you want me to come?" she asked. I rolled on top of her and pinned her hands above her head.

"I do," I said. "Please."

"Well," she breathed. "Since you asked nicely."

I leaned down and kissed her slowly, firmly. She hitched one of her legs around my waist and gave my bottom lip a soft bite.

Fuck.

I kissed her harder and let her hands go so I could use mine to roam her body—her fucking insane body that was basically the sum total of everything I'd ever found attractive. I felt her fingers run up and down my back before slipping under the waistband of my briefs.

"Ada," I growled against her mouth. She giggled innocently, and it shot straight to my dick. That sound was just for me. "Don't start something you can't finish."

"Believe me," she said, "*I* can finish it."

Before I had a chance to make her prove that to me, one of our phones started buzzing. I looked over at the nightstand. It was Ada's. I reached over and grabbed it so I could hand it to her.

"Who is calling you this early?" I asked.

"It's probably Evan," she said. It was Evan's last week on-site, so I knew there were probably a lot of things the two of them needed to address together.

Ada looked at the screen, and I watched the color drain from her face. "That . . . that can't be right," she murmured. I don't think she meant to say it out loud.

"Is everything okay?" I didn't like the effect whoever was calling was having on my girl. It was jarring to watch her go from playful to blank within a few seconds.

Ada didn't answer. She just held her phone and watched

it ring. It wasn't until it stopped that she spoke. "That was my ex-husband," she whispered.

Okay, well, fuck that guy, I thought.

"Are you guys in contact?" I asked. Not because it bothered me—I was secure enough about myself that it didn't. The call didn't make me uneasy, but the effect it had on Ada did. I didn't know much about her ex, but I knew he'd made her feel trapped, and that was enough.

Ada shook her head. "No, not at all." She was staring blankly ahead. "The last time we talked, I told him good night. When I woke up the next morning, he had left. I got the divorce papers in the mail a week later."

Shit. That was brutal.

I wrapped Ada in my arms and felt relief wash over me when she leaned into me. "You didn't deserve that," I said into her hair.

"I know," she said. "Thank you for saying so." I rubbed my hands up and down her arms. I didn't know whether I was trying to soothe her or myself more. "Can I tell you something?" she asked.

"Anything," I said.

"That day we went out, you told me you wanted to know something no one else knows." I remembered saying that. I wanted to know everything about her. "When I woke up and he was gone, I felt relieved. I was deeply sad afterward, but not because I was grieving the relationship. I was grieving all of the parts of myself that I lost or gave up in the name of comfort because I would rather have been comfortable than happy. I chose to prioritize my false sense of security instead of me."

She took a deep breath before continuing. "I was ashamed of myself. I let him control every aspect of my life because I didn't have the confidence to do it. I didn't have a sense of ownership over anything in my life, so the fact that I was completely dependent on someone else didn't matter to me. I didn't even know our debit card PIN."

I tried to imagine a different version of Ada—one less fierce and fervent—but I couldn't. Now I admired those qualities even more because I knew that everything she was, was on purpose.

"I think"—she sighed—"I think Chance wanted power over somebody, and I mistook that for being cared for."

My chest ached. All I could do was hold her tighter, so that's what I did. We stayed in our bed awhile longer, and I tried not to think about how empty my arms would feel without her.

Chapter 26

Ada

Ryder Day was shaping up to be one of my favorite days ever. After an unexpectedly emotional start, Wes and I reluctantly got out of bed and started our days. He was going to check on Loretta and help Gus with a few things around the ranch before both of them came back to the Big House to celebrate the Ryder family holiday.

While Wes and I were getting dressed, he asked me if I wanted to call Chance back, and if I wanted him there while I did. I would be lying if I said I wasn't curious about why Chance had called me, but I wasn't curious enough to call him back.

I told Wes no.

If there was something pressing or urgent—I couldn't imagine what—he would call again or text or find some other way to get in contact with me.

A few months after everything went down, I thought about what I would feel if Chance ever reached out to me. I'd tried to get in touch with him in the weeks immediately after the divorce papers showed up in my mailbox, but I was never successful. He didn't want to talk to me—until now, apparently—nearly two years later.

Back then, I thought I'd be comforted by some sort of closure from him. Now I thought the closure that I'd established for myself over the last year was more important.

So what did I feel about the unexpected phone call? Shocked. And I had every right to be.

What did I feel about the man making the phone call? Nothing. It wasn't an empty nothing or a hurt nothing, it was an . . . indifferent nothing.

It was the opposite of what I felt when I thought about Wes, but I wasn't ready to dive into that train of thought yet, especially with the Arizona offer looming over me.

I walked into the kitchen and saw Amos. He was reading the paper and drinking a smoothie that I assumed was healthy based on the fact that it was the color of dirt.

When I walked in, he said, "Good morning, Ada."

It was rare for me to see Amos in the mornings—I swear the man woke up at three. "Good morning," I replied. "Or should I say happy Ryder Day? Is that a thing?"

Amos chuckled. "Happy Ryder Day."

"What made you decide to create your own holiday?" I asked with a smile. I was genuinely curious, and I liked listening to Amos talk.

He smiled back, and it was warm and kind. He slid a cup of coffee across the counter to me. "You know," he said, "you're the first person who's ever asked me that."

"Really?"

Amos shrugged. "My kids don't know a life without Ryder Day, so I don't think they've ever thought about the why—maybe just the what and the who."

I sat on the chair next to him and took a sip of my coffee. "I'm listening."

"It was Stella's idea," Amos said thoughtfully. Stella. Amos's late wife, Wes's mom. Amos leaned back in his chair. "When I was a kid, my father had Ranchers Day, which was just a day he took off from work, basically. He had . . . different priorities than me." Amos's mouth turned down slightly. "He wasn't a kind man. He wasn't faithful to my mother, he didn't care much about me or my brothers, so when I inherited Rebel Blue—which wasn't supposed to happen because I was the youngest—I decided I didn't want to do anything that he did.

"Stella knew that," Amos continued. "So on our first anniversary, she pitched Ryder Day—a day to celebrate us, the family we were building, and the place that we took care of and that took care of us." Amos's eyes had gone soft, and his tone was ardent. I used to doubt that Wes was as good as he seemed, but the more time I'd spent around the Ryders, the more I realized that all three of them—even Gus, who was a lot grumpier than the other two—were the product of a devoted father, who loved them so loudly they couldn't help but be good people.

"That's beautiful," I said. "Thank you for letting me join in the fun." I hoped I sounded as sincere as I felt.

"We're all happy to have you," he said. "You're a part of Rebel Blue now." Amos's words burrowed their way into my heart, and I wanted to keep them there forever. He said I was a part of Rebel Blue, but I felt like Rebel Blue was a part of *me*.

It was weird. I'd spent my entire life feeling like I didn't belong—not because I didn't fit in or because I was lonely, but because I felt like I just belonged *elsewhere*.

But I hadn't known where.

I think I might have been homesick for Rebel Blue before I knew it existed.

A few hours later, Emmy and I set the table outside and pulled out more Adirondack chairs from a storage shed to put around the fire pit. Emmy was wearing a red sundress that looked like it was made for her. As we were setting up, she had turned on a Bluetooth speaker and there were some country songs playing that I didn't know.

"Is it a requirement at Rebel Blue to like country music?" I asked jokingly.

"Kind of, yeah," she replied. "And old-school rock and roll."

"See, that I can do." I waved my hand toward the speaker. "But this is not my jam."

"Hmm. We'll see how long that lasts," she said with a smile. It was going to last forever, but I didn't have the heart to tell her that. I would not become a country convert.

Even though some of the songs were pretty catchy.

Brooks and Amos started bringing food out to the table. Amos had been cooking all day, and Emmy had joined him pretty early. I popped in and out of the kitchen as they worked, listening to them talk and occasionally jumping into the conversation. Luke had shown up about an hour ago and joined in.

I hadn't seen Wes since this morning, but he'd texted me and told me he and Gus would be there soon.

"Hello, Ryders!" Teddy's voice came from the back door. I looked over from where I was placing the silverware next to each plate to see her standing in the doorway. In front of her was a man in a wheelchair, who I assumed was her dad, Hank. His gray hair was pulled into a ponytail, and he had a long beard. I could see from here that his skin was covered with tattoos—including his hands. He was wearing a black Led Zeppelin T-shirt that looked like it was straight out of 1972.

In short, he looked badass.

He had a guitar case and a cane across his lap.

Everyone gave Teddy and Hank a wave, and Luke went to the doorway to help get the wheelchair safely down the step.

I watched Amos walk over to him and shake Hank's hand. Emmy gave him a kiss on the cheek. Teddy pushed Hank to the head of the table, near where I was, and introduced me to her dad.

"Dad," she said, "this is Ada. She's the interior designer who's helping Wes."

"Ah." He nodded. "The one Wes is smitten with." Yeah, there was no question that this man was Teddy's father. I felt my eyes widen. I didn't know how to react to that.

"I swear to God," Teddy said with a groan, "I'm never telling you anything ever again."

Hank's eyes twinkled. They were the same color as

Teddy's—a silvery blue. He reached one of his weathered hands out to me. I noticed the tattoos on his knuckles but couldn't read them. "Nice to meet you, Ada. I'm Hank."

"*Now* he's got manners," Teddy muttered. She looked at me and mouthed "Sorry."

I shook Hank's hand. "Nice to meet you," I said with a shy smile.

"Teddy's told me a lot about you."

"Clearly," I said with a chuckle. "But I'm not sure 'smitten' is the right word," I added, trying to downplay what I was feeling.

"I am." That was Wes's voice. When I turned around, he was walking toward me, Waylon in tow, from the back door. I hadn't heard him arrive. When he got close enough, he put a hand on my lower back and kissed my temple. I was so focused on his touch and the electric current it sent through me that I barely had time to worry about the fact that Wes was touching me, kissing me, in front of everyone.

Or the fact that I liked it. A lot.

Gus appeared in the doorway with Riley on his shoulders. When she saw me, she waved and called, "Hi, Ada Althea Hart!"

Damn—good memory on that kid. "Hello, Riley Amos Ryder," I called back. Gus lifted Riley up and over his head so he could set her down.

"Uncle Wes brought a calf home the other day," he said, ruffling her hair. Riley's eyes widened adorably. "She's in the pasture on the other side of the house. Why don't you go say hi?"

Riley didn't even respond—she just took off like a shot.

Gus joined our circle and offered Hank his hand. Hank took it. "Good to see you, Gus," he said.

"You, too," Gus replied, and I could've sworn he smiled—just a little bit.

Teddy turned to me. "Ada," she said, "can you pinch me really quick? Maybe punch me in the face?" My brow furrowed. *What?* "That guy talking to my dad looks a lot like my sleep paralysis demon, and I need to wake up before he gets any closer."

Gus rolled his eyes. "I don't want to hear about the dreams you have about me, Theodora."

"Nightmares," Teddy corrected.

I looked at Hank, who was looking from his daughter to Gus and back with a small smile.

"Is Cam coming?" Wes jumped in. I'd learned that if someone didn't cut Gus and Teddy off, they'd just keep hurling insults at each other.

"No," Gus said with a sigh. "Something came up. She didn't sound good on the phone, and she asked if I could keep Riley for the weekend." Gus shook his head. "Honestly, I'm worried about her."

"Did she get her bar results back?" Teddy asked him. The sarcastic and condescending tone she normally employed when speaking to Gus was gone—concern for Cam took over.

"She hasn't mentioned it," Gus said. It was obvious that Gus cared about Cam as more than just the mother of his child. From what I'd observed, the two of them were friends.

Teddy reached her hand out and squeezed Gus's arm.

Gus looked at her, but by the time I'd blinked, Teddy's hand was back at her side and Gus was looking away. I could've imagined the whole thing.

"I'm sure she'll be okay," Teddy said to no one in particular. At least, I think that's how she wanted it to seem. I made a mental note to text Cam tomorrow and see if she was okay.

"Dinner's ready!" Emmy called. She, Amos, and Brooks brought out the last platters of food and set them on the table.

There was so much food—I had no idea how we would eat it all. Potato salad, roasted carrots, grilled zucchini and corn. Deviled eggs, fruit, and homemade rolls. The meal was rounded out by barbecued grilled chicken. Everything about it felt perfect—the food, the setting, the people.

We all sat. Amos and Hank were at the heads of the table. Gus was next to Amos, Riley was next to him, and then came Emmy and Brooks. On the other side of the table, Teddy sat next to her father. Then there were me and Wes, who had one of his hands on my thigh under the table for all of dinner, which didn't escape Emmy's notice.

I tried not to think about what she'd said while we were riding—that I shouldn't treat Wes like a final destination if I was planning to move on. I knew what she meant, but nothing about Wes felt temporary, and I didn't know how to treat him like he was.

But that didn't change the fact that this wasn't permanent.

That thought made my stomach curl, and I set down my fork abruptly. There was a lot of chatter going on, so no one noticed—except Wes.

He always noticed.

"You okay?" he whispered. I just nodded and gave him the best smile I could muster. I could tell he didn't believe me, but he didn't push it. He just gave my thigh a reassuring squeeze.

Dinner stretched until the sun started to set. The sky was vibrant with orange, pink, and purple. I'd seen a lot of Wyoming sunsets over the past few months, and it felt like every single one was more beautiful than the last.

After dinner, Wes, Brooks, and Gus cleared the table and returned with blankets and supplies for s'mores.

We moved to the chairs around the fire pit. "So," Wes said as he draped a blanket over my lap, "how has your first Ryder Day been?" The way he said "first," like there would be more, made my heart jump, then fall.

"I think I love Ryder Day," I said. Wes looked at me the way I looked at the sunset, and I wanted to run and hide. There was just so much . . . feeling when he looked at me.

I turned away and grabbed a marshmallow out of the bag that Teddy handed me. Hank started strumming his guitar as the fire crackled. I was surprised at how skilled he was. The song he was playing was soft and beautiful, almost wistful.

I felt like it was wrapping itself around me.

"What song is this?" I asked Wes, who was lighting his marshmallow on fire.

"Let Me Call You Sweetheart," he responded without a thought. My throat tightened, and even though Wes was just answering my question, it felt like more.

Wes felt like more.

This place, this family—it all felt like more. In that moment, I could almost see it—the future I wished I could have. A future where I got to sit by this fire next to Wes while surrounded by people I was starting to feel close to.

My heart ached for a future that wasn't beholden to my past.

The past that gave me an interminable urge to run just to avoid feeling stuck—even if running made my heart blister and my soul weary.

I couldn't be here right now.

"I—I'm not feeling well," I whispered to Wes. "I'm going to go to bed."

"Are you okay? Do you want me to come with you?" he asked.

"Yeah," I said. "I'm fine. Just need some rest."

I stood up. My head had the same feeling it did when Emmy found me on the path—like it was full and could spill at any moment.

"Tapping out?" Teddy asked. "Aggie and Dusty haven't even shown up yet."

I nodded. "I'm not feeling well," I repeated. "Thank you for letting me be part of your day," I said. "It was wonderful." And it was, but wonderful things didn't last. I walked toward the door, trying not to let anyone see that I was falling apart.

"Let us know if you need anything," Emmy called after me. I didn't respond. I just kept walking. I didn't stop until I made it into the room and shut the door behind me.

My back against the door, I sank to the floor. When I looked up, I realized I'd gone to Wes's room instead of my own.

I sighed. I couldn't stay in here, so I got to my feet. I was about to open the door and head to my room when I saw a notebook on Wes's bed. I recognized the brown leather. It was his sketchbook.

I didn't know what possessed me to cross the room and pick it up—much less open it. Curiosity, maybe. Or maybe it was because he wasn't here to comfort me and this felt like the next best thing.

Either way, I flipped it open. It landed on a page near the middle of the sketchbook. I'd never seen any of Wes's sketches up close—just in passing—so I didn't know what to expect. The first thing I thought was that the sketch I was looking at was beautiful.

Of course it was.

It was a string of roses, thorns, and leaves. They were shaded beautifully, boldly. The style looked familiar to me, but I couldn't pinpoint why.

I turned the page to find a similar drawing, but the roses on this one were colored. The red was vivid.

Again I turned the page, and again I found roses, thorns, and leaves. Again, and again, and again.

Every page looked familiar to me, as though I'd seen it before. But it wasn't until I flipped the page again and the roses, leaves, and thorns were drawn onto the sketch of an arm and shoulder that I realized why these images looked familiar.

It was because I saw them in the mirror every day.

Just then, the door opened, and I froze.

I didn't turn to look at him. I didn't close the sketchbook. I just stood there staring down at the drawings.

The door clicked shut, and within a few seconds he was behind me—so close I could feel his breath on the back of my neck. Every nerve in my body was firing little bolts of lightning.

"These sketches," I whispered. "Are they . . ."

"Yeah," he breathed before I could finish.

"Why?" I said softly.

"You know why," he said. I squeezed my eyes shut. This was too much. "Sweetheart, what's wrong?"

It's not what's wrong, I thought to myself. *It's what's right.* But that's not what I said. "I can't do this," I said as I turned to face him.

"Tell me why," he said.

"Because I'm leaving in a few weeks, Wes. This was never going to be anything but temporary." My voice was hollow. It wasn't convincing. "We never should have started this," I said.

"You want to call it quits because of a little distance?" he asked, like it was ridiculous.

"I'm going to Arizona," I blurted, even though I hadn't accepted the job or even responded to Irie's email. "I got an offer. They want me to start in August."

Wes's face looked stunned and then hurt. "Why didn't you tell me?"

"Because it has nothing to do with you," I said. The words tasted like bile. "You're my boss. I'm contracted for a project. Once that project is complete, I'm done. I move on. I get a new boss."

Wes's features shifted from hurt to anger. "So that's all I am to you, then?"

"That, and a good lay." I shrugged, trying not to show how much I was hurting. *What the fuck is wrong with me?*

Wes laughed, but there was no humor in it. "Oh, so that's what you're trying to do, push me away." *Yes,* I thought. "Well, guess what, sweetheart? You can push all you want, but I'm not going anywhere."

"But I am," I said. "I'm leaving, Wes. What don't you get about that?"

"And I'm so fucking proud of you," Wes said. "You deserve that job. I want you to take it. I'm not going to hold you back from following your dreams."

I blinked slowly. That was . . . not the response I was expecting.

"I can see you're confused." He stepped closer to me. "So let me break this down for you: I fucking adore you, Ada. You are, without a doubt, the most brilliant and purposeful woman that I've ever met, and I would be the stupidest man alive if I let something as stupid and surmountable as distance take you away from me."

"You don't even know me," I said.

Wes took a deep breath. "I know that your feet and hands are always cold no matter the weather. I know that you prefer to wake up early on the weekends because you would rather take a nap in the afternoon than sleep in. I know you love sour candy and hate repeating yourself. I know you're always on time, and I know you're lying about hating country music." He paused for a minute before saying, "I know you."

"No, you don't. Those are all little things. Tiny things."

"The little things are the big things, Ada. They're the things all the big things are made of. I might not know you all the way, but I want to, and I'm just asking you to give me a chance to do that."

I shook my head. "You don't want me that way, Wes. You might think that you do, but you don't. I'm not the woman for you." My heart broke as I said it, and I had to look down at the floor. If I looked at him, I would start crying. "Once I leave, you'll realize it. And then you'll find her—someone as warm and bright as you."

He was quiet, and the silence allowed me to feel the weight of my words. They were heavy enough to crush me. After a few moments, I felt Wes's finger snake under my chin, forcing me to look at him.

I thought he would look angry, but he didn't. He looked sincere as he said, "You say you're not nice, or warm, or bright, or any of these other stupid fucking words that people use to describe the sun, but I never asked you to be the sun." I rolled my eyes, trying to move them in a way that would stop the tears from falling. "I would rather have the moon anyway."

I scoffed at him then. Acting like he was being ridiculous was my only defense mechanism. "I'm the moon?" I asked sarcastically.

"You're the moon," he said. "And I'm the tides. You pull me in without even trying, and I come to you willingly. I always will."

The tears finally spilled over, and I collapsed onto the floor. Wes knelt in front of me. "I need you to be honest with me, sweetheart," he said. "Do you want this? Do you want me?" I felt like he already knew the answer to that question but wanted to make sure I knew it too.

I nodded, not trusting my voice.

"Then we owe it to each other to try." I stayed quiet, letting tears stream down my face. "Please, Ada, tell me we can try."

"Okay," I said so softly I didn't even know if he could hear me, but he must have because he wrapped me in his arms, and I let myself melt into him. Even though I'd started it, I didn't want to have this fight. I just didn't know what else to do.

When I fell asleep in his arms later that night, I let myself believe that maybe, just maybe, things could work out.

Chapter 27

Wes

I've always had a thing for adrenaline—for the things that make me feel indestructible. I felt like I didn't have anything to lose. Because of that, I used to be fearless.

Until I met Ada Hart.

Now I had something that I was terrified to lose.

And with a little less than a week until Baby Blue was finished, we were getting closer and closer to a point in our relationship where losing her was a real possibility.

I wasn't worried about distance or the job in Arizona, but I was worried about the way Ada thought about the distance—like she thought that's all it would take for me to give up on her.

I didn't know how to prove to her that this was for real.

After Ryder Day, we agreed to try, and things had been good. Great, even. I felt like this was our beginning—like we were on the edge of something big.

It was after seven, and Ada was still at Baby Blue. I had come back to the Big House after my workday to grab her something to eat and take it down to her. I hadn't seen her yet today.

I was packing up a sandwich, Doritos, some Sour Patch Watermelons, and a Diet Coke when my dad came into the kitchen.

He still had his workwear on, including his signature black cowboy hat.

"Weston," he said. "Do you have a minute?"

"I was going to take some dinner down to Ada..." I started, but my dad put his hand up.

"It won't take long," he said. "I promise." So I nodded and waited for him to continue. He pulled out a chair across the counter from me and sat down.

"When I decided I was going to build this house"—my dad motioned with his hands, referring to our home—"all I wanted to do was knock the old Big House to the ground." That surprised me. My dad put so much effort into maintaining many of the original structures on the ranch. It was important to him that we didn't build new things just to do it or let something fall into disrepair because it might be easier than taking care of it. "But I couldn't bring myself to do it, even though I don't have the fondest memories of it.

"You saw something in that house that I never could," my dad continued. "And I am so proud of you." As he said it, he pulled an envelope out of his denim jacket and slid it across the counter.

I picked it up. "What is this?" I asked, opening the seal.

"A deed," he said.

I froze. Did I hear him right? "A deed?" I asked slowly, unsure.

"In your name. For that house. And the fifteen acres around it." My throat tightened, and I clutched the envelope in my hands. "Your own piece of Rebel Blue." I felt water pricking at the backs of my eyes.

"Are you serious?" My voice was shaking.

"If my life had gone according to plan, Rebel Blue wouldn't have been mine," he said. "And a life without Rebel Blue . . ." My dad's voice trailed off. "Isn't much of a life.

"Someday, August is going to run the ranch, and he's going to be excellent," my dad continued. I nodded at that. Truer words had never been spoken. I'd never wanted to run Rebel Blue—that was Gus's dream. But I wanted to be a part of it. "You deserve a piece of it too."

Slowly, I opened the envelope and pulled out the papers and saw my name. It really was mine. I looked up at the ceiling, trying to blink the tears away.

I felt I'd proved to myself that I could do something that I and my family could be proud of.

"Thank you, Dad," was all I managed to get out. "This is . . . this is just . . . Thank you."

"I'm proud of you, Weston." His voice was gravelly. "Your mom would be too." Well, damn, wasn't that just a shot to the heart. When my dad brought up my mom, I knew he was at his most earnest.

I stayed in this moment with my father for a little bit longer until he nodded at the food I'd gotten out for Ada. "Don't keep her waiting," he said.

I smiled. He didn't have to tell me twice.

★

When I got to Baby Blue, Ada was taking the plastic off a large mirror that had just been mounted on the living room wall. Even without all of the plastic off the mirror, I could tell that it made the room feel much bigger.

It was beautiful in here, but everything paled in comparison to Ada Hart. She was wearing a pair of worn-out overalls and a black tank top.

She saw me in the mirror, and her reflection smiled at mine. I loved that I was the only one who pulled smiles out of her. "What are you doing here?" she asked.

"I brought you dinner." I held up the bag.

"And what's with the goofy smile on your face?" she asked. I set the bag on the ground and walked up behind her. "Seriously," she said. "You look like your cheeks are going to explode."

I wrapped my arms around her waist, and she leaned into me. I kissed her shoulder—right in the middle of one of the roses. "I'm happy," I said. I pulled the envelope out of my back pocket and handed it to her. Her eyes narrowed as she took it from me. I watched her open it in the mirror, and I saw her eyes widen when she read it.

"Wow," she said. "Wes, I'm so happy for you." Her eyes were so bright it was almost blinding.

I peppered her shoulder and cheeks with kisses and squeezed her sides. She squirmed and laughed. "Wes!" she squealed. God, I loved it when she said my name. I dragged my hands down her body, and when our eyes met again in the mirror, something changed. I was suddenly very aware of the fact that the most beautiful woman in the world was pressed up against me and that her chest was heaving.

Our eyes stayed locked. My hands stopped at her hips, and I pulled them back into mine. I was already hard for her. I watched her brown eyes widen and her mouth part.

I brought my hands back up her body and over her breasts, which I couldn't help but squeeze before I unbuckled one side of her overalls and then the other. The straps fell off her shoulders. I pushed them down her body. I had to kneel so she could step out of them.

God, her skin was so fucking soft. I lightly trailed my fingers up the inside of her leg as I stood—goose bumps followed me, and I grinned with satisfaction. When I made it to the hem of her shirt, I pulled it up over her head and threw it to the ground.

I slid my fingers under the waistband of her panties at her hips and looked at her in the mirror. Her face was already flushed and her eyes were glassy. "You're devastating," I whispered.

She turned away from the mirror to face me. Her hands slid under my T-shirt, and I had to stifle a jump. This woman and her cold fucking hands. She gave me a knowing smile. "Are we about to fuck in your brand-new house?" she asked coyly, even though the bulge in my jeans should've given that away.

"God, I hope so," I groaned as she dragged her nails down my back. I cupped the back of her head and pushed her back against the mirror as I brought my mouth down on hers. As soon as our mouths met, both of us moaned. Ada clutched at me, and I used my other hand to move her panties to the side. Fuck, she was wet for me. It was like the more comfortable we got with each other, the more our bodies responded—which was saying something, because I'd never been with anyone who made me crazy like this.

I slid two of my fingers inside her, and she bit my bottom lip. From the way she was gripping my shoulders, I knew her nails were going to leave a mark.

I couldn't fucking wait.

When my thumb brushed her clit, she sighed my name. I needed more.

I slid my fingers out of her, and she whined. I gripped her ass hard with both of my hands—hoping I would leave my own mark—and picked her up. I walked us over to the couch and laid her down. I kissed my way down her body, stopping to take off her lacy white bra. I sucked her nipple into my mouth and her back arched beneath me.

"Can I go down on you?" I asked against her skin.

"Wh-what?" she asked as she lifted her head. She looked dazed.

"I want to go down on you, sweetheart," I said. "I will sign the deed to this house over to you right now if you let me go down on you." I might have been kidding, but I didn't know for sure.

"You're ridiculous," Ada breathed. I was. She made me that way.

"Tell me yes, sweetheart," I said as I kissed her right below her belly button and brought my hands to her hips, then I kissed her over the fabric of her underwear and she moaned.

"Yes," she said. "Please, please, please," she chanted.

"I'm the luckiest man alive," I groaned. I pulled her panties down her legs, and when I threw them across the room, I saw something out of the corner of my eye.

It was us. In the mirror. *Hmm.*

I made my way off the couch and dragged Ada to the edge of the couch as I went. "What are you—" Ada started.

I knelt in front of her. I pulled my shirt over my head and said, "Look up, sweetheart. Take in the view."

Her legs were slung over my shoulders, and I pulled her toward me so I could take a long, languid lick up her center. She let out a surprised "Oh," and I smiled against her. It was then that I knew nothing was ever going to be enough when it came to us.

My dick was already painfully hard in my jeans, and I'd barely even touched her.

I licked her again and then I stopped holding back. I buried my face between her legs, and I devoured her like I was starving.

And I was. For her.

"Oh my god, Wes," Ada moaned. "Oh my *god.*" She knotted her fingers in my hair, and her thighs closed around my head. I used my hands to force them back open. I sucked her clit into my mouth and her hips rolled.

I looked up at her. Her eyes were glued to the mirror behind me. *Fuck.* I sucked on her clit harder. I watched her mouth fall open and her head fall back. Her breaths were coming quicker now. I knew she was close.

I started fucking her with my fingers as I tasted her. She started to buck, and her grip on my hair tightened. What started as her chanting my name dissolved into a string of moans and sighs.

Her pussy tightened around my fingers and her body went rigid. I felt her come on my tongue and continued to wring her orgasm out of her. It wasn't until she collapsed back on the couch that I sat back on my heels.

Ada's eyes were on me, and they tracked my every movement as I brought my hand up to wipe her off my mouth before I licked her off my fingers.

"Fuck," she whispered. I fully intended to crawl up beside her on the couch and lie with her for a while, but Ada had other plans. She grabbed my face and pulled my mouth back to hers. I wondered if she could taste herself.

"Wes, I want you inside me," she said against my mouth. "And I want to watch again." *Jesus Christ.*

I pulled my mouth away from hers, and she started kissing and biting at my neck as she went to unbuckle my jeans. It was my turn to groan.

"Sweetheart," I moaned before I uttered the worst five words in the entirety of the English language. "I don't have a condom." Why the fuck didn't I have a condom?

Dumbass.

"I don't care," she said, and I went still. "I'm on birth control, both of us are clear."

"Ada . . ." I hesitated. I didn't want her to feel pressure or do something she regretted in the heat of the moment.

"Please, Wes." She pushed my jeans down my legs and cupped my dick over my briefs. "I want to feel you."

"Are you sure that's not just the orgasm talking?" I managed, lucky I was even able to get words out when she was pulling down my briefs and wrapping her hand around my cock.

"Orgasm or no"—she licked her way up my neck and bit my earlobe, and she was lucky I didn't fall to my knees—"it doesn't change the fact that I want to feel your cock inside me. Without anything between us."

Fuck. I loved every part of Ada, but I especially loved this part. The bold part. The one that kissed me at the bar, that argued with me, the part that pushed and shoved and brought me to my fucking knees every time it came out to play.

I kissed her then, hard and hot. "Are you sure?" I asked.

"Yes, you have my enthusiastic consent." I felt her smile against my mouth, and I started walking her back toward the mirror.

When we were close, I turned her around. "Hands on the mirror, sweetheart," I said into her ear, and then I bit her neck.

Ada leaned forward and her palms landed on the mirror just before our eyes met in the reflection. "Spread your legs," I said. I trailed my hands down her back and gripped her hip for leverage as I guided myself inside her.

I went slow. Both for her sake and for mine, I wanted this to last. Ada watched me the whole time. Her entire body was flushed.

"You feel," she moaned as I pushed further into her, "*big.*" My hips rolled involuntarily, and now I was fully seated inside her.

My breath was ragged. I put my head on her shoulder and closed my eyes. *Breathe.* "Look at us, Wes," Ada sighed, and I lifted my head. "Look at how good we look."

I almost blurted it out then—how I felt about her—but I bit my tongue. Instead, I started to thrust in and out of her.

Again. Again. Again, and again.

Ada's moans turned into screams, and we didn't take our eyes off each other as both of our bodies started to shake. "I'm close, Wes. I'm so fucking close." I thrusted harder but kept the same pace, and Ada's eyes glazed over.

"Tell me where to come," I said. We only talked about the beginning—not the end.

"In-inside me," Ada stammered.

"Fuck," I grunted. Ada's eyes started to roll back, so I reached my hand around her and gripped her chin. "Eyes on me, Ada." Her brown eyes snapped forward. "I want your eyes on me when I fill you up."

Ada's body went rigid, and I felt the walls of her pussy squeeze around me. Both of us were careening toward the edge, and I pounded into her recklessly. We were lost in a sea of sighs and moans.

Our bodies shook and went still as both of us hit our peak.

A little while later, Ada and I were wrapped up in each other on the couch. I had one of my hands in her hair and was massaging her scalp. Her eyelids were at half-mast.

"Mmmm," Ada sighed. "Did you say something about dinner?"

I chuckled. "Glad to see your brain's still working. I'll get it." I untangled myself from her and stood from the couch to grab the bag off the floor.

When I looked back at Ada, my heart did the wild horses thing again.

She looked warm and satisfied. I felt something primal

and possessive in my chest knowing that I was the one who made her feel that way.

When I walked back to her, I set the bag next to her on the couch, knelt in front of her, and put my head in her lap. She stroked my hair.

"Ada . . ." I started. My heart was pounding, and my feelings were climbing up the base of my throat.

"What's up, cowboy?" she asked.

"I'm going to tell you something." My head was still on her lap. I knew if I didn't say something, I'd regret it. Because I knew that I'd rather wait for Ada Hart than be with anyone else.

"Okay . . ." Ada's voice sounded worried.

I took a deep breath and lifted my head so I could look at her dark and soulful eyes. "I'm not going to say what I want to say because I know you're not here yet, but I want you to know that I'm here. And that I'm waiting."

Her eyes searched my face, and I could see her fighting her impulse to run. That was a good sign—that she was fighting it.

I put my head back on her lap, giving her room to breathe. She started stroking my head again. "Okay," she whispered. It was the best response I could've gotten, and it made my heart swell.

"Okay," I responded.

Chapter 28

Ada

Today was the day. Baby Blue was going to make her debut, and I was trying—and failing—to be cool. I always got a little nervous when I showed a finished project, but this one felt different.

It *was* different.

This project was important to me. It was my way out of California and a springboard into my career. But it was also much bigger than me.

Baby Blue was a part of a family. It was a dream come true for the man I . . . liked. A lot. The man who told me he felt something big for me and was willing to wait for me to get there too.

I couldn't tell him that I was already there.

Because if I was there, that meant that I could stay here, and staying here scared the hell out of me.

I knew if I stayed here that I would never leave. I could almost see it. Wes and I would redo one of the little houses on his part of the property. We would listen to vinyl records on Sunday mornings, and he would draw while I found something to do with my hands. I'd sit with Loretta while he played fetch with Waylon. On the second of June every year, we would go to the Big House and be a part of Ryder Day.

I would never have to wonder what it was like to be loved, because Weston Ryder would love me all the way.

I shook myself out of that train of thought. I could not spiral—not today. I splashed water from the bathroom sink on my face. I grabbed a washcloth from the cabinet to dry it.

When I looked in the mirror, it reminded me of the other night at Baby Blue. First I thought about Wes kneeling in front of me, watching the muscles in his back flex as he devoured me. *Look up, sweetheart. Take in the view.* Then I thought about how we looked together in the mirror and how he felt inside me. *I want your eyes on me.*

I watched a blush creep up my cheeks in real time. Jesus Christ, I felt like Wes.

Okay, Ada. Get your game face on. I jumped up and down a few times and shook out my shoulders. It didn't help.

Everything felt weird today, like I was on the edge of something. It was the same feeling I'd had when I walked into Baby Blue for the first time three months ago.

It was also the same feeling I'd had when I saw Wes for the first time in the bar. I just didn't recognize it then.

There wasn't a huge difference in my appearance since I came to Wyoming. My hair was a little longer, and a few freckles had popped up from spending time in the sun.

Even though there wasn't really anything tangible that had changed about my appearance, I looked lighter—happier.

I'd spent the past three months doing a job that I loved, and right now I was trying to tell myself that that was the only reason. Because I could do the work that I loved anywhere, so if I believed that that was the only reason I looked—and felt—happier, then it would be a lot easier to leave for the job in Tucson.

Fucking hell. Why was I having so many feelings? This annoying internal monologue while looking at myself in the bathroom mirror had to stop.

I left the bathroom before I could have another deep thinking session.

The room I walked into wasn't the one I'd been spending every night in. Honestly, I didn't remember the last time I'd slept in here.

The thought of sleeping in a bed without Wes made me sad. He was always so warm, and he never got mad when I put my frozen feet on him.

Nope. Don't go there. No more deep thinking.

I slid on a pair of jeans and a plain black short-sleeved shirt. One thing was for sure about Wyoming, I'd never experienced so many seasons within such a short period of time—sometimes they hit all four seasons in a day. The decent amount of snow that remained when I got here was long gone, and everywhere I looked it was lush and green.

It made me want to know what it all looked like in the fall.

If everything worked out, I'd be in Arizona, working on a delightful little bed-and-breakfast. My shoulders noticeably drooped, which is the opposite of what they should have been doing. Since when was I not excited about a delightful old bed-and-breakfast?

Since Weston Rhodes Ryder. That's when.

He'd said a lot of things that had made it abundantly clear

how he felt about me, but when I thought about them now, my heart started to kick.

Not in the good way.

Everything he'd said—distance not being important, that he'd wait for me, that I was the moon—was hitting me all at once, and my head started to spin.

The timing could not be more inconvenient.

My brain was starting to take his words and warp them into something they weren't, into something I'd heard before. From someone else.

Someone who'd made me mistake control for care and dependency for love. All of a sudden, all of these false parallels were knocking around in my head like a pinball machine. The truth was in there too, but everything was going so fast that I didn't know which was which.

Did I get out of a situation where I was completely and solely dependent on one man just to get into the same situation less than two years later? Did I leave the place that felt like a cage just to get locked in a new one?

I sank to the floor and pulled my knees to my chest.

When I looked up, I saw my car keys on the nightstand. The keys to the car that still didn't work.

Wes had told me he was going to fix it, but he still hadn't done it. I knew it was because he'd been busy, and when he asked me if I wanted him to fix it, I told him not to make it a priority. But when I thought about a car that I couldn't drive, all I thought about was the life I'd had before Rebel Blue, and the life I'd had before the family that came with it.

Wes was good. He was gentle. So why the hell was I freaking out?

Because once I got the urge to run, I couldn't stop it. Wes could, but he wasn't here right now. Before I knew what I was doing, I stood up and grabbed my small duffel off the back of the bathroom door.

I was calm as I walked down the hall and opened the garage door. My mask was on, and I knew from experience that it wasn't going to slip.

Wes's old truck, the one I didn't know how to drive, was unlocked, and the keys were on the seat.

I guess it was time to see if those stick shift lessons held up.

Chapter 29

Wes

I knew I had the stupidest smile on my face, but I didn't care. Today was my fucking day, and nothing could ruin it.

Seriously, the sky could fall right now—the titan that held it up could collapse, and I wouldn't care.

Because who needed the sky when I had Ada Hart?

She hadn't let me see Baby Blue for the past couple of days because she wanted the almost-finished product to be a surprise. There were a few things she had left to do—a few pieces of furniture, linens, things like that—but both of us wanted the family's input to see if there were any other parts of Rebel Blue that they wanted represented in there.

I rode Ziggy back to the Big House and put him in the smaller pasture next to the house. Ada might have gone riding with Emmy, but she'd never ridden with me. And ever since I first had that mental image, I was trying to create an opportunity to make it happen.

Today felt like the perfect time. Riding through Rebel Blue with my woman to the place we'd built together? And it was on my property? Yeah, I could get into that.

Plus, I was so proud of Ada. She was so good at what she did—talented as hell—and I couldn't wait to show her off. Honestly, I was excited for her to go to Arizona and work her magic there too.

Yeah, we had to work out a plan. The guest ranch wouldn't open until next summer, so I could visit her while she was in Arizona, and she could always come back here whenever she wanted.

I didn't want it to be that way forever, but it was worth it to make a short-term plan for a long-term relationship.

When I walked in the front door to the Big House, something felt off, but I didn't know what. "Ada?" I called.

No answer. Huh. I checked both of our rooms. No sign of her.

I thought she'd be here already.

The front door opened, and I heard footsteps. I made my way down the hall to meet whoever it was in the kitchen.

". . . you're seriously putting in a mechanical bull?" That was Gus.

"Yeah, I've gotta do some rearranging, but we've got that whole second floor." And Brooks.

"I pity the first person who has to walk on that second floor, though," Emmy said. "We should probably put them in a harness and bring in one of those giant pads that stunt people use."

"There are a million boxes up there," Brooks countered.

"And I bet the floors are substantially less sticky," I said as

I came into the kitchen. "Hey," I greeted everyone, and Emmy came and gave me a quick hug.

"Hey, stranger," she said. "I feel like I haven't seen you in years." It had been a while since I'd seen Emmy. My work didn't overlap with hers a lot, but we did talk almost every day—she mostly sent me harassing messages about what was going on between Ada and me.

When Emmy came home last year, it took a second for me to adjust to having her back. For Gus and me, it was like we were both waiting for the other shoe to drop—waiting for her to leave again. I was really happy she hadn't. The three of us balanced one another out.

"Hey," Brooks said. "That part you had me order for Ada's car got here. It's out in my truck."

I felt bad that it'd taken me so long to fix Ada's car, but I'd needed Brooks to help me diagnose the problem because car engines were like his Rubik's cube, and he loved to fix shit. There's a reason he was always handymanning on the ranch. Turns out we needed a part, and parts for an early nineties Honda weren't in ready supply in Meadowlark. "Thanks, man. I appreciate it."

"Where's Dad?" Gus asked, looking at his watch. It was ten minutes before the hour, and that qualified as late for Amos Ryder.

And Ada Hart.

"I'm right here," my dad's voice came from the back door. "I got an older filly today. I was just getting her settled in the stables."

"Dad," Gus groaned. "If you got Riley a horse, I swear to God."

My dad grinned. "Actually," he said, "I rescued those three senior horses, and there happened to be an older filly that needed a home too." Whenever we had extra room in the stables, Dad liked to fill them. Usually he filled them with horses that needed a beautiful place to live out the rest of their days with a lot of love and sunshine.

Gus's eyes narrowed. "And this has nothing to do with the fact that both you and Emmy"—he shot my sister a look—"have told me in the last week that Riley should have her own horse."

"None at all," my dad said, "but I couldn't leave her there, and if Riley accepts my offer to start helping me take care of her, that's her choice."

"Both of you"—Gus motioned to my dad and my sister—"are ridiculous." When Gus turned away, I saw my dad shoot Emmy a wink. I wondered what those two were up to.

"So," Emmy said, changing the subject, "are we ready to go?" I looked down at my watch again. It was time.

"Ada's not here yet," I said.

"Are you sure she's not meeting us down there?" Emmy asked.

"I'm sure." And I was. I'd watched Ada put today in her calendar—time and location included—and she lived by that thing when it came to her job. I pulled out my phone to call her. I walked away from my family, and they continued to talk.

Her phone rang. And rang. And rang. It went to voicemail. I tried again and the same thing happened.

Try one more time before you freak out, I thought.

So I tried one more time. Again it went straight to voice-mail. No rings, which meant she'd turned her phone off.

I felt my shoulders drop. Or maybe it was my heart—I couldn't tell.

She ran.

"Did you get ahold of her?" Emmy asked. All I could do was shake my head. I took a breath before I turned around and faced my family.

As soon as Emmy saw my expression, her face fell. "Wes, I—" I shook my head before she could finish. I didn't need her to say she felt sorry.

I needed to get out of here.

So that's what I was going to do. Everyone but Emmy looked confused as I grabbed my hat off its hook and headed for the garage door.

"Are you going after her?" Emmy called.

"No," I said. "I'm going to wait for her." When I opened the door to the garage, I saw that my old truck was gone.

The one with the stick shift.

That's my girl.

Chapter 30

Ada

It would've been a hell of a lot easier to drive this stupid old truck out of town if I didn't hear Wes's voice in my head say "*Clutch, sweetheart*" every time I had to shift or stop or do anything with the stupid fucking clutch.

It also would've been easier if I'd had the foresight to turn my phone off before Wes started calling me.

I thought about Wes, standing in the kitchen with his family and having to tell them I wasn't there and that I wasn't coming.

I was just about to pass the WELCOME TO MEADOWLARK sign, except now I saw the back of it. The sign informed me that I was now leaving Meadowlark.

My whole body reacted as I passed the border. It shuddered and went weak.

Even though I really didn't want to, I thought about what Emmy had said—not to treat Wes like a final destination if I was going to leave anyway.

My heart lurched in my chest because that's exactly what I'd done.

I'd spent the last few weeks falling deeper and deeper into whatever it was between Wes and me when I should've been trying to keep some distance between us.

Because leaving him fucking hurt.

Why hadn't I done what I said I was going to do? Why hadn't I just stayed away from him? Why had I gotten us into a situation where both of us were going to end up hurt when I left?

Because I wanted Wes. Even if it was just for a short time.

But in that short time, I'd gotten more than I'd bargained for.

So I'd left without a word.

Just like Chance had done to me.

I hadn't realized that that's what I was doing. I didn't think I was doing it on purpose, but in the quiet cab of the truck, with only the sound of the engine and my heartbeat to keep me company, I started to feel like the worst person alive.

By leaving without telling him, I didn't have to endure his fighting to keep me. I could get the best of both worlds, and I wouldn't have to pick up any of the pieces.

This way, the wreckage that I left behind wasn't my responsibility.

That thought hit me like a freight train, and it *hurt*. The realization that I was doing to Wes what someone had done to me made me want to vomit.

I pulled the truck off the road onto the dirt shoulder. I forgot to push the clutch in when I stopped, so the truck shuddered and died—fitting for how I was feeling.

Tears leaked out of my eyes like a badly patched roof, and I collapsed, my head landing on the steering wheel.

My body was racked with sobs. How could I fuck things up so royally in less than a few hours? How did I go from wanting someone to leaving him? From feeling at home to fleeing? From happy to brokenhearted?

Was I really so scared of my feelings for Wes that I was willing to become a person I didn't like? Did I really want to live with the fact that I'd abandoned the man that I loved because the possibility of my happiness looked different than I expected it to?

No, I didn't want to live with that.

I wanted Wes.

I didn't want to call him out of the blue nearly two years later and hope that he answered. I still didn't know why Chance had called me—I didn't care—but I hated that he felt like he could. I didn't want to be that person for Wes.

And this was the shittiest part of it all: When it came down to it, I knew Wes would forgive me. I knew if I left now and showed back up in a few months, a year, he'd forgive me. He would take away the burden and the guilt that I felt for leaving by giving me absolution.

He'd let everything be okay.

Because he was deeply caring, kind, and gentle. He often carried the things that were too heavy for others by himself. Not for any sort of recognition or praise—simply because he cared.

I couldn't let him do that. Not for me, not for this.

Because this—leaving—was the dumbest thing I'd ever done.

Wes once said to me that I was the moon, and I'd scoffed

at him. But he was right. I was the moon, and the moon couldn't glow without the sun.

And my sun was in Meadowlark, Wyoming.

This was a mistake.

I had to go back. I couldn't follow through on leaving him. I didn't want to.

Rebel Blue Ranch was my home now. It was the first place that had ever felt like it, and I was an idiot for even thinking about leaving.

I pushed in the clutch, started the engine, and whipped the truck off the shoulder. Dirt and rocks went flying, and I sent a silent thank-you to the sky that I'd never once seen a cop car in Meadowlark.

Once I was headed in the right direction, I took a second to admire the world around me. The mountains and trees in Wyoming felt like my friends. It felt like they were cheering for me—that they'd told the wind to blow behind me so I could get to Wes faster.

I'd made it farther out of town than I thought. It took nearly thirty minutes of mountains and the sun setting behind them for me to see the WELCOME TO MEADOWLARK sign in the distance.

As I approached, I noticed a familiar truck right in front of the sign.

It couldn't be.

But it was. A cowboy was sitting on the hood of the truck, and a ball of white fluff was sitting on the ground next to him.

I'd know that cowboy, and his dog, anywhere.

For the second time today, I pulled the truck onto the shoulder. As I brought it to a stop, I could feel Wes's eyes on me.

I took a deep breath before I raised mine to meet them. I was worried he would look angry or sad. He didn't.

He was smiling. Dimples on full display.

I got out of my truck at the same time he slid off the hood of his, and Waylon ran toward me. When he got to me, I reached down to scratch his big, fluffy head.

"He has a thing for beautiful women," Wes said, still smiling.

I remembered he'd said that the night we met, so I responded the same way I did then: "Has that line ever worked for you?"

"You came back, didn't you?"

We didn't run to each other. We didn't collide in some extraordinary cosmic moment. We took slow, ordinary steps toward each other, and we met in the middle.

"Hi," I breathed.

"Hi." He was still smiling.

"What are you doing here?" I asked. There was no way he could have known I would come back.

"I was waiting for you." But somehow I guess he did.

I didn't know what to say, so I figured I'd start with an apology. "I'm sorry I ran away." Wes nodded but didn't respond right away.

His smile faded a little. He looked like he was thinking—a small line formed between his brows. "Ada"—his voice was hesitant—"I'm sorry if I made you think that I was the type of guy who would be okay with you not doing something you wanted."

Now I was the one who probably looked confused.

"I want you to go to Arizona. I want you to take that job if that's what you want," he said.

I did want that. I felt like I'd learned so much at Rebel Blue, and I wanted to try to do the same thing somewhere else. I wanted to bring things back to life and create spaces where people felt like they could belong.

But there was something else I wanted more.

"I want you," I said. "I want to be with you."

Wes studied me like he didn't understand. After a few beats, he said, "You can have both. You don't have to choose between me and the job. You don't have to give something up to get another thing in return."

I blinked slowly.

"You can go to Arizona. You can go anywhere you want," he said. "And I'll come to you when I can. And then, when your project is over, you can come home—like everyone else does when they're done with work."

"We can't do that forever," I said, letting him know that I wanted to be with him that long.

"I know." He nodded. He lifted his hand to tuck a piece of hair behind my ear. "Something will have to give eventually, but it doesn't have to give right now, so there's no need to force it to."

I threw my arms around him. He held me there, a hand cupping the back of my head. "Do you mean that?" I said into his shoulder.

"Every word," he said. I felt his lips in my hair.

I pulled back and looked up at Wes. Before I could stop myself, I blurted out, "I love you," and as soon as the words left my mouth, I felt shock color my features.

Wes's dimples grew and his green eyes glittered. "I wanted to say that first," he said.

"You didn't have to say it." I shrugged. "You showed me."

He kissed me then, slowly and deliberately—like we had all the time in the world. And in so many ways, we did. Because this was the start of my life. This was what I was on the precipice of when I came to Wyoming.

We pressed our foreheads together, and Wes said, "I love you, Ada. I'll keep showing you, but I needed to tell you too." I kissed him again. "And if you ever feel like you need to run again," he said, "can I request that you at least stay inside the county line?"

I laughed. From the first time our eyes met at the bar, I felt like Wes could see me in a way that no one else could, and that question proved it. He knew I was scared, and he loved me anyway.

He saw me for exactly who I was, and he loved me because of it, not in spite of it.

And as far as lifetimes went, basking in the warmth of the sun seemed like a pretty damn good way to spend one.

Epilogue

Eight Months Later
Wes

I waited for Ada in the Jackson airport. I was bouncing on the balls of my feet, twiddling my thumbs, and constantly adjusting my hat. It had been about two months since I'd seen her—the longest we'd gone since she left Rebel Blue for Tucson in July.

Since then, she'd also completed projects in Utah and New Mexico. All of them were hospitality projects—inns, B&Bs, that sort of thing. She'd found her niche, and she was damn good at it. I'd gone to see her a few times at each place, which meant I'd been leaving Wyoming more than I ever had in my life.

In Utah, we'd even had a long weekend to explore a few national parks—Bryce Canyon was my favorite.

The places we went were beautiful, but Wyoming was always going to be my home, and Ada knew that. She also knew that when she was ready, Meadowlark and I would be here waiting to welcome her home for good.

Ada came back to Rebel Blue for the few weeks she always had in between jobs. I'd started renovating a cabin on the far side of my piece of Rebel Blue with her in mind. I still switched back and forth between there and the Big House. When my dad asked me why, I told him it was because the new house didn't feel like home without Ada there.

God, I missed her.

We did what I said we were going to do. We made it work. But goddamn, it wasn't easy. When Ada was gone, there was a hole shaped like her in my life and my soul.

But I filled it with memories of her and us. I filled it with pride in her chasing her dreams and doing what she wanted. I filled it with a love that felt both perfectly ordinary and extraordinary at the same time.

I'd been waiting for Ada my whole life. I had three decades of wondering why I couldn't or didn't want to fall in love under my belt. Thirty years of waiting was a lot, but I'd do it all over again to have her at the end of it.

And I did. Have her.

We were a forever sort of thing.

That was the thought that ran through my head when I saw an unmistakable mane of shiny black hair and my favorite roses running toward me. Before I could brace myself, she'd dropped her bag, jumped into my arms, and wrapped her legs around my waist. I stumbled a little bit but recovered quickly.

We didn't kiss. Not yet.

I held her tight and buried my face in her neck and she did the same. We stayed there for a second, breathing each other in. Every time we saw each other, it was like we had this moment of remembering that the other was real.

"I missed you," she whispered.

"Welcome home, sweetheart."

She pulled back and her brown eyes met mine. We stared at each other the way we always did. She'd come from New Mexico and must've been spending a lot of time outside because her freckles were back.

Her eyes searched mine for a second before she planted a firm kiss on my mouth. There was something about her making the first move that just fucking did it for me. It took me back to that night in the bar when she'd fisted my shirt and crashed her mouth into mine.

What are you doing to me? I remember saying.

I'd known her—"known" being a strong word, I realize—for five minutes and she'd already had me by the balls.

We kissed long enough that we started to get a few hoots, hollers, and whistles from passersby. I knew I was blushing, but I didn't care.

When she finally pulled away, I mourned the loss of her mouth against mine, but I guessed her forehead against mine would have to be enough for now.

"I missed you," she said again.

"I love you," I responded. "And I missed you like crazy."

"Let's never go that long again, deal?"

"Deal," I said. Easiest deal I'd ever make in my entire life. She tightened her legs around me one last time before unwrapping them and dropping to the ground.

I picked up her bag and slung an arm over her shoulder as we walked toward the baggage claim—my girl did not pack light. "How many bags this time?" I asked. Sometimes she brought a lot of stuff home—antiques and shit.

"Just two." She smiled up at me. I recognized her first

bag—it was the same one she'd brought to Rebel Blue—when it appeared on the carousel. Now it was marked with one of the airline's orange "heavy" tags.

She pointed at her next bag, which had the same tag. *Jesus.* I made a mental note to lift with my legs before I grabbed them both.

They were heavy as hell.

"You know," I said, "if your plane fell out of the sky, it would be your fault because of these two monsters."

Ada waved her hand like that wasn't a big deal. "The rare vintage set of Pyrex mixing bowls that I got for our house was worth the risk."

Our house.

It wasn't the first time she'd said it, but every time she did felt like the first time. I didn't think I'd ever get over the fact that Ada Hart was mine and I was hers.

"I'll take your word for it," I said as I opened my truck's passenger door for her. She gave me a quick kiss before she hopped in. I rounded to the other side and got in. Ada swiftly slid across the bench seat to saddle up next to me, which was just the way I liked it.

I turned on some James Taylor, and we started the three-hour drive back to Meadowlark and Rebel Blue. We talked about Ada's last project and her newfound love of incorporating found rocks into design elements like backsplashes and shower floors. I told her about the wranglers we'd hired to guide our rides at Baby Blue this summer.

Baby Blue, which was now the guest ranch's actual name, would officially open on June 15 and run weeklong trips through the last week of August. Our guests would have the option to ride every day, hike, fish, and hopefully relax too. Every week was already booked solid. Ada's social media sent a lot of people our way.

The seasonal wranglers and guides we hired were great, and we'd mapped out the trails they would use around Rebel Blue that wouldn't interfere with the ranch hands' work, but the likelihood that guests would come in contact with some stubborn cows was still pretty high.

All part of the ranch experience, I guess.

"Do you think you'll be around for the opening?" I asked, trying not to give away how much I wanted her there, even though she probably already knew.

She pushed up and kissed my cheek. "I wouldn't miss it for anything," she said. "Plus, I need to make sure the inside looks perfect."

Relief and joy washed through me. She would be there to welcome people to the place we'd built together. The place that had springboarded both of our dreams.

After Ada had returned from her short-lived getaway, we showed my family Baby Blue. They loved every square inch of it. Especially the painting that now graced the entryway. It was one of my mom's. It was big—probably four by six—and it depicted the Rebel Blue Ranch headgate at sunset.

My dad teared up when he saw it. So did Emmy and Gus.

"So," I asked, "when do you head back out? Do you have your next job lined up?" I realized we hadn't talked about it yet. She'd never brought it up in any of our FaceTimes, phone calls, or messages. Normally, she lined the next job up about two months before the end of the current one.

Instead of answering, she just said, "Pull over," which was

odd, but I did what she said. Once the truck was stopped on the dirt shoulder right outside Meadowlark, Ada turned her body toward me and put a hand on my face.

"I'm not," she said. "Heading back out."

My heart thundered in my chest. Was she saying what I thought she was saying?

Her brown eyes were soft as she said, "You told me you would never stand in the way of following my dreams. You're my dream, Wes. You, and Waylon and Loretta and Baby Blue." My breath caught in my throat. "I reached out to the Poppy Mallow Inn. I'm going to renovate a few of their rooms. I followed my dreams, and they led me back to you."

I kissed her then. It was frantic and full of disbelief. She was staying.

For good.

Ada wrapped her arms around my neck and pulled her body into mine. Our kisses turned from frantic to needy as she started to unbutton my shirt. I slipped my hands under her tight black T-shirt and rubbed them up and down her back, reveling in what it was like to touch her again.

Fucking heaven.

I slid my tongue into her mouth and she moaned. God, I missed her sounds. I loved them. I loved everything about her—her body, her mind. She brought her hands to my belt. "Ada," I warned.

"I need you," she breathed. "I love you, Wes." I wasn't ashamed to admit that my dick got hard every time she said my name, and I hoped it would be that way forever. I kissed my way down her neck and bit the base of her throat.

The wild horses in my chest broke into a lope as I laid her back on the bench seat. I lifted her T-shirt so I could see her perfect tits heave as I slid into her. I watched her eyes roll back and her mouth fall open.

"Fuck, Ada," I groaned. "I dream about you all the time. About the way you feel when we're together." Her breaths were fast and strangled. "My dreams don't even come close to the real thing."

She pulled me down to kiss her, and I went to take my hat off, but she stopped me with a hand on my chest. "Leave the cowboy hat on," she said with a wicked smile that made my hips roll.

I kept the hat on.

It was almost two hours later when we rolled into Rebel Blue. The sun was setting behind the mountains, and I felt like I was on top of the world.

"I hope we didn't miss anything," Ada said worriedly. "I will feel terrible if we missed their entrance."

"If we did," I said with a grin, "it's your fault." Even though I knew we hadn't missed anything. We wouldn't have time to go and drop Ada's stuff at our house like I'd planned, but Brooks and Emmy wouldn't be here for another fifteen minutes.

I pulled the truck to a stop in front of the Big House. It looked like Teddy, Gus, and Dusty were already here. When we got out of the truck, I laced my fingers through Ada's.

Inside, some soft old country was playing. I could hear

voices over the music and I could smell all of Brooks and Emmy's favorite foods: smothered chicken, mashed potatoes, fresh bread, honeyed carrots.

All the good stuff.

When Ada and I walked into the kitchen, we were met by my dad, Hank, Gus, Riley, Teddy, and Dusty. There were smiles and hugs and "Welcome homes" for Ada. I watched her hug everyone. Her smile was genuine—I couldn't remember the last time I'd seen the tight professional smile she met us all with at first.

Ada belonged here, and everyone knew it.

"Cutting it kind of close, aren't you?" Gus said.

"What were you two crazy kids up to?" Teddy asked with a wink. Before either of us could answer, the front door opened again and all of us went still, waiting for Brooks and Emmy to appear in the kitchen.

When they did, both of them were glossy-eyed and looked happier than a horse in an open field. Their smiles were so big that their cheeks probably hurt, and they just got bigger as they looked at all of us. Seeing Emmy and Brooks this happy made my heart soar.

"So?" Teddy asked, and Emmy giggled as she unlaced her left hand from Brooks's and held it up for all of us to see.

My mom's ring, a simple gold band inlaid with small diamonds, now graced her ring finger.

I'd known that Brooks had that ring in his possession since about a week after Emmy's last race of her barrel racing career.

Cheers erupted and there were more hugs and tears. My

dad kept scrunching his nose—his telltale sign that he was an emotional mess.

Emmy was glowing and Brooks was basking in her glow. I was so fucking happy for them. There were more hugs, more tears, and more laughter. Gus gave Brooks a clap on the back, and Teddy hugged Emmy close and kissed the side of her head.

When things had settled a bit and we sat down to dinner, Ada leaned in and whispered, "I think I'd like to do that someday. With you." I looked at her questioningly. What did she mean? She must've seen it on my face, because my entire world stopped for a minute when she said, "Get married, I mean."

I kissed her temple and said, "Yes, ma'am."

Acknowledgments

Writing a book is hard. Writing a second book is really hard. There were so many times while I was writing *Swift and Saddled* that I wondered if I was cut out for this. I feel humbled and deeply grateful to be surrounded by family, friends, and readers who pushed me to write a book that I am proud of.

Many things have changed since I wrote my acknowledgments for *Done and Dusted,* but one thing that will never change is my gratitude and love for my parents—my black cat mom and golden retriever dad. I am what I am because of you two, the way you love each other, and the way you love me. Thank you for overcoming all of the odds.

Many tears were shed while I was writing this book, but Stella caught them all. Thank you, my angel.

This wouldn't be a Rebel Blue Ranch novel if I didn't thank my Lexie gal. You're right next to me as I write this, and you don't even know. On the darker days, your faith in me feels like sunshine. Thank you for telling everyone we've ever met that I wrote a book.

To Sydney, thank you for never being too busy to listen. Thank you for helping me sort through the wreckage of my thoughts in order to create something beautiful.

To Candace, for sticking with me since the beginning. You have become my rock, and I am so grateful to know you.

Tayler, I am so incredibly grateful for the opportunities

I've had to work with you. You are kind to me on the days that my brain isn't, and I can't thank you enough for loving Rebel Blue as much as I do. Thank you for welcoming me into your family.

Angie, you continue to support me in ways that I never could've imagined. "Thank you" isn't enough, but I hope it will do for now.

Austin, you amaze me. Thank you for sharing your talent with me and my stories. The covers you create are my favorite things.

Jess, I'm not kidding when I say that I think you are the best agent ever. Thank you for showing up for me, for looking out for me, and for believing in me. This career can be scary, but you make it less so. Thank you for making it look like I sort of know what I'm doing.

Emma, thank you for seeing something in me that I've never seen in myself. You changed my life. I can't wait to welcome you to Rebel Blue with open arms and a pair of cowboy boots.

And most important: Thank you, my readers. Whether you've been here since the indie days of Rebel Blue or if this book was your first adventure into Meadowlark, I am so happy you're here. This has been the ride of a lifetime, and I am the luckiest gal alive because I get to share it all with you.

I hold each and every one of you close to my heart. You all have shown up for me in a way that can only be described as miraculous. Not only do so many of you read my books, but you also recommend them to your friends and use them as inspiration to make beautiful things! It makes me very emotional! An emotional mess! Thank you for loving my books and for loving them loudly. My heart beats for all of you, and of course for Rebel Blue.

Finally, a yeehaw to Huey, Thumper, Brindle, Spanky, Jewel, and the entire Absaroka Ranch family. Thank you for cheering me on. Hitting Send on this story while I was surrounded by all of you, the mountains, and the big blue sky was a moment that I'll never forget.

SWIFT AND SADDLED

LYLA SAGE

Dial Delights

*Love Stories
for the
Open-Hearted*

Wes's Spanakopita
(Spinach Pie)

Recipe directly from Mama Sage's mouth
(she has never measured a thing in her life)

Ingredients:

1 package phyllo dough

2 pounds spinach, chopped (Mama Sage likes it chopped so it's easier to eat)

3 green onions, chopped (the whole thing—green and white parts)

½ cup parsley, chopped

8 ounces feta (she feels the need to say "good feta" here)

3 eggs

Salt

Olive oil (again, she feels the need to say "good olive oil" here)

Directions:

1. Preheat the oven to 350°F.

2. Wash your spinach, onions, and parsley and dry them thoroughly. Start by combining most of the filling ingredients (chopped spinach, green onions, parsley, eggs, and salt to taste) in the biggest bowl you own. This is controversial, but Mama Sage doesn't wilt the spinach first (don't tell my grandma that, though).

3. After that's combined, add in ¼ cup (good) olive oil and crumble in your feta cheese. Combine again. Mom says it's best to use your hands.

4. Grease a 12" x 9" baking pan with (good) olive oil.

5.   Pour some of your (good) olive oil into a small bowl. You'll use it to brush the sheets of phyllo before you lay them in the pan. Phyllo is a tricky pastry. To keep it from breaking, once you get it out of the package and unfold it, cover it with plastic wrap and a kitchen towel.

6.   Brush a phyllo sheet with olive oil and lay it in the baking pan. You want a few inches hanging over the edge of the pan. Continue this process until the bottom of the pan is covered with phyllo and you have a border of phyllo.

7.   Pour your filling into the pan and spread it evenly.

8.   Brush more phyllo sheets with olive oil and use them to cover the filling. Once the filling is covered, take the phyllo that's hanging over the edge of the pan and fold it up. This makes the ends of the spanakopita crispy. My family fights over these pieces.

9.   Brush the top of your spanakopita with (good) olive oil. Sometimes my mom adds a little butter, but that's the American in her.

10.   With a sharp knife, gently score your spanakopita into squares. This makes it easier to cut after baking, and it helps the steam release while cooking.

11.   Bake for 30–45 minutes. (Yes, that's a large margin between cooking times, but it's the best I could get out of my mom.)

12.   Enjoy!

Keep reading for an exclusive sneak peek

at the first chapter from

LOST AND LASSOED,

the next book in

the Rebel Blue Ranch series!

Chapter 1

TEDDY

Nothing said "good morning" like the smell of stale cigarettes and spilled beer. Walking into the Devil's Boot at night was one thing; honestly, it was one of my favorite things. But during the day, it was an assault on the senses. I could almost feel the ghosts of bad decisions clinging to my suede jacket (cream-colored, vintage, covered in fringe, totally adorable yet badass).

So why was I walking into Wyoming's dingiest dive bar at seven o'clock on a Sunday morning? Because my best friend asked me to, and there wasn't anything I wouldn't do for her.

Emmy Ryder and I had been friends since birth—literally. My dad started working on her family's ranch when I was only a few months old and Emmy was only a couple of months older than me. My first memory is of the two of us jumping over one of the skinnier parts of the stream that cuts through Rebel Blue Ranch. We went back and forth until Emmy slipped and fell into the stream. I can still hear the splash and the clattering of river rocks that accompanied it. Almost immediately, her ankle swelled up like a balloon—even at five or six, I knew that was not what an ankle should look like. I helped her out of the stream, and she leaned on me the whole way home.

We'd been leaning on each other ever since.

Her fiancé, Brooks, was the owner of the Devil's Boot. He'd inherited it from his dad a few years ago, and he was actually kicking ass as its proprietor. Brooks had a lot of dreams for the bar. His biggest one was installing a mechanical bull—no, I'm not kidding—which is why I was about to spend my Sunday sifting through boxes and sweeping up layers of thirty-year-old dust and grime and God knows what else to clear the way for it.

I didn't mind, though. Plus, I kind of owed him, considering I'd kicked him out of his and Emmy's bed last night so she and I could have a sleepover.

Emmy and Brooks were standing at the bar talking with their heads close together. I'd left their house earlier to grab some coffees and give them a chance to have some alone time, which they probably used to have sex in the shower—horny little shits.

Sometimes I wanted to get a spray bottle so I could spritz them—you know, the way you do with a cat or dog when it's being bad?—when their public displays of affection got a little too intense.

But Emmy and Brooks were made for each other, and I loved them both. A lot. I loved Emmy more, obviously, but Luke Brooks had grown on me over the past couple of years. It was kind of a beautiful thing to watch your best friend be loved in the way you know she deserves.

"Coffee's here," I said, announcing my presence.

Emmy turned to me. "Oh, thank god, you're a hero." She was wearing the tank top I got her for her birthday and a pair of black leggings. The top said "Luke Pillows" right across her boobs.

It occurred to me that I was probably overdressed for a day of cleaning out the Devil's Boot's second floor—Wrangler's, black tank top, and the jacket, obviously. But I liked clothes, the way I felt when I put together an outfit I liked, and I really liked this one. Clothes were like armor, and armor would be needed if a certain older brother of Emmy's was going to show up today.

Not Wes. I loved Wes.

I handed over her cup, which she took gratefully. She curled her fingers around it and took a sip. The gold band that now adorned her left ring finger glinted in the light. She looked down at the cardboard drink holder I was carrying. It had two more cups in it—an iced brown sugar latte for me and a black coffee for Brooks.

Emmy arched a brow at me. "Funny," she said. "I remember asking you to grab a cup for Gus too."

"Huh," I said, shrugging my shoulders. "Must've forgot." Gus was Emmy's oldest brother, Brooks's best friend, and, most important, my arch nemesis.

Small towns wove complicated webs.

It wasn't that I hated Gus ... Well ... Actually, scratch that. I did kind of hate him. I don't remember how it started (that's a lie, but it's not important). Mostly, I just always felt like he didn't like me, so I didn't like him, and then it spiraled into us being delightfully mean to each other all the time.

He was just so ... grumpy. Men who are that good-looking

should not be allowed to be such big assholes. It was false advertising.

And it was getting worse with age.

Emmy sighed. "How do we feel about trying to be nice today?" she asked.

"Not great," I said. Brooks laughed from his spot at the bar. I walked over to him and handed him his cup. He lifted it in a cheers motion.

"Thanks, Ted," he said. "Gus won't be here for a little bit, so you've got time to prep your verbal arsenal."

"See?" I said, looking at Emmy. "He gets it."

Emmy shot Brooks a pointed look, but he just winked at her. I watched her soften a little after he did it. "I just thought it would be nice if our best man and maid of honor didn't hate each other," she said. The words "maid of honor" sent a little pang through my sternum.

Of course I was thrilled to be Emmy's maid of honor. I was excited about her wedding, her life, everything. But sometimes, when the topic of the wedding came up, I got sad. Not inconsolable or anything, but it felt like my happiness for my best friend and my sadness for myself were both staking claim in my chest, punching each other as hard as they could to see who would get knocked out first.

It was a reminder that we were in different phases of our lives, and it scared me. Emmy had always needed me. We were each other's number one. Now she had Brooks, and I was terrified that she wouldn't need me the way she used to—that she wouldn't need me the way I needed her anymore.

Talk about a bummer.

"Then maybe Brooks should pick a best man who isn't so hateful." I shrugged my shoulders and looked over at him. "She's got two brothers, you know."

All he did was smile and say, "Noted."

Emmy sighed and moved on. She tried to get Gus and me to get along a couple of times a month. It never worked, but I admired her persistence. My best friend never gave up. She led me back over to the bar where she and Brooks had laid out a checklist for the day. The goal was simple: Get all the trash out of the second floor and the basement and move anything that was going to be saved to the basement.

Brooks and Gus would take the basement, which was okay with me because that place was straight out of a horror movie, and I wasn't really in the mood to get possessed by a demon today. Unless it was a hot demon; then I could be persuaded.

Emmy and I would take the second floor. Brooks's eventual plan was to put a smaller bar and new seating up there and remove some of the seating on the first floor to make room for the mechanical bull.

Once we were armed with garbage bags, gloves, and cleaning supplies, Emmy and I started toward the rickety stairs that led to the second floor of the Devil's Boot. The back door to the bar opened then. Gus Ryder sauntered in, and I could feel my blood pressure rising.

He was wearing a tight faded blue T-shirt, gray joggers, and a Carhartt baseball cap that covered his dark brown hair, which was longer than I'd seen it in a long time. Last year, he had started sporting a mustache instead of the short, neatly trimmed beard he'd adopted in his twenties. The mustache was still going strong, and even though I thought it looked good on him, the first thing out of my mouth was "Hey, Porn-stache. Nice of you to join us."

"Fuck off, Theodora," he said without even glancing my way. His voice was bored. The way he said my full name made me grind my teeth together.

"Did you steal that shirt out of Riley's closet?" I asked, gesturing to his tight blue shirt. Riley was Gus's six-year-old daughter, and the way his shirt was hugging his chest and biceps, it looked small enough to be hers.

"You know," he said, finally casting his emerald eyes to me, "the way you're ogling me is making me uncomfortable."

"Well, the way I can see your nipples through your shirt is making me uncomfortable," I countered. "Brooks," I said, glancing over at him. "I can't work in these conditions."

Brooks shrugged and said, "Take it up with the boss," nodding toward Emmy, who was looking at Gus and me. She was unamused.

All she said was "Gus, you and your nipples are in the basement. Ted, let's go." I followed her up the stairs but turned back toward Gus to give him a wave.

He flipped me off.

I hope he gets eaten by a demon.

A few hours later, Emmy and I were in the double digits of full garbage bags, and I felt the grime of the Devil's Boot like a film on my skin. I had severely underestimated the muckiness of the bar's second floor. I'd had to drop my suede jacket over a chair and cover it with a plastic bag in hopes of keeping it unaffected. On the bright side, I'd found a few old vinyl records that Emmy said I could take home. I texted my dad and told him we were going to have a Tanya Tucker and Willie Nelson listening party tonight.

I continued to sort through the boxes I was working on in the corner. I found a bunch of what looked like old newspapers. I pulled one out; it was a story in the *Meadowlark Examiner* from 1965 featuring the Devil's Boot as one of Wyoming's best bars.

"Emmy," I called. She looked up from where she was pulling a dirty and wet-looking piece of fabric from the other corner of the room. "Have you seen these?" I asked, gesturing to the newspapers.

"More newspapers?" she asked.

"Yeah," I responded. "Are there more than these?"

Emmy nodded. "We found a few boxes in the basement. Luke wants to keep them. I think he wants to frame a couple of them. You and Ada could probably come up with something cool to do with them too." Ada was Wes's girlfriend. She was an interior designer and impressively creative. I liked to paint and do things with my hands, so she and I got along.

"They're really rad," I said, thumbing through more of the papers. There were stories about the Devil's Boot and pictures of it throughout history. A copy of the *Jackson Hole News* named it the most unique bar in Wyoming.

"Will you take that box to the basement? There's a small closet at the end of the hall where we put all of the others."

"You know how I feel about the basement," I whined.

Emmy laughed and said, "I guess this is your chance to live out that demon romance you told me about last night."

I let out a huff. I couldn't believe she was using my book recommendations against me.

"Fine," I muttered. "But if I get murdered down there, or brought to some evil dimension, you're going to feel really bad for making me do this." I slid on my jacket; I didn't want to let it out of my sight. Plus, I had to look cute in case the hot demon came through.

Emmy put a hand over her heart. "I promise to throw you the best funeral that Meadowlark, Wyoming, has ever seen," she said.

"Don't forget, I want to be cremated and shot off in fireworks," I responded.

"While KISS performs 'I Was Made for Loving You,'" she said with a wave of her hand. "I know, I know." I'd decided on that when Emmy and I were in sixth grade. Talk about going out with a bang, am I right?

I picked up the box and started down the two flights of stairs. The basement was dark. This was the first time I'd made it all the way down here, and it was seriously creepy. Where were Brooks and Gus?

The smell of cigarettes and stale beer wasn't as strong in the basement. It mostly just smelled old. It was also a lot cooler—probably because of all the paranormal activity that was lurking in the nooks and crannies. The floorboards creaked under my feet. Just when I started to relax a bit, a loud bang startled me, and I ran toward the closet at the end of the hall.

I needed to get out of this creepy basement immediately— hot demons be damned.

When I got to the closet, my jacket snagged on the doorknob, slamming the door shut behind me and leaving me in total darkness. I dropped the box of newspapers and heard a frustrated grunt.

There was someone else in the closet.

I turned back to the door, trying to unsnag my jacket and get the door open. I succeeded in untangling my jacket, but I could feel a tear where it had gotten caught on the door. The door, on the other hand, wouldn't budge.

"What the fuck, Theodora?" came a deep and angry voice from right behind me.

And that's how I locked myself in a closet with Gus Ryder.

Well, shit.

LYLA SAGE lives in the Wild West with her loyal companion, a sweet old blind rescue pitbull. She writes romance that feels like her favorite things: sunshine and big blue skies. She is also the author of *Done and Dusted*. When she's not writing, she's reading.

@authorlylasage

Books Driven by the Heart

Sign up for our newsletter
and find more you'll love:

thedialpress.com

 @THEDIALPRESS

@THEDIALPRESS